Bolan left the cockpit and moved quickly along the cargo area.

Mitchell was pressed against the side of the fuselage. As Bolan reached her, he felt the plane sideslip. The nose began to drop, the aircraft starting to veer off course. They needed to get out fast.

"Now," he snapped and saw Mitchell's eyes shining bright. Fear. Her face was white, drained of blood.

She reached out and slid her hands through the straps across his chest, gripping tightly. Bolan grabbed the door release handle and activated it.

As the slipstream caught the edge of the door it was dragged free, swinging back against the exterior fuselage. Bolan felt the powerful drag of air tearing at them. He didn't fight it, simply let his body fall free.

The slipstream caught them and they were flung away from the plane, bodies helpless as they fell, turning over and over. Bolan heard Mitchell's scream of pure terror. He concentrated on clearing the aircraft as it wheeled over, free from any control, and then he sensed its bulk swinging overhead....

DON PENDLETON'S MACK BOLAN®

CHAIN REACTION

A GOLD EAGLE BOOK FROM

WORLDWIDE®

TORONTO • NEW YORK • LONDON
AMSTERDAM • PARIS • SYDNEY • HAMBURG
STOCKHOLM • ATHENS • TOKYO • MILAN
MADRID • WARSAW • BUDAPEST • AUCKLAND

Recycling programs
for this product may
not exist in your area.

First edition October 2014

ISBN-13: 978-0-373-61572-8

Special thanks and acknowledgment to
Mike Linaker for his contribution to this work.

CHAIN REACTION

Printed in U.S.A.

When justice is done, it is a joy to the righteous but terror to evildoers.
—*Proverbs* 21:15

I do what I do not for personal gain, but for true justice. My war is against those who turn their back against civilized society for their own ends.
—Mack Bolan

PROLOGUE

The big Desert Eagle boomed as the black-clad women
fired twice. Her shots forced Mack Bolan to duck, giving
her a few seconds to make a grab for the bag on the table.
She caught hold of it in her left hand, pulling it with her
as she fired again at Bolan before making a direct run
for the window.

The Executioner pushed upright, bringing his submachine gun into target acquisition.

The woman had covered her face with her right arm as
she hit the glass. It shattered as she burst through it, long
legs powering her forward.

Bolan's finger stroked the trigger. The P-90 fired its
remaining rounds before it locked on empty.

The dark-clad figure twisted to one side as a single slug
clipped her left arm. Her grip on the bag slackened and
it fell free, hitting the frame of the window and dropping
back inside the room.

Then she was gone, in a shower of glass fragments and
splintered window frame, landing outside. It seemed she
was about to fall but with a supreme effort she righted
herself and vanished from sight.

By the time Bolan reached the window she was almost
out of sight, dodging between the parked cars. Bolan had
other priorities. If he hadn't, he would have pursued her
to find out who she was and the nature of her involvement
with the criminal group he knew only as Hegre.

CHAPTER ONE

Jack "Boomer" Rafferty, six foot three and powerfully
built, released a string of colorful curses as he worked the
wheel of the massive diesel truck and swung it off Route
N87. Dust boiled out from beneath the huge tires of the
Kenworth "road train" truck as Rafferty took the rig along
the soft shoulder, red dust clouding in its wake. Air brakes
hissed as the assembly came to a halt. Rafferty pulled on
the handbrake and sat back, still cursing to himself. He
cracked open the door and hauled his bulk off the seat
and out of the cab. As he hit the ground, he felt the blast
of superheated air wrap around him. The forty-five-year-
old Australian native, his exposed skin burned brown by
constant exposure to the sun, still found the extremes of
Australian weather challenging. Right now he was also
frustrated by the double-blowout in a pair of his rig's rear
tires. He expressed his anger by kicking out at the offending wheels. Both tires on the right-hand set at the rear of
his rig were flat, the side walls shredded. Rafferty had
never seen the like of this damage before; blowouts were
not unheard of, but the extent of the damage to the rubber
gave him the impression that someone had deliberately
tampered with the tires.

"What the hell, Boomer?"

Rafferty saw the face of his co-driver and partner peer-
ing at him from the cab window. Lou Douglas, a leaner,
balding version of Rafferty, had a sour expression on his

bearded face. He had been taking his turn in the sleeper unit behind the cab. Disturbed by the lack of motion, he had woken and was ready to challenge why the vehicle had stopped.

"Problem, mate," Rafferty said. "Couple of flats and they don't look right to me."

Mumbling to himself, Douglas worked his way forward, then out of the cab. He followed Rafferty's pointing finger, leaning over to peer at the shredded tires. He moved from one to the other, fingering the shredded rubber. When he turned from his inspection, his weathered face was creased by a disbelieving scowl.

"Those aren't regular bursts," he said. "Christ, Boomer, those tires have been shot to ribbons. And I don't think by accident."

Rafferty didn't appear to be listening any longer He had turned away and was staring skyward. His attention had been taken by the silver-and-blue helicopter swooping in low and landing on the road a couple of hundred yards behind the stalled rig. Red dust spiraled up from the rotor wash, briefly obscuring the helicopter and the men who had climbed out to move quickly in the direction of the rig and its operators.

Four men.

All armed.

They moved to confront Rafferty and Douglas.

Three of the newcomers were holding MP-5 submachine guns. The fourth carried a large, long barreled rifle with a telescopic sight unit attached. A powerful sniping rifle.

The explanation as to how the tires had been shot out, Rafferty realized.

"You've got be joking," Douglas said, his face flushed with anger. "A heist?"

One of the armed men laughed. "Never thought of it like that. Now just take it easy, boys, and we'll be done in a minute." He looked toward two of his crew. "Go fetch it. Then we can be out of here."

Rafferty raged on the inside, but he knew there wasn't a thing he could do. Not with those autoweapons pointed at him and Douglas. He'd served his time in the Australian Army and he knew the sort of damage the weapons could do; he wasn't about to risk his life for the cargo he was hauling. He wondered what these men were looking for.

He watched the two walk the length of the train, counting off the container boxes until they reached the one they were looking for. A minute or two later he heard a soft crack of sound and spotted a plume of smoke at the rear of the container. He figured the sealed and secured doors had been breached.

The leader of the hijackers smiled at Rafferty's expression.

"Working it out, smart boy? I like a man who thinks on his feet."

"What I can't figure is what you want. That container is full of dry goods for stores in Alice. Nothing else."

Rafferty was referring to the town of Alice Springs. Set in the geographic center of Australia, in the Northern Territory, and known as *The Alice,* it lay around three hours' drive from their present position and had been the truckers destination for this section of the journey.

"Maybe I collect dry goods," the man said.

"Don't bullshit me, mate," Douglas snapped. "You figure we just fell off the turnip truck?"

"Lou," Rafferty said. "Just leave it."

"Do what your mate says."

Douglas stepped forward, brushing off his partner's warning hand.

"I'm not listening to this bastard," he yelled.

Douglas was known for his explosive temper and lack of caution under pressure. It had gotten him into trouble on a number of occasions.

This time it got him more.

"No," Rafferty yelled, realizing what was about to happen.

Douglas had taken only a few steps, raising his fists, when the MP-5 crackled. The burst was short, sending a volley of steel-jacketed 9 mm slugs into Douglas's torso. The force of the burst stopped him in his tracks as the bullets cored into his lean body, shattering ribs and tearing through his heart and lungs. Douglas took a step back, eyes suddenly wide with shock. He lost coordination and dropped to the ground, clutching at his punctured chest. He squirmed in short movements before his body shut down. Blood trickled from his slack mouth.

"People never learn," the shooter said.

Rafferty was frozen, staring between his dead partner and the man who had just murdered him.

The two men who had opened the container appeared, hauling a battered metal box between them. It looked like a well-used tool box. They placed it on the ground.

"That was all we wanted," the shooter said. "Nothing else."

"What?"

The shooter grinned. "Bloody hell. You had no idea." He kicked at the box. "Diamonds. Contraband from the mines up north. You've been hauling millions in uncut stones. Put on board your train to be picked up by us. We snatch the box and fly away. By the time the cops show up there's nothing to find."

Rafferty felt a chill invade his body. There would be nothing for the police to go on because the only witnesses wouldn't be able to point a finger. He looked beyond the strip of road. At the wide and empty blue sky and realized it would be the last time he saw it.

"Bloody shame, mate, but that's the way it goes."

The MP-5 crackled a second time. Rafferty felt the first impact as the burst of 9-mm slugs entered his body, then he was falling. He hit the ground on his back, eyes seeing the bright day fade into darkness. Then nothing.

"Let's go, boys," the shooter said.

The metal box was picked up and the hit team retreated to the idling helicopter. It rose quickly, circling the scene once before it cut off to the west. It flew steadily to its destination where it eventually touched down and the metal box was transferred to a waiting SUV. The team quickly changed into civilian clothing. The pilot took the helicopter back into the air, quickly vanishing from sight.

With practiced coordination the team quickly stripped down their weapons and placed them in a large canvas bag. A deep hole was dug and the weapons buried, along with the clothing they had worn during the hijack. All signs of the buried equipment were obliterated once the hole was refilled. The rear of the SUV was loaded with luggage and cameras all part of the team's cover as a group of traveling tourists. The metal box was placed underneath the bags.

When everything had been organized, one of the team took the wheel and the SUV was turned around and made its way to the main route back along the highway.

Their destination lay just over two-thousand miles away at the coastal town of Port Hedland. For the next twenty-four hours the team would take turns at the wheel, stopping only for refueling and refreshments. The highway meandered through an empty landscape, with few outposts. Planning had established the places where gas could be obtained. Similarly, every food stop had been marked on the map they carried.

They reached Port Hedland twenty minutes after the anticipated arrival time, midmorning, and parked near the harbor.

Phil Durrant, the team leader, looked out over the water. He spotted the ship he was looking for and pointed it out to his people.

"All ready and waiting for us," he said, glancing at his watch. "Our boy should be waiting in the café just along the way. Let's do this."

The driver backed the SUV into the parking spot next to the café, alongside an older, open-backed and paint-faded Australian-made Holden 4x4. The café's blue-and-white structure had wide windows overlooking the harbor, and as he climbed out of the SUV Durrant spotted their contact sitting at one of the booths. He leaned back inside the SUV. "Let's go."

Durrant turned and made his way into the café, leaving his team to handle the quiet transfer of the metal box into the 4x4, next to the clutter of tools and marine equipment. Durrant made silent contact with the waiting man who would take over the next stage of the delivery.

With the transfer complete the crew entered the café, where they joined Durrant at his table. None of them spoke to the contact man. Durrant and his team ordered food and drink. The contact man finished his own meal before paying at the counter and leaving the café. He climbed into his truck and drove away from the café.

The guy's name was Karl. None of the men had ever met him, and identification was made from the photo image that Durrant had received over his cell phone.

Committing the face to his memory Durrant had erased the photo.

All Durrant knew was that they were associates of the Hegre organization.

KARL DROVE DOWN the road, turning into the marine yard after showing his ID to the security guard at the gate. He was known as a regular in his position as a maintenance man working for one of the companies that serviced sea-going vessels using the Port Hedland facility. After a couple of minutes talking to the security guard, Karl drove on, along the dockside. He parked and hauled a couple of toolboxes from the back of his vehicle. One of the boxes contained the stolen diamonds that had been transported two thousand miles across the country by Durrant and his team.

As he made his way to one of the berthed ships, Karl acknowledged passing associates. He walked up a short gangway that allowed entry to the ship through an open cargo hatch, nodding to the crewman standing just inside.

"Just coming to fit that faulty pressure valve before you push off."

The man nodded. "You know where to go."

Karl nodded and continued on his way into the ship. He took a companionway that led belowdecks. Just before he reached the engine room he diverted and walked into the ship's maintenance store. The guy in charge, known to Karl, took the stolen toolbox and vanished from sight behind the metal racks of parts where he opened the box, removed the heavy leather satchel holding the diamonds and placed it in a large metal locker. He returned to where Karl was waiting and handed back the toolbox, now considerably lighter. He had the replacement pressure valve ready, and Karl took it with him and left.

An hour later Karl left the ship and carried his toolboxes with him as he returned to his pickup. The toolboxes went into the back. Karl drove off the dock and picked up the road into Port Hedland.

In town he parked and sat behind the wheel as he made a quick phone call. When his contact picked up, he delivered the arranged confirmation.

"New pressure valve fitted."

TWO HOURS LATER the ship left the harbor and headed out to sea. It was heading for Hong Kong and the harbor at Kowloon. When it docked a few days later, the consignment of diamonds was left in the locker while the ship was unloaded and the crew went ashore for a break. The crewman assigned to handle the diamonds would soon leave the ship and deliver them to the arranged place farther along the dock—a local fish cannery owned in part by Hegre, a legitimate business conglomerate that had a flourishing criminal element.

Lise Delaware received news of the imminent delivery. From Kowloon the satchel would be sent to Hegre's agent in the Philippines. Once the deal had been completed and the money passed to Hegre the next part of the process would be negotiated and arrangements would be made for the contracted merchandise to get under way.

CHAPTER TWO

Washington, D.C.

Special Agent in Charge Drake Duncan stood at the window of his office in the FBI's J. Edgar Hoover Building. A gray drizzle of rain drifted past the glass. Dark clouds were coming in over the city. The weather matched Duncan's mood.

He was in charge of the task force investigating the Hegre organization. It was still causing the FBI man sleepless nights. Since becoming involved in the virus investigation a while back, when he had first realized the reclusive nature of Hegre, Duncan had accepted that even the combined resources of the agency were having problems. Now, months following the original investigation, the FBI was seeing only scraps of information. Leads had taken them in a hopeful direction, only to fade away to nothing. He was beginning to understand just how complex the criminal group was. From what had come to light during the virus affair—the involvement of an FBI agent who had been bought off and the existence of a member of the CDC in Atlanta who had handed Hegre samples of the smallpox—Duncan had accepted he was combating a criminal conspiracy with a far-reaching network of contacts. Hegre bought and paid for the best help it could find. And it was obvious the organization was not held back by moral concerns. Hegre was in the business of making money. It didn't make judgments on the consequences of its operations as long as it profited. It operated on a simple, cold blooded premise: if a venture made money Hegre was interested. Right now Duncan had a problem on his hands, which was the reason for the call he was making to the one man who could help him.

Matt Cooper.

Duncan was the first to accept that Cooper's direct involvement in the Hegre-North Korea operation had resulted in the curtailing of the incident. Despite Cooper not being part of the FBI, or any agency Duncan knew about, the man obviously had top-ranking backup. And if it hadn't been for the man's selfless resistance, more people would have died and the lethal strain of adapted smallpox could have resulted in countless deaths.

SAC Drake Duncan was a dedicated agent, who had the strength of the FBI to back him. Yet here he was calling on a man who worked by a set of rules far beyond the FBI's agenda. He was doing it because an agent was dead, another missing and Duncan was placed in the position of not trusting the people around him. It was a sad, but undeniable fact.

Hegre had breached the FBI previously. Duncan had the nagging feeling that might have happened again, because the dead agent—Ray Talbot—had been operating under deep cover, his actions sanctioned by Duncan himself, with very few people aware of the fact.

The FBI worked on a mandate of loyalty, with each and every agent sworn to uphold the law and deliver unbiased and corruption-free service. On the other side of the coin was human frailty, the probability that certain individuals could fall into the dark side of life. It had happened over the years, luckily on a small scale, but no organization was immune.

Duncan had built his team by handpicking each member. Yet even that did not preclude someone slipping inside who had a less-than-honest mandate. Ray Talbot had been working in the field under the charge of Duncan's most trusted—and in this case there was no chance of any suspicion—team leader. Special Agent Sarah Mitchell, early thirties, was a young woman who had come up through the ranks as a Duncan protégée. Smart and capable, she had sailed through FBI training and once in the field had exhibited a natural resourcefulness in her work. Intuitive, she saw things that others might easily miss, and she picked up on the minutia of operating procedure with ease. She also had a willful nature that sometimes got the better of her. Not deliberately smart-mouthed, she could exchange banter with the best, and on more than one occasion her eagerness almost got the better of her.

Duncan found her refreshing. He would have willingly put himself on the line for her, knowing that in any situation she would always have his back. In terms of the physicality of FBI work she was hard to beat. Her marksmanship, with a variety of weapons, was always at the top of the score card.

He had put her in charge of the current phase of the Hegre investigation. She had taken a keen interest in the matter, to the point that Duncan had to remind her to treat it like any operation. He understood her frustration. Sarah Mitchell hated being beaten and no matter how sophisticated Hegre appeared to be, to Mitchell it was simply another criminal organization and as such she channeled her energy toward bringing it down. SAC Duncan had laid out her assignment, then given her free rein to run the operation on her own, with his overall supervision.

The past week had brought nothing. Duncan sensed, from her emailed reports and his talks with her via phone, that Mitchell was becoming frustrated at the lack of progress. And as time went by Duncan himself started to experience concern. In part that was because of his suspicion there might be a Hegre mole within the unit. He was searching to uncover evidence that would expose the traitor, hating the thought that Mitchell and her team might be in harm's way.

He avoided voicing his concern. The problem with unearthing an insider was the undeniable fact that bringing his thoughts into the open might simply play into the guilty person's hands. At worst he might find himself talking to the traitor without knowing. It was one of those situations where unburdening himself might come back to bite him. He needed to move slowly, keep his wits about him, and not show his hand.

But now he needed a presence on the case, an independent presence not part of the FBI, but with a feel for Hegre and the ability to move in ways that weren't possible for Duncan's people. A man he *could* trust.

Matt Cooper was free of any inside influence, a man who could move through the morass of regulations as he homed in on the perpetrators.

Duncan's personal cell phone connected and the voice he remembered from their last meeting came through.

"SAC Duncan, Cooper. Hal Brognola told me you could be reached at this number. Are you free to talk?"

"Yeah, he mentioned that you needed to reach me. You sound like a man with a problem, Duncan."

"Damn right. And it's the same problem that brought us together last time."

"Hegre?"

"Yes."

"They operating again?"

"You know we've been working on cracking their cover

since the smallpox affair. And we've barely scratched the surface. Then we got a break. Not a massive one, but enough for me to send in part of my task force to check it out. Up in the Northwest. A couple of my people vanished. Now one of them has turned up dead, tortured before he was killed."

"Sorry to hear that, Duncan."

"The agent's name was Ray Talbot. He was young and a real go-getter. His partner Jake Bermann has vanished. There are two other agents on the team, and they're looking for him—my case agent Sarah Mitchell and the fourth member of the team, Joseph Brewster."

"Lots of open country up there," Bolan said. "It would be easy to get lost."

"I received an email from Ray. It must have been caught up in some sort of server glitch because it was sent a couple of days ago, about when he vanished off the radar. So we lost any chance of getting to him before he died."

"I'm guessing you haven't told the rest of the team that he's dead. There must be a reason."

"You remember we had a leak during the smallpox operation?"

"And you identified him. Are you saying you might have another leak?"

"I'll give you a clue, Cooper. This call is being made on my personal cell."

"Understood."

"You told me to contact you if there was a new lead. That's what I'm doing. I need an outside source. Someone off the record and with the know-how to work on his own."

"I'm listening."

"I can send you the coordinates Ray Talbot attached to his email, a location in the area where he was investigating. I'll pass it along to Mitchell, but give you the chance to reach the area first." Duncan paused. "Cooper, I'm asking a lot for something that's not strictly your responsibility, so if…"

"You lost people the first time round," Bolan said. "Talbot now, and maybe your agent, Bermann. From what we understand about Hegre, those people have no respect for anyone in their way. They need to be stopped."

"Use this number if you need to get through to me, Cooper."

"I'll let you know when I have something."

CHAPTER THREE

FBI Agent Sarah Mitchell crossed the parking lot outside the diner, balancing two paper cups of coffee and a couple of sandwiches in her hands. Her partner, Agent Joseph Brewster, saw her and quickly climbed out of the Crown Victoria. He moved around the car to relieve her of the load.

"You always do things the hard way."

"You noticed."

"Funny lady."

They climbed back inside the car, closing the doors against the rising chill.

"This is one cold place," Brewster said. He glanced across at his partner. "You sure you didn't specially ask for this assignment?"

Mitchell took her time drinking her coffee before she looked at him.

"Why would I do that, Joe?"

"I can think of one reason. You have a weird sense of humor, and landing me here in the back of beyond would fit that."

"You think I'd put myself through all this just to get a laugh?"

Brewster placed his coffee in the cup holder and proceeded to unwrap his sandwich. He checked the filling, nodding when he found it was beef.

"If I was playing jokes," Mitchell said, "would I have brought your favorite kind of sandwich?"

"I guess not."

They had just completed their meal when Mitchell felt her cell phone vibrate in her pocket. She took it out and checked the caller ID. She was disappointed it wasn't from Ray Talbot, or his partner Jake Bermann. The call was from SAC Drake Duncan, her FBI superior.

"Sir?"

"You're not going to like this, Mitchell."

"Talbot?"

"He's been found. It's not good."

Mitchell touched her partner on the arm.

"I'm putting you on speaker, sir."

"Talbot has been found," Duncan repeated for Brewster's benefit.

"Not alive?"

"No. The body is about thirty miles from your current position in a place called Treebone. Some locals found the body, which had been dumped in a creek."

"You want us to check it out?"

"Yes. I want an FBI presence in place. I want you to find out what happened. One more thing, Mitchell. Just remember Bermann is still missing too. I'll get back to you with details."

"Leaving now, sir," Brewster said.

He gunned the Crown Victoria, tires skidding against the loose gravel as he swung back onto the highway.

Neither of them spoke for the first few miles. They had been expecting Duncan's news. Agents Talbot and Bermann had been missing for a few days, and it hadn't been looking good. Ray Talbot had always been an independent type of guy, liable to go off without keeping his teammates informed. It was the way he had operated, and he had always brought in good results. Even so, receiving the news of his death had been a shock.

It was Mitchell who broke the silence. She leaned forward and slammed her clenched first on the dash.

"*Damn, damn, damn.* What the hell is going on, Joe? This is crazy. When Ray stopped checking in, I should have figured something was wrong"

"There's no logic to it. They vanish, disappear for a few days then Talbot shows up dead."

"Now I know Hegre has to be responsible for this."

Mitchell felt Brewster's eyes flick her way for a few seconds.

"Not that again," he said.

"Yes. *That again.* We were getting too close."

"Sarah, we have no real proof. It's all…"

Mitchell rounded on him, her hazel eyes flashing with barely concealed anger. Frustration.

"What were you going to say, Joe? It's all in my head? I'm imagining it?"

"I understand how you feel, Sarah, but we have to go with real proof. We're FBI. Not freelance cowboys with guns."

"And a dead agent is proof we've made waves. How many more before you believe?"

"Procedure," Brewster said. "We're supposed to get local invitations before we walk over their jurisdiction."

Procedure.

It was word Brewster used a lot, something he pushed every time they came up against a problem.

Hell, Joe, I hope we never get in a tight spot and you won't move if it goes against procedure, Mitchell thought.

SAC Duncan called her again just under an hour later.

"An email showed up on my computer. It was from Ray Talbot, dated almost two days ago. It had been delayed because of a server glitch…"

"Our system?"

"Unfortunately. Ray's message got snarled up so it's only just come through."

"That leaves us at a disadvantage."

"Don't remind me."

Duncan held back from telling Mitchell that he had delayed informing her until he had contacted Matt Cooper. Talbot had already been dead and Duncan wanted more feet on the ground. And he was still nervous concerning the possible leaks. Hence his call to the *unofficial* Matt Cooper.

"Is his message going to help, sir?"

"I'm downloading it to your cell, Agent Mitchell. I'll let you make a decision. Your call on this, Sarah. But keep me in the loop."

Mitchell sat back. A simple technical delay had held back Talbot's email and now he was dead.

Had the delay been the reason he hadn't survived? Unable to have his message picked up quickly. Had it been that simple?

Had Talbot died waiting for his FBI response?

A response that hadn't come.

The thought sickened her, made her determined to find out what Talbot had been trying to pass along.

Her cell phone pinged. She opened the downloaded message and scanned Talbot's email.

Info panned out. Have located Hegre base. North of town of Treebone. Am about to check it out. GPS location attached to this message. Talbot

"Ray sent a location. He was going to check it out."

"Just him and Bermann?" Brewster snapped. "Damn stupid move. He should have—"

"Christ, Joe, if you mention procedure again I'll scream.

Ray is dead. Jake is missing. I don't give a rat's ass about the rule book right now."

"I—"

"Just drive, Joe. No talking. Just goddamn well drive."

She threw her cell phone onto the dash in frustration, then tapped the GPS coordinates into the vehicle's navigation system.

Her emotions were a mess. The Hegre investigation, missing agents and now Ray Talbot's death. She knew her FBI training had taught her to maintain objectivity, but how could she not be affected by such things? The day she became that hardened she would hand in her badge and gun and walk away.

She stared out through the windshield, the road curving away in front of the speeding car. Tall trees edged the route on both sides and in the far distance the were hazy outlines of mountains under the blue sky. Mitchell felt the sting of tears, angry at her emotions, but just as sad at the loss of a young life.

They reached Treebone an hour later, Brewster driving through the isolated community.

"We'll bring the locals in after we check out this location," Mitchell stated. "See if we can locate Jake without sirens screaming and lights flashing."

Twelve miles on the northern side of the town, the GPS informed them they were a half mile from their destination. The display on the screen indicated a right turn ahead.

"Keep going," Mitchell said. They drove by the dirt road. After a quarter mile Mitchell told Brewster to pull off the road.

He pulled the Crown Victoria onto a fire road and nosed it into the timber, undergrowth rattling against the side of the car until Mitchell told him to stop.

She pulled out her Glock pistol, checked it and kept it in her hand as she opened her door.

"Sarah…don't…"

Mitchell glanced across at her partner. He was staring at her, face taut with anger.

"What the hell, Joe?"

"You know we can't do this. Not without proper sanction. It's too risky."

"Not your damned procedures again. Agent Brewster, I am up to here with you and your rules. Ray is dead. Jake is still missing. He could be dead too by now. Ray left us a message directing us here, offering us a chance to catch up with this Hegre group. And you want to play the protocol rule. Well, the hell with your uptight games. I can't wait."

Brewster stiffened. "I can't stop you, Sarah. You're my senior agent. But I won't follow until I have clearance. This is wrong. We need to call it in. Get Duncan's authority. Call in backup. Too risky otherwise."

Mitchell stepped out of the car, turning to look back at her partner.

"Those people could be moving out. They may have already. I can't let that go unchecked."

"Not until we have Duncan's say-so."

"Duncan said it was my call."

"He didn't mean this action."

"Then stay put. I'm not sitting around here."

Mitchell moved away from the car, into the thick foliage, feeling the close-ranked trees crowd around her.

She knew it was her impulsive nature making her go ahead. But there was the loyalty she had to Ray Talbot. That hot-blooded combination made her push through the forest, back toward the location Talbot had sent before he died.

CHAPTER FOUR

The thick mulch underfoot deadened any sound she might have made. The close branches overhead broke the daylight into ragged patches. Undergrowth tugged at her FBI windbreaker. She held her Glock close to her chest as she traveled. She scoured the way ahead, moving steadily, but with caution. Her eyes probed the tall trees, the tangled undergrowth. This wild country was new to her. Sarah Mitchell would admit to being a city girl. Tall buildings and concrete she knew. The sights and sounds, the smells of urban life were her familiars, not greenery and timber. The forest with its own scents offered unknown challenges. She had been on the move for roughly twenty minutes when she glimpsed her target directly ahead, its dark bulk showing through the trees. She advanced, taking a slower pace until she could see the full outline of the structure.

A four foot stone wall ran around the property. Mitchell moved up to it so she could see the building clearly. An unpaved road led up to the house, and a pair of high-end SUVs were parked at the front entrance. She could see a number of wood-framed windows, but from her position she was unable to see inside. The whole place reeked of decrepitude. Mitchell crouched, trying to formulate her approach and aware that once she cleared the wall she would be pretty well exposed if she made for the house.

Mitchell heard a faint sound then and realized she was

not alone. She gripped the Glock tighter, feeling a slick of perspiration on her palm.

She had been sure she had slipped in unseen.

Something told her that it was not Brewster who had made the sound. Her partner would not have come in so close without identifying himself to her.

She flattened against the stone wall, straining her ears to pick up any more sounds. She stayed put for a while, listening, but picked up no more noise. That didn't comfort here. For all she knew there was someone close by doing exactly the same thing.

Now, she thought, *was where things could get really awkward.*

What would the FBI manual tell you about things like this? She knew the answer straightaway. *Don't get yourself into tricky situations in the first place.* Right now that was of no damn use at all.

Sweat beaded Mitchell's face. She had gotten herself into this position, so she had no choice other than getting herself out. All because of her impetuous nature. That and being mad with Brewster.

Mitchell turned slowly, searching the shadows. She probed the air with her pistol.

Nothing.

So why was she so worked up?

Because something didn't feel right.

Mitchell almost gave a yell when cold metal pressed into her neck.

"Give me the gun," a quiet voice said.

No threat. Just a commanding tone that made Mitchell pause and consider her actions.

"Finger off the trigger and just let go."

She felt a hand close around the Glock and push the barrel down.

"Let it go, Agent Mitchell."

FBI rules stated not to give up her issued weapon, but the insistent pressure of the man's gun made a powerful statement that instantly wiped protocol off the board. Mitchell let go of the Glock and felt it drawn away.

"That wasn't hard, was it?"

"My boss might not agree."

"At least you're still alive to argue the point."

Mitchell turned to face the newcomer.

He was tall, well over six feet, with black hair, and steady blue eyes that held her defiant gaze. The first thing she saw was his combat blacksuit. The muscled body beneath showed broad shoulders and a lean, well-defined torso. His calm demeanor was unthreatening, but Mitchell sensed that deceptive calm could turn quickly. He wore a shoulder rig, probably for the Beretta 93-R he held in his fist. A gun belt around his waist held a second high-ride holster holding a .44 Magnum Desert Eagle. Whoever he was, Mitchell decided, he had come loaded for bear. There was even a sheathed knife on his left hip.

"Three words," the man said. "SAC Drake Duncan."

"Okay. I'll make a calculated guess you're not part of Hegre," Mitchell said.

The faintest of grins etched his lips briefly.

"FBI training is getting sharper."

Mitchell inclined her head. "Is my badge showing?"

"No, but the way you reacted shows agency training. And that Glock is standard-issue."

Mitchell stepped back and looked him over a second time. There was a military bearing about him. The way he held himself spoke of self-control and a dedication to what he was doing.

"Special Forces?" she asked.

Mack Bolan shook his head. "Not in the way you're

thinking. I don't have affiliations to any agencies you can think of. But I'm on your side. My name's Matt Cooper."

"Matt Cooper? SAC Duncan mentioned your involvement in the smallpox investigation."

"That's why I'm here. Duncan asked me to run background interference because he has concerns about your safety. He has suspicions there might be a leak in your department."

"Damn. This isn't the first time." Mitchell thrust out a hand. "Special Agent Sarah Mitchell."

Bolan took her hand. As slim as it was against his own, he felt the firm grip.

Her handshake gave Bolan the opportunity to take a closer look at the woman. He noted she was tall, and had an athletic build. The eyes that studied *him* were bright, a shade of green and amber that instantly drew attention to her face, and alert. They were set in a face that could only be described as beautiful. She wore her dark hair cut chin-length. There was a determined air about her that told Bolan she was not a person likely to be intimidated. He gauged her age to be early thirties, and the way she had handled herself told him she was far from being a novice.

"Nice to meet you Agent Mitchell." He handed her Glock back. "I suggest we get out of here so we can discuss things in more secure surroundings."

They retreated, drawing away from the wall. Bolan led the way, Mitchell keeping up with his ground-eating stride.

"So how did you get here?" she asked. "Not by taxi seeing the way you're dressed."

"A private fast flight and rented wheels."

He offered no more of an explanation and Mitchell didn't query. This man plainly had good backup whoever he was.

Bolan guided her into the tree line to where his hired

SUV was concealed in the thicket. She looked over the vehicle and the camouflage Bolan had constructed.

"And you?" Bolan asked as they settled inside the vehicle.

"My partner brought me as close as was safe, then we parted company. Right now I have no idea where he is. For all I know he's somewhere putting his case to Duncan."

"Is that the way the FBI is running surveillance now?"

"Agent Brewster doesn't approve of my methods. Now I like him, but the guy is so anally retentive he lives and breathes the FBI manual. After a time it became a pain in the ass. SAC Duncan set us on the tracking of this group we believe is part of Hegre. We got his far but Brewster refused to carry out a close visual on them. Said he needed to get permission from Duncan before we did anything. We got to arguing in the car. I climbed out and told him to go get his permission and walked off into the forest."

"He didn't come after you? That doesn't seem like the best behavior for a partner."

There was a trace of suspicion in Bolan's voice that Mitchell failed to pick up.

"I guess I can be difficult to work alongside, Cooper. Duncan is always telling me to cool it." She waved her hand in a frustrated gesture. "What the hell, I'm supposed to be going after the bad guys, not checking the FBI workbook every five minutes."

"So what brought *you* here?" Bolan asked.

"Two missing agents who were part of my team. Then the news that one of them, Ray Talbot, had turned up dead. And Duncan calling me with the news that a delayed email from Talbot had a location. This location."

"Right now we backtrack to your vehicle. Go talk to your partner. Assess how things stand before we take any action. Agreed? Let's add your partner to the mix. It gives us one more body."

Mitchell hesitated but reluctantly nodded.

They retreated, Mitchell giving him directions to the Crown Victoria. Reaching it, they found the vehicle empty. There was no sign of Mitchell's partner.

Bolan's intuition was warning him of something not quite right in the situation. This whole setup with Mitchell and her reluctant partner did not gel. He decided to play along until he could work out just what was going on.

CHAPTER FIVE

"This whole thing was based on small leads," Mitchell said. "Enough to have us make a move. Our analysts have been working their way through names and contacts that have any link to Hegre. Duncan gave me a small team to follow up any leads we got. Hegre is smart. They cover their tracks well, and use local assets to do their dirty work so they can stay out of the spotlight. We got lucky and picked up a couple of very thin leads and started to track the links. One of the cell phones we picked up from the smallpox episode had a list of numbers on it. There were tracked calls to this location. Our people have been watching those numbers, and one of them recently showed activity. We pulled a message that gave a location and it showed up as the being a remote address. The one we just left. Confirmation came when the same location was provided by Ray. I hadn't had contact for a couple of days. That wasn't like Ray. The guy *always* kept in contact."

"So you decided there was a link."

Mitchell nodded. "Duncan said that Ray had been found dead near the town of Treebone. Brewster and I had been on the lookout for him. That delayed email Ray sent had the GPS location for this place. Brewster figured it was tenuous at best but as I am higher up the pay grade he went along until I decided to go take a closer look. That was when he dug in his heels and started to quote protocols.

Duncan gave me free rein, but Brewster wanted a directive. Now we have another missing agent."

"You wanted to find out if your missing guy was around?"

"I couldn't waste time. Ray was dead. Jake Bermann could be in danger. Waiting wasn't an option."

"I can't fault that, Agent Mitchell."

"Look, Cooper, I don't have time to debate this. If Brewster has gone to call in the troops we could be waiting for a couple of hours." She hesitated. "How long does it take to kill someone? For all I know Bermann could already be dead, but I'm damned if I can just wait around." She took a breath to calm herself. "What I can't figure is where Brewster is. The man is no Eagle Scout. Not the type to go wandering around in the woods."

Bolan understood her reasoning. He could accept rules of engagement. But he could also see it from Mitchell's viewpoint. If her teammate, Bermann, was in enemy hands his life expectancy could be counted in hours...maybe minutes. As she had also said the FBI agent might already be dead. It was an unenviable position to be in, and Bolan could sympathize with her predicament.

"What were you planning before I showed up?" he asked. "You looked about ready to go storming in on your own without any intel about how many you might be up against."

"I was hoping my partner might join me...*oh hell*...I know I didn't think it through. But I can't simply do nothing. And now Brewster is missing."

The haunted expression in her eyes made Bolan aware of the depth of her feeling. Sarah Mitchell was impulsive, but caring. Her need to locate one of her own had overridden her FBI protocols.

"We'll do this," he said, "but you follow my lead. No questions. Okay?"

Mitchell nodded.

"Where the hell is Brewster?" she asked again.

Bolan had been asking himself that question. There was still that faint but nagging suspicion tugging at him. The more he thought about it the stronger his suspicion became. Until he had proof one way or the other he would not voice his thoughts to Mitchell.

"We need to move back to the house. Check it out before we decide what to do."

Mitchell nodded again, said, "It's time I called in and found out what's happening." She searched in her jacket for her cell phone. "Damn, I left my cell in the car. I argued with Brewster and tossed it on the dash before I headed out. Losing my cool again…"

She got in the car and leaned forward to grab her cell phone, but it was not there.

"Let me do that," Bolan said. "My cell is on a higher security setting than yours anyway."

"You think mine could be compromised?"

"Think about it. If it's missing, who has it?"

Bolan took out his cell phone and called Stony Man, getting Aaron Kurtzman on the line.

"What can I do for you, big guy?"

"I need you to contact FBI SAC Drake Duncan. Ask him if he's had a call from Agent Brewster on Agent Sarah Mitchell's team asking for help."

"Something you're not happy about?"

"You could say that. I just need clarification."

"I'll call back ASAP. Anything else?"

"Any more intel on Hegre?"

"We're making some headway."

"Keep me posted."

"I'll let you know what Duncan says."

Mitchell was watching Bolan intently. "Well?"

Bolan lowered the cell phone. "My contact will get back to me when he has something."

"So what do we do in the meantime?"

"What we were going to do. Only now we watch our backs."

Mitchell leaned back in her seat, slowly shaking her head. The thoughts inside her head translated to the expression on her face. A particular thought had pushed its way to the surface.

"My God, you think Brewster has sold out. Right? Damn it, Cooper, you do."

"Let's say I have a doubt about him. A partner bugging out and allowing his teammate to go in alone. I may be wrong, and if I am I'll be the first to say sorry. We let my people make contact. And we handle things my way."

"*Brewster?* He's sold out."

"I only have a vague feeling at the moment. That's why I wanted to check it out. I could just as easily be wrong, so we hold our judgment until confirmation one way or the other. Let's say I have a suspicious nature. Reserve judgment until we have proof positive one way or the other."

Bolan walked a few steps and waited for Mitchell to join him.

"Cooper, I hope you're wrong," she said.

"So do I."

They retraced their way back to where Bolan had come up on Mitchell. A couple of minutes in and Bolan felt his cell vibrate in his pocket. He took it out and answered the call.

"Striker, Duncan has not had a call from Agent Brewster," Kurtzman said. "He's not a happy camper. What's going on out there?"

"Nothing good. But at least the picture's clearer. Thanks for the intel."

Bolan cut the call. He felt Mitchell's eyes on him.

"Brewster didn't call Duncan."

"Then you could be right about him," Mitchell said. "Looks like he had me fooled. Had us all fooled."

"Don't beat yourself up about it, Agent Mitchell."

"Hey, if he didn't call it in, what the hell *has* he been doing? Maybe he got taken himself. Have you thought about that, Cooper?"

"It crossed my mind. I won't dismiss it as a possibility."

Mitchell had the same hope. It didn't quite add up though. The more she recalled her last conversation with Brewster she had to admit his attitude had been evasive. She hadn't caught on because of her own eagerness to move on the location.

Bolan's keen instinct for situations had him checking their position as they walked. And that instinct alerted him to a shadow of movement to their right, within the overhanging bushes by the tree line.

They weren't alone.

The subdued gleam of metal reflecting light brought the Executioner full circle. The people out there were not showing themselves as being friendly. Bolan and Mitchell were being stalked.

A sudden acceleration in movement confirmed that notion. The figures were closing the circle, shortening the distance between them.

Not friends by any means.

Enemies.

"Down, Mitchell. *Now,*" he snapped, reaching out to give her a none-to-gentle push that took her off balance and to the ground. Bolan followed, sliding his Beretta 93-R from leather as he dropped, swiveling it to line up on the shooter who had emerged from the trees. Bolan heard the crackle of autofire, felt the hiss of slugs passing over his falling body. His finger stroked the 93-R's trigger and the Beretta fired a triburst. Bolan had gone for the chest, but his fast release, as he dropped to the ground, was off target.

The 9 mm slugs struck the shooter in the upper left shoulder, creating a significant wound as they hit bone, shattering it as they flattened and tearing at muscle and flesh. The guy stumbled, crying out in pain as his shoulder was mangled severely; losing a flap of torn flesh and spouting blood. He lost all interest in the battle as he went to his knees, letting go of his submachine gun, his attention focusing on the pain that engulfed him. Incapacitated, he was an open target for Bolan to make his follow-up shot. The soldier drilled a 3-round burst into the guy's head. This time Bolan's aim was on target. The dead man flopped over onto his back, his skull split and bloody.

Mitchell's tumble occupied her for the seconds it took her to hit the ground. She managed a clumsy recovery, her right hand automatically snatching at her holstered Glock, dragging it free. Her training kicked in. She threw out her left hand to take her weight as she pulled herself to one knee and focused on the area beyond where Cooper had been firing. She caught a fleeting glimpse of the first shooter falling and saw movement beyond that.

Two more gunners concentrated on their position. The closer man was hauling his weapon into the firing position.

She raised the Glock, two-fisted, and brought the muzzle on line, her finger easing the trigger back. She felt the reassuring kick as the pistol fired, repeating the gesture to launch a second slug. Both slugs hit center-mass, and the would-be shooter fell back, slamming to the ground. The moment she triggered the pair of shots, Mitchell pulled her Glock round to the second man, locked on him and fired another double tap.

Bolan had already resighted his 93-R and fired simultaneously. His slugs were a fraction behind Mitchell's and hit within a half-inch of hers. Struck by the lethal combination of 9 mm and .40-caliber slugs, the guy went down fast and hard.

"You hurt?" Bolan asked.

"Only my pride," Mitchell said. "Cooper, you picked up on those guys fast."

"I have a suspicious nature."

They fell into a team position, each checking opposite directions, tracking their weapons across the area. As they studied the area, they watched for further movement, easing into the cover provided by the trees.

"I hate to even think this," Mitchell said, "but Brewster could have been directing those shooters."

"There's only one way to find out," he said, and pulled her deeper into the foliage.

They were heading directly for the Hegre stronghold.

CHAPTER SIX

The bulk of the house spread before them, partly obscured by the overgrown network of trees and undergrowth. The access road was little more than a rutted track. Two vehicles were parked in front of the building. Bolan and Mitchell crouched against the perimeter wall.

"Not exactly a Realtor's dream property," Mitchell whispered.

"Ideal for these guys," Bolan said. "Out of sight, out of mind. It's somewhere they can carry out their work in safety."

"I'm not sure I like what you're suggesting. What work?"

Bolan checked his Beretta.

"No time for chitchat," he said. "We can't be sure we dealt with the whole of the search team back there. We need to go in now."

Bolan led them across the low wall. They skirted the bulk of the house and pressed against the side wall. A number of boarded windows were set in the wall. With Mitchell at his back, the soldier moved to the rear corner, crouching to peer around. Thirty feet from the back of the house were more trees and a heavy spread of undergrowth that almost reached the rear of the building.

They observed more closed-off windows on ground level and the upper floor; a derelict outhouse; a single wooden door that would allow access to the interior.

"Our way in," Bolan said quietly.

Mitchell tapped his shoulder in agreement.

"Stay sharp," Bolan said and moved to the door.

Mitchell checked back the way they had come. There was no movement but she was aware how quickly a situation could change.

"Clear," she said.

Bolan examined the door. Wood, the panels cracked and warped. Whatever paint had once coated it was long gone. He set himself, knowing that wooden barriers could be deceiving.

"No walking through walls?" Mitchell said. "I'm disappointed, Cooper."

Bolan set his distance and drew back his right leg, then launched a powerful kick that planted his boot over the lock. Wood splintered. The door flew open, crashing against the inside wall. Bolan went through, breaking to the right. Mitchell copied his move, going left. They both swept the empty room. Nothing save dust and scattered detritus.

Beyond the room they heard voices raised in anger.

"We disturbed someone," Mitchell said.

They crossed the room and went through the door on the far side, which revealed a wide passage with stairs to one side.

"Shooter," Mitchell yelled as a moving shape emerged from the shadows ahead.

A slim guy in shirtsleeves opened up with a squat SMG, a line of slugs punching into the wall to one side. He seemed to fire more for effect than to seek a definite target. Bolan turned and cut loose with the Beretta, catching the guy in the side. The shooter slammed against the far wall, clutching his side as blood began to soak his shirt. Bolan put a triburst in the gunner's skull. The guy sagged to his knees, then toppled over.

Mitchell caught sight of a second shooter, taking a side step to avoid his falling partner. She took advantage of the man's hesitation, leaning out from behind Bolan. She settled her aim without hesitation and punched a pair of .40-caliber slugs in the guy. Chest high, over the heart, the solid impact of the slugs knocked the target off his feet. He took an awkward fall, slamming to the floor on his face and rolling against the wall, his body in spasm just before he died.

A shadow materialized along the passage, weapon up and firing. The burst of autofire came close. Bolan held his ground, the enemy fire bypassing him as he raised the Beretta and triggered a burst. The distant figure staggered as slugs ripped into his body. He refused to go down until Mitchell fired a .40-caliber round through his throat. This time he dropped without a sound.

CHAPTER SEVEN

"Cover me," Bolan said as he dropped the exhausted magazine and rammed home a fresh one from his pouch. As he activated the 93-R, he felt the heat from Mitchell's close fired Glock as she took down a second gunner emerging from an open door. The .40-caliber slugs ripped into the target's chest. He dropped his weapon. They moved in unison, clearing the foot of the stairs and aiming for the door the shooters had come from.

Mitchell turned to check the stairs, scanning the shadowed landing. As Bolan cleared the doorway, he found a large room spread out in front of him. The large windows looked out on the front of the house and the pair of parked vehicles. Bolan took in the room at a glance and what he saw was imprinted on his vision like a vivid snapshot.

A half-naked figure was strapped to a wooden chair, the exposed chest and torso a mass of bloody wounds. Enough blood had been spilled to soak the man's pants to midthigh. His head was thrown back, his throat slashed wide and bloody. Bolan's gaze dropped to the bound man's bare feet. Most of the toes on the left foot were gone, leaving ragged and bloody stumps. The blood was dry, indicating that the man had been dead for some time.

Mitchell had remained at the entrance to the room, keeping a lookout for any interference. She took a quick look inside, saw the bound man and Bolan heard the shocked gasp when she recognized the victim.

"It's Jake Bermann."

"Mitchell, don't lose it. Not now," Bolan snapped.

Her face registered surprise as she looked beyond Bolan to the farthest reaches of the shadowed room. Her Glock arced to one side, finger closing on the trigger.

"Down," she yelled, stepping in through the doorway.

Bolan dropped to a crouch, turning.

A pistol fired, the shot going over Bolan's head.

Mitchell's Glock cracked twice, flame spouting in the shadowed room.

As Bolan came around, he saw an armed man jerk as Mitchell's .40-caliber slugs hit. The target cried out in pain as he fell back, the weapon clutched in his sagging right hand firing a shot into the floor. Light from the closest window set him in clear sight.

"It's Brewster," Mitchell said.

Bolan crossed the room in long strides, the 93-R trained solidly on the hunched-over figure. Brewster was on his knees, clutching his midsection. His Glock hung from his fingers, loose and presenting no threat. Bolan took it from the man, holstering his Beretta and holding the Glock.

Brewster, moaning, moved so he could sit awkwardly, still clutching himself. Blood soaked through his shirt in a continuous flood, turning his shirt and pants a glistening red.

"I'm calling this in," Mitchell said.

Bolan handed her his cell phone and she keyed in a number. Standing at the doorway, she stared at Brewster as she raised her phone.

"SAC Duncan, this is Agent Mitchell. We have located Agent Bermann, sir. He's dead. And we have Brewster. He tried to shoot us. It was Brewster who gave us up to Hegre. He's down. We have the situation under control. Yes, sir, Cooper is with me. We need backup at the location you gave me. You can send in the troops now. Yes, sir, we'll stand fast."

Bolan saw the spread of blood as it pooled under Brewster's slumped body. He grabbed cushions off armchairs pushed to one side of the room and laid Brewster down with one of the cushions under his head. The man stared up at Bolan. His face was sickly white and glistening with sweat.

"He's in a bad way," Bolan said over his shoulder.

"Good," Mitchell snapped back. "Don't expect any kind of help from me, Cooper. You see what they did to Jake?"

Her voice rose in anger. "You see what they did, Brewster. To one of your own. And Ray."

"What did they want from him?" Bolan asked.

"Information," Brewster said. "Hegre was concerned the FBI was getting too close and starting to unravel how it worked."

Blood trickled from Brewster's mouth, frothy and constant.

"You were helping them?"

Brewster nodded. Life was slipping away. His hands covering the bullet wounds in his body were wet with blood.

"They offered so much money," he said, his voice weakening. "A million. It seemed so easy at the time. I took it because I was greedy. No other word for it. I was living above my means, seeing all kinds of perps with money coming out of their pockets. I was risking my life for nothing while they had it all." Brewster began to cough up more blood. His face twisted in a spasm, then formed a crooked smile. "When Hegre made the offer, I just couldn't refuse. You know the funny part? I never got the chance to spend any of it."

"Where's the woman?" Bolan asked. "Delaware?"

Brewster's head moved from side to side. "Lise? She moves around. She's hard to pin down." He fixed his gaze on Bolan. "She wants you, Cooper. You killed Rackham, burned her with a bullet and wrecked their Korean deal. She *will* come after you."

"I'll try not to lose too much sleep over that."

Behind Bolan, Mitchell's Glock cracked once—twice.

"Incoming," she called, and Bolan moved to her side. He saw shooters moving along the hallway, weapons up.

Bolan snapped up the Glock and started to lay down offensive fire. As the Executioner drove the shooters back, Mitchell ejected her empty magazine, reloaded and brought her weapon back online. Together they covered the hallway with a powerful curtain of .40-caliber fire. Two men went down, one screaming wildly.

Retreat became the order of the day as the Hegre crew backed off. Bolan refused to let it end there and he tracked the hallway, sending more deadly fire at the enemy as they pulled away. When the Glock locked back empty, Bolan snatched the 93-R from its holster and continued to fire. The interior of the house echoed with the constant stream of gunshots. The last man in the group reached a door and kicked it open. Before he could clear the opening, Mitchell's Glock fired twice and the guy's head was hammered by a pair of .40-caliber slugs. They cored in through his skull and blew a portion of brains out through the bloody exit wound.

Mitchell slumped back against the wall, Glock sagging in her two-handed grip. The weapon had locked on empty, smoke still curling from the barrel. Bolan saw her shoulders moving as she trembled in the aftermath. He could see the rage seeping away, and he knew in her mind she would be seeing the image of her tortured, dead FBI teammates.

Ray Talbot.

Jake Bermann.

Mitchell would be taking on the blame because she felt a responsibility toward her team.

It wasn't enough they had found Bermann.

They had arrived too late.

Bolan watched her, seeing her expression and feeling for the FBI agent. There was not a thing he could do for her.

His thoughts turned to another female.

Lise Delaware.

The woman would seek revenge, would attempt to even a perceived score with Bolan. Somewhere along the line that need would be addressed.

CHAPTER EIGHT

"One way or another, Cooper, I'm getting to the bottom of this."

The determination in Mitchell's voice told Bolan all he needed to know. The FBI agent was not going to stop until she had the answers she wanted. She had good reasons.

Mitchell reloaded automatically as she voiced her thoughts.

"They don't do this and not pay."

Her partners had been killed because they had been betrayed.

And Mitchell's own tenacious nature would not allow her to ignore facts.

"The Bureau is in a good position to run some checks on Brewster's recent history," Bolan said, then added, "second thoughts. Go careful. Hegre appears to have deep contacts. It could be they might get wind of anyone looking too close at their business."

"Are you saying they might have someone else in the Bureau? That's crazy, Cooper. This is the FBI were talking about. Hegre doesn't own it."

"Agent Mitchell, I've been up against this group before. They had a pretty good reach last time around. I can't do anything to stop you from checking them out. Just be careful is all I'm saying."

Mitchell understood his concern. And as much as she even hated the thought there might be some other kind of leak within the FBI, her good sense cautioned against being careless.

She only had to remind herself what had happened to Joe Brewster. He had been a careful man, never one to even think about taking unnecessary risks. He was a stickler for obeying the rules. She had believed him to be an upstanding FBI agent who played by the book.

She had been wrong there. Brewster had stepped outside the circle and accepted Hegre's money. He had been turned. In Mitchell's eyes, if Brewster had been corrupted, it could happen to anyone.

Mitchell was at the room's front window, keeping watch, waiting for backup to arrive. Her initial anger when she had realized Brewster had betrayed them had ebbed, leaving behind a dull ache. It wasn't every day she had two friends die and witnessed another partner selling her out.

Glancing over her shoulder, she saw Cooper crouching over Brewster's prone figure, talking quietly to the wounded man. Cooper fought with the dedication of a professional, yet now he was speaking to the man who had tried to kill them with the compassion of a priest taking confession. In the brief time she had known the man, Cooper had shown her many facets of his character. She found herself drawn to him, fascinated by his powerful presence and the deadly skills he used so well.

"Game's over," Bolan said to Brewster. "You rolled the dice and ended up with snake-eyes. A low roll. Whichever way you look at it, you don't come out with any kind of winning hand."

"So this is where I open up and admit the error of my ways?"

"Hegre isn't going to come to the rescue."

"But you are? You'll offer me absolution if I confess before I die?"

"I'm no priest," Bolan said. "But I'm open to offers."

Brewster was bleeding from the mouth now, his breath ragged.

"If Mitchell was in your place right now, she would be pulling a trigger on me."

"She lost friends over this. You were one of them. Do the right thing and at least offer her something in payback." Bolan held the man's gaze. "Or don't. It makes no difference to me, Brewster. I'm tracking Hegre however long it takes."

Brewster's eyes rolled, and for a moment his stillness made Bolan imagine he was gone. Then he took a breath, his gaze focusing again.

"Hegre has a deal with some high-ranking Iranian group, brokering them uranium for their enrichment program. All illegal. It's coming out of Kazakhstan. And diamonds to finance it from Australia... Cooper, remember what I said about Delaware. She's crazy mad for what you did to their last big deal...losing the North Korean game cost Hegre a lot. Too much for them to ignore. Cooper, you're top of her Most Wanted list."

Brewster clutched at Bolan's sleeve as a spasm of pain coursed through him.

"Hegre has this deal all worked out. They plan to transport the diamonds to Hong Kong...pass on to an end buyer in Philippines...make a killing...that's all I overheard."

The effort pushed Brewster over the edge. When he fell silent this time, Bolan found his vital signs had flatlined. Pulse and respiration gone. He rose to his feet and turned away, catching Mitchell's gaze. He shook his head.

"Did he say anything?" she asked when he joined her.

"A lead. Maybe."

Bolan called Stony Man on his secure cell phone. Price answered and Bolan picked up on her concern.

"I'm fine," he said in answer to her question.

"You would say that if both your arms had been blown off."

"I can tell you they're both intact and in good working order. Now patch me through to Bear."

"Kurtzman here. Fire away," he said. Then added, "Sorry. In your circumstances that may have been an inappropriate remark."

"Make up for it by doing some hard checking. Anything and everything concerning Iran and uranium from Kazakhstan. And look into any intel on a diamond heist in Australia."

"Slightly bizarre combination but interesting. I guess you want the express response?"

"Don't I always?"

"I'll put the Boy Wonder on it. Nothing he likes better than a puzzle request."

Bolan knew the cyberteam would work its magic. If anyone could pull digital rabbits out of imaginary hats, Kurtzman's people would do it.

THE FBI DESCENDED within a couple of hours, a pair of Bureau helicopters swooping in and disgorging armed agents. They surrounded the house and swept the area. Mitchell went out to brief them. SAC Duncan had given the order she was still in charge. Bolan stood back and watched her direct the clean up operation. She handled it with confidence, and he could see why Duncan had so much faith in her abilities. The only moment she faltered was when Jake Bermann was removed from the house, even though the man was in a closed body bag. She showed no remorse at all when Brewster was taken out; she had made her stance known and refused to think any differently; Bolan could sympathize with her—Brewster had turned against everything the FBI stood for, had betrayed his fellow agents by accepting money from the very criminal organization the Bureau was fighting.

Duncan called, informing Bolan he was already inbound from Washington and would attend the scene ASAP. An FBI regional mobile-command center had shown up, establishing a base for the FBI teams working the scene, and once that was in motion Bolan and Mitchell stood down. She designated one of the agents to handle things while she took a break. Despite her professional attitude, Bolan could see she was under some stress though she was attempting to conceal the fact. He had one of the agents drive him to his vehicle and recover Mitchell's. They returned them to the crime scene. The area was a hive of activity as the Bureau teams processed the house and surrounding grounds. The FBI worked with practiced efficiency, the next couple of hours full of activity.

Bolan kept an eye on Mitchell. She was back directing operations, but a couple of times he noticed her standing alone and looking a little lost. The violent action of their encounter was most likely the worst incident of her Bureau career. High-intensity shooting matches were not an everyday occurrence in the FBI.

Bolan had a quiet word with one of the agents. The man saw Bolan's point and told him he would step in until Duncan showed up. The Executioner spoke to Mitchell. At first she refused to leave the site, but eventually she gave in to his persuasion. He drove them back along the highway to Treebone. Mitchell sat quietly beside him, gazing out the window and not saying much. Bolan parked up at a local diner, overrode her protests and made her go inside for a coffee and some downtime. She made a half-hearted objection but that didn't last long once she smelled the aroma of coffee.

Bolan had removed his tactical gear, stowing it in the rear of the SUV, pulling his leather jacket on over his black clothing and Mitchell had produced a plain wind breaker from her SUV so they at least *looked* like an ordinary couple in need of a break.

Bolan ordered coffee for them as they settled in an empty booth. He sat across from Mitchell and watched as she buried her head in the mug, savoring the hot brew. As she set the mug on the table and leaned back, Bolan could see the tension slip away. She glanced up at him, a tired smile on her lips.

"Yeah, okay, that coffee was just what I needed."

Bolan nodded. "Always take the doc's advice."

"So now you're a doctor. Anything else I need to know about you, Cooper?"

"All in good time," Bolan said.

Mitchell ran a finger across the rim of her coffee cup, knowing what she wanted to say, finding it hard to say. She had always followed Bureau lines, stayed within the parameters the FBI hammered into its agents. But right now she had to step beyond them because there was something going on that transcended normal policy. The recent events had made her lose some degree of faith in her profession. She admitted she was probably overreacting, but she was unable to push aside what Brewster had done. Bad enough he had worked against the FBI. The deaths of two of her team, men she had worked with and had trusted, had compounded that betrayal. It had made her see the world from a different angle.

Apart from SAC Duncan, the only man she could trust right now was Cooper.

Matt Cooper had already saved her life, kept her alive and had talked a lot of sense.

"This can't end here, Cooper. Hegre is still operating.

Still out of our reach. And I'm not so sure, right now, that the Bureau is capable of doing anything about that."

"The FBI makes its decisions based on the rules. I don't. I work my side of the street by acting on intel, sometimes hunches. Duncan believes I break every rule that exists. He's probably correct, but my approach gets the results I need."

"Cooper, you're just a Lone Ranger at heart."

"I forgot my mask today. Hey, I need to make a call," Bolan said. "If there's something to uncover, we'll find it."

"Should I close my eyes and look the other way? Hands my over ears while I sing *la-la-la?*"

"Only if you want some funny looks. Order some more coffee. Maybe something to eat. I'll be back."

Bolan slid out of the booth and walked to the door, retrieving his cell phone from his pocket. Mitchell watched him go, a thin smile on her lips. She caught the server's eye and beckoned to her.

"Two more coffees. What's the best thing on the menu?"

"Honey, the boss would tell you everything on the menu is the best. Take my advice and stick to steak, eggs and hash browns. Those he can cook."

"For two," Mitchell said. "And thanks for the advice."

BOLAN HAD KURTZMAN on his cell phone.

"Any results, Bear? You guys worked your magic yet?"

"Akira's trawling picked up on that Australian angle. There was a recent theft of diamonds from one of the mines in the Northern Territories. One hell of a haul. At a conservative estimate the cops figure the haul to be worth in excess of $80 million in uncut stones. Akira hacked into the police database and found out there was a hijacking on the highway between the mining area and Alice Springs. One of those Aussie road-trains was stopped on the road, the crew gunned down. The doors on one of the containers were blown open. Nothing on the manifest was taken.

"Then the local police at the mining company homed in on one of the employees taking off unannounced. He must have panicked when the cops started questioning employees. They picked him up on the highway, chased him and the guy lost control. He ended up in the local hospital with two broken legs, smashed ribs and a fractured shoulder. They found a stash of uncut diamonds in his luggage. His pay for the job. It seems he'd been contracted by Hegre to filter off diamonds from a number of batches between being lifted from the mine and weighed up. He was a production foreman and had a gambling and drinking problem. In debt up to his ears. Hegre paid him to arrange the thefts. He hid the cache in a metal toolbox and had it added to the road train cargo. All this came out in the hospital. The guy couldn't wait to confess once the cops confronted him with the evidence."

"How were the diamonds taken out of the country?"

"The guy came clean on that. Pretty slick operation. The heist team simply drove across country. Two thousand miles plus, to the coast and the diamonds were to be placed on a freighter out of Port Hedland on the Australian West coast."

"Any trace on where the cache was heading?"

"The guy didn't know that. Or the name of the ship."

"Damn."

"Don't give up so easily, Striker. I have more."

"You found the ship?"

"Don't sound so surprised, my friend. Our young master of the cyber universe ran checks on all the vessels that left Port Hedland in the timeline we had and has come up with the answer you will love."

Kurtzman explained how the tracking had been

achieved and Bolan chalked one up to Akira Tokaido, the youngest member of Kurtzman's cyberteam.

"Only three ships left the port in the timeframe we were looking at. Akira ran in-depth checks on them. Ownership. Destinations. Arrival dates. Two were quickly discounted. The third turned out to be the one we wanted. The *Echo Rose,* registered in Manila. She's had more owners than you can shake a stick at. The tramp of all tramp ships. She carries mixed cargoes of every shape and size all round the region. When Akira ran his check on who has her papers currently, he hit a spiderweb of fake titles and shaky companies. All covers for the real owner of the *Echo Rose.*"

"Hegre?"

"Very loose connection, but the buck does stop at the Hegre corporation. Akira logged into the ship's manifest. The *Echo Rose* was on a cargo run that would take her up through the Timor Sea, delivering cargo all the way up to Hong Kong and Kowloon."

"Ties in with what Brewster said before he died. Hong Kong and Kowloon."

"Brewster?"

"A bought agent. Joseph Brewster. We might be looking at other leaks."

"Other insiders?"

"Anything and everything, Aaron. We have names from last time around. Start to pull strands together."

"On it."

When Bolan went back inside, his food had just been delivered. He glanced at the enormous platter then across at Mitchell. She was enjoying her meal.

"Are we eating for the whole diner?"

Mitchell smiled. "A big guy like you needs his food."

"Let's hope we don't have to do any running for the next couple of days."

"So?" Mitchell asked.

Bolan knew what she was angling for. It was time to update her on his talk with Stony Man.

CHAPTER NINE

"Hegre is involved in a deal to supply uranium for the Iranians. I don't have the full details, but it looks likely the stuff came from Kazakhstan. Hegre will do the deal on behalf of the Iranian connection. Iran finds it difficult to buy uranium on the open market, especially since the nuclear deal it struck with the six world powers. Once Iran's name comes up, most countries back away. Hegre steps in and does the buy for them, shunts it around locations until they can finally ship it to Iran undercover. The stolen diamonds help Hegre raise plenty of cash for working the deal, and they'll get it back in triplicate once the client pays up." Bolan added, "Hegre lost a big load of cash when a North Korean deal went sour. The diamond heist will have helped boost their reserves."

"Not if we could take it away from them," Mitchell said.

Bolan did not fail to pick up on the *we*. The look on Mitchell's face told him that she was not joking. The FBI agent, already deep into the Hegre mythology, was as committed to the organization's downfall as Bolan. She had already proved her worth under fire and she had a sharp brain. Her unflinching attitude was well suited to Bolan's way of operating.

"Hong Kong isn't downtown U.S.A.," he pointed out.

"Don't you believe I can handle it?"

"I do. I'm not so sure China can."

Mitchell smiled across Bolan's shoulder as she spotted a familiar figure crossing the diner's parking lot.

"Here's someone else who probably feels the same," she said, watching as SAC Drake Duncan pushed open the door and stepped inside.

He spotted them and made his way to where they were sitting.

"Sir," Mitchell said.

"They told me you two had headed out for some peace and quiet," Duncan said, not unkindly.

"That was my idea," Bolan said.

"I'm not complaining." Duncan surveyed the meals they were eating. "Looks good. I haven't eaten all damn day."

Bolan waved the server over and ordered a meal for Duncan, adding a request for more coffee.

"Coffee would be good," Duncan said. "My head is still reeling after that flight from Washington. I got the go-ahead to get a flight courtesy of the Air Force. And I thought regular airlines moved fast."

Bolan ran through what they had learned about Hegre, the diamonds and the uranium. Duncan listened patiently.

His coffee arrived and he sipped it.

"Good," he said. He looked from Bolan, to Mitchell, his thoughts almost visible as he digested the information. "I am getting the feeling there's something unspoken, and I'm certain I'm not going be too happy about it."

To his credit SAC Duncan did not explode with righteous anger as Bolan brought him up-to-date. He remained silent as Bolan gave him the details of Stony Man's revelations, though he refrained from revealing his information source. The FBI man only glanced at Mitchell a couple of times as he absorbed what Bolan had to say, especially when the soldier asked for Mitchell to be allowed to accompany him on the mission.

Mitchell remained silent, for once holding back from making any kind of remarks, facetious or otherwise. She realized the big man was in her corner and his quiet stating of the facts got his request listened to and considered without there being any raised voices or impassioned pleading.

When Bolan had finished Duncan leaned back, catching the server's eye and asked for more coffee.

"I need this," he said when the coffee had been delivered. "Truth be told I could do with a splash of whisky in it."

"If we want to take advantage of this," Bolan said, "we need to move. A flight to Hong Kong should allow us to be there when that ship docks."

"To do what?"

"Ideally take that cache of diamonds away from Hegre, stop them from rebuilding their cash stores and try to get a line on where the uranium is."

"That all sounds damn fanciful to me."

"There's always Lise Delaware," Mitchell said quietly.

"I understand your need to settle this because of your dead teammates," Duncan said. "The FBI does not go in for personal vengeance, Agent Mitchell—Sarah."

Mitchell took a breath. "Sir, Hegre is the cause of those deaths. They need to take responsibility for them. In a court of law if possible. We're talking about a major criminal organization here. One that uses bribery of law enforcement officials and anyone they can get their hands on to protect their interests. Who murder at will."

"You make a good case," Duncan said. "You have the means to get to your destination, Cooper?"

Bolan nodded. "Yes."

Duncan shook his head. "I must be crazy to allow this. If it backfires, Sarah, we'll both be out of a job. If anyone asks, you're on special assignment, undercover and out of contact." He threw up his hands. "What the hell am I doing? Just get out of here, the pair of you, before I get all righteous and lock you both up."

MITCHELL DROVE WHILE Bolan contacted Hal Brognola, director of the Sensitive Operations Group, whose base was at Stony Man Farm.

"Are you sure about this?" Brognola asked after Bolan had laid out his next move.

"Hegre is leaving a trail of bodies while they wheel and deal. FBI agents, truckers in Australia, and there's the possibility of a deal with Iran for uranium. Hegre needs to be shut down, put out of business for good."

"I should know better than to even question what you're up to. Tell me what you need. Barb will arrange to have tickets ready for you at Seattle-Tacoma airport. We have your photo, and Aaron will access Mitchell's from the FBI database. I'll have passports couriered to you by first thing tomorrow morning and left at the hotel desk."

"Hotel?"

"We'll book you in for an overnight stay. Details on which hotel will follow."

"Have Andy Chen meet us at the airport in Hong Kong. We'll have to leave weapons behind. In the SUV. I'll leave the key at reception."

Chen was a contact Bolan had used before.

"Don't worry about that. I'll have a pickup arranged. Chen will be able to get you ordnance once you arrive and a satellite phone."

"Thanks."

"Keep in touch, Striker. You know how Hegre operates, so stay on your toes."

"I have good backup on this."

"And more at home."

"Watch yourselves."

"Good backup?" Mitchell said as Bolan ended the call. "Was that about me?"

"Do you always eavesdrop?"

Mitchell smiled. "Only if it matters."

"It matters."

"Then thanks."

"Keep your eyes peeled for a shopping mall," Bolan said.

"Why?"

"If we turn up at the airport dressed this way, someone is going to think it's a SWAT raid. We need clothes to fit the role of tourists."

They rolled into the parking area of a mall twenty minutes later. Mitchell led the way and they hit a couple of stores, using Bolan's Stony Man issued credit card to buy what they needed. A quick visit to restrooms and they emerged dressed in casual outfits more suited to the roles they were about to play. They would leave the soiled clothing in the SUV. The only item Bolan retained was his leather jacket.

Bolan had purchased a couple of lightweight carryalls for the change of clothing they had bought. He added a third bag for the weapons they would leave behind. Before they drove away from the mall they placed their weapons in the third bag, wrapped in the clothes they were abandoning. Bolan stowed the bag in the SUV's trunk, out of sight.

Minutes before they arrived at the airport Bolan's cell rang. It was Barbara Price, Stony Man's mission controller.

"A king guest room was booked for you at the Seattle Airport Marriott. The reservation was made for Mr. and Mrs. Hamilton. That's who you are on your new passports. You look like a nice couple."

"Thanks. I'll talk to you later."

"Your friends interest me," Mitchell said.

"Interesting is one way to describe them. Head for the Seattle Airport Marriott hotel. It appears we're booked in as a married couple. The Hamiltons. Passports should arrive before we fly out tomorrow at 11:00 a.m."

"Whoever you friends are they have good taste," Mitchell said as they reached the hotel.

She drove the SUV into the parking lot and they made their way inside the hotel.

Mitchell wandered around the large room, checking the facilities.

"Is this your usual standard?"

"No. Sometimes only get a single bed."

"Cooper, do you mind if I crash? The day's catching up on me. You know what I mean?"

"You go ahead."

Mitchell took a fast shower, wrapped herself in a bathrobe and climbed into the bed.

"Just wake me in time for breakfast," she murmured.

WHILE BOLAN AND Mitchell slept, a Stony Man courier arrived in Seattle at 6:35 a.m. He handed over the sealed package at the desk of the Marriott, picked up the keys for Bolan's SUV and drove out of the parking lot. He drove to a small private airport where he transferred to an aircraft for his return flight to Washington, taking with him the carryall containing the ordnance Bolan had left behind.

AT 8:00 A.M. Bolan picked up the package waiting at the hotel reception desk. It held the Stony Man–prepared passports for himself and Mitchell. They looked well used and were stamped with entry and exit visas from a number of countries.

When he showed the passports to Mitchell, over breakfast, she was impressed.

"I may keep this," she said. "It would be very handy if I want to take a quiet trip somewhere."

"What would SAC Duncan have to say about that?"

"That would be telling." Mitchell regarded him across the table. "And speaking about telling, what about you and the mysterious Lise Delaware? What do you have to tell me about her…?"

CHAPTER TEN

As they settled in their seats for the flight to Hong Kong, Mitchell leaned over and said, "I still don't have the low-down on Delawar"

"First time we met she tried to kill me. I screwed up a big deal for Hegre and grazed her arm with a bullet. From what I've learned she doesn't let it go when she's been bested."

"You must have gotten to her, Cooper."

"What can I say. And all *I* know is her name…"

WHEN LISE WAS fourteen years old, she came home from school and found her mother dead in the bathtub. The cold water was tinged pink from the blood that had streamed from her slashed wrists. It was later confirmed that Rose Delaware had also swallowed every pill in the house. It was a final act of desperation, brought on by the severe depression she suffered from. She had struggled with her condition for a number of years, fighting a slow, losing battle. Rose's ongoing condition had only been relieved by the presence of her daughter, and she fought against it every day. She kept her apartment clean and provided a loving environment for her daughter, Lise.

Things she kept from her daughter only came to light after her death. The thing that pushed her over the edge was the final chapter in the long-running battle with her husband. He had wanted a divorce. Rose had denied him that, but he continued to fight her and had finally gotten what he wanted by citing her unreasonable attitude and deliberate obstruction when he told her he wanted to re-marry. It had cost him a lot of money, but he was wealthy and the financial cost meant nothing to him. The divorce papers were found on the bathroom floor where Rose had dropped them.

The trauma of finding her dead mother affected Lise badly. She fell into an almost vegetative state and had to be hospitalized. She was given the best care available, a pri-vate room and around-the-clock care. Her father chose not to visit her. They had never been close. Work had always been his top priority. It took nearly six months before she began to come out of her shell and respond to attention.

Three weeks later a man came to the hospital. She vaguely recalled his face. He had visited her mother some years back. Lise remembered how he had been with her mother. He had offered to help, but for some reason her mother had turned him away. She couldn't understand why. Her mother refused to talk about it. Now on the day he vis-ited her, she sat and stared at him, still cloaked in despair at the loss of her mother. When he came back days later, he brought a woman with him. They spoke with the people in charge and later that same day she was removed from the hospital. There was a large car outside and Lise was placed inside, with the man on one side and the woman the other. They drove for what seemed a long time.

Lise watched through the car window until fatigue took over and she slept.

When she awakened, she was dressed in warm pajamas and tucked in a soft bed.

In the days and weeks that followed, Lise came to know the woman, who was with her most of the days. She brought new clothes. And food. The room she was in was large and bright, filled with good things. The woman—she found out her name was Claire—looked after her. Lise was taken from the room, down the wide staircase and through a door that led outside into a wide, attractive garden.

The house was where Lise would spend the next few years. In comfort and surrounded by people who cared for her and ensured she lacked for nothing. Not once did she inquire about her father. He was responsible for her mother's death. He was dead to her.

The house and grounds were spacious. There was a swimming pool and a wide patio. Claire and Lise spent many hours in the warm sunshine. There were a number of staff in the house who fetched and carried, doing anything Claire requested. Lise did not see the man for a few weeks. When she finally asked where he was, Claire simply told her he was away on business, but he would come to see her when he came back. Claire was her constant companion, and through her kindness and patience Lise was gradually drawn out of her solitary mood. Sometimes at night she would lie in her bed and think about her mother, trying to bring back the good times. Then her mother had been strong and beautiful. But the dark memories kept overshadowing the good times. Lise would lie and stare into the shadows, brooding. Thinking about the bad times, struggling to banish them. Gradually the memories faded, but never completely. They always hugged the deep corners of her mind. Lise learned to keep them buried because she didn't want to disappoint Claire, who devoted her time and patience to the girl.

When the man came back to the house, Lise learned his name was Julius Hegre. He spoke to her gently. Explained to her that her mother had been his sister, and he wanted to take care of Lise now.

When Lise asked why her mother had refused his help, he told her she had not approved of his business.

Hegre had smiled his distant smile and told her when she was older he would explain.

The explanation did not come for eight years.

Lise was twenty-two years old when he had explained the mystery behind his business affairs. Watching her face as she absorbed his words, Hegre saw not shock, but a spark of interest that only grew as he revealed his true occupation.

She began, from that day, to immerse herself in his business, always asking questions, wanting to know everything he could tell her. There was a confident spirit emerging and the revelation that his business was nowhere near lawful only intrigued her more. She was like a young child again, full of curiosity, eager to run before she could walk. Hegre could never tire at the bombardment as she badgered him with more and more questions.

Lise threw herself into the physical interests her lifestyle allowed her to pursue: horseback riding, swimming, a growing interest in shooting—using every kind of firearm she could get her hands on. She excelled at martial arts— her instructors were always having to rein her in as she pushed herself harder. She revealed a ruthless streak, and many of Hegre's hardened crew found themselves challenged when faced with her in the dojo. She was as hard on herself as she was any opponent.

Her companion had left by this time. There was nothing more she could do for the young woman who faced life with a confidence bordering on arrogance. The child had long since disappeared, and the full-grown woman had become a stranger to her tutor.

Lise's change revealed itself in a traumatic event that occurred one day when she returned from riding across the wide estate. She left her horse at the stable, then made her way through the stand of trees to the house. She entered through the kitchen, riding boots clicking on the tiled floor. From the kitchen she made her way down the wide hall, wondering why the house was so unusually quiet.

No one was about, which she found strange. There should have been at least a couple of Hegre's bodyguards in sight.

Lise sensed something wrong.

As she passed Julius Hegre's study, she heard voices. One belonged to Hegre. The other she didn't recognize.

She neared the closed doors and heard the unknown voice suddenly rise.

She hesitated for no longer than a couple of seconds before instinct took over. The situation was not right. She knew that for a fact, though she couldn't put her finger on why. All she sensed was Julius being in danger, and she had to do something about it.

The voices rose higher.

Accusations.

Anger.

Then there came the muffled sound of a shot from behind the doors.

She hit the closed double doors with her left shoulder. They flew open.

Julius was down on one knee, right hand clasped to his right side. The bright color of blood seeped through his fingers.

One of Julius's bodyguards was sprawled unconscious on the floor, a deep gash in the side of his head streaming blood.

Ten feet away was a man she recognized as Peter Karpov, a business rival of her uncle's. He held a large pistol in his left hand, a Desert Eagle, already bringing it back on target.

Karpov half turned as Lise crashed into the room, made

to twist the pistol in her direction. She didn't break stride, just kept moving, and Karpov had no chance to avoid her. She slammed into him bodily, the force of her forward motion knocking him off balance. As she struck him, she clamped both hands around his left wrist, twisting against the bone until it snapped. Karpov squealed at the burst of pain, And he felt himself going down. He slammed to the floor, the impact knocking the breath from his body, leaving him momentarily stunned. The pistol was jarred from his grip. It struck the floor, bouncing end over end, and Lise took a long stride toward it. She snatched it up.

The weapon settled on Karpov as he rose to his knees, gripping his broken wrist. He saw the black ring of the muzzle pointing at him. It was the last thing he ever saw.

Lise's finger squeezed back on the trigger.

The pistol bucked in her grasp as it fired. Before the shell case hit the floor she fired a second time.

The slugs slammed into Karpov's head, entering just above his left eye. They cored in, shattering bone and cleaving through his brain, before erupting in a bloody shower from the back of his skull. The impact threw Karpov off his knees and dropped him to the floor. He landed hard, the looseness of sudden death having removed any physical control. He sprawled on his back, half of his head missing.

Lise stood upright, the heavy pistol sagging toward the floor. Breathing deeply, she turned, her first impulse to check on Julius. She felt only concern for him. The fact she had just killed someone had no impact on her. There was no revulsion.

No regret.

Nor was there any kind of vicarious thrill. It had simply been something that had to be done.

"Are you all right?" she asked. Then gave an embarrassed smile. "Of course you are not all right. You have just been shot."

She moved to be closer to him. It was then she became aware of the pistol in her hand. The Israeli Desert Eagle was a .357 Magnum. It would become her personal weapon of choice from that day on. She stared at the pistol for a moment. Then she moved to place the weapon on Hegre's desk before she turned her full attention to him.

"Let's get you into a chair," she said.

Lise helped him into one of the leather armchairs. She stripped off her riding jacket, took off her white shirt, folded it and wadded it over Hegre's wound, pressing it tight. She slipped the jacket back on and buttoned it as she heard footsteps approaching along the corridor. Moments later Dominic Melchior, her uncle's lawyer and friend, stepped into the room. He was closely followed by a couple more of Julius's men. Melchior was unarmed, while the others carried handguns.

Melchior took in the scene quickly. He raised a hand to the men.

"Get on the phone. I want the doctor here ASAP to attend to Julius, a cleanup team to get rid of that mess on the floor and attention for Hendly. Do it now."

One of the bodyguards turned and quickly left the room, closing the doors behind him. The other man took up a position close to the door.

"He shot you, but you still got the drop on him?" Melchior said to Hegre.

Hegre shook his head slowly.

"No. Not me. It was Lise."

Melchior looked across at her. She returned his stare with unflinching steadiness.

"She tackled him. He dropped the gun and she picked it up and shot him," Hegre said.

Melchior looked from Lise to the bloody corpse on the floor. A spreading pool of blood had fanned out from beneath Karpov's shattered skull.

"It looks as if all those martial arts and shooting lessons are paying off," he stated.

"They will from now on," Lise replied. "I intend to be his personal bodyguard. Where he goes, I go. Argue with me, Dom, and I'll pick that gun back up and shoot you, too."

Hegre raised his head and looked at Melchior.

"I wouldn't argue with her, Dom."

Melchior nodded. "I believe you. And I believe *her*."

"Where were you all? Lise demanded, her voice taking on a hard tone.

"Karpov's people came in from the garden, taking us by surprise," Melchior said. "They had us under their guns before we could react. No excuses, Julius, they caught us off guard. Two of our people are dead. They shot them in front of us."

Lise glanced at Hegre. He had a pale sheen on his face.

"My fault," he said. "I should have read the signs earlier. Karpov has been threatening to move on us for months. I didn't believe he would do it in such a crude way."

"They shouldn't have been able to get so close," Lise snapped. "Things have become slack around here. Everyone has become complacent and let security slide. That won't happen again."

"I have to admit she is right, Julius," Melchior said.

Dominic Melchior had been with Hegre from day one. He was, apart from being the organization's lawyer, Hegre's consigliere, and the man who often acted as Hegre's conscience. Slim, gray-haired and always dressed impeccably, Melchior offered counsel to his friend, uttered the words that could calm Hegre and make him see the right path to choose. He had an uncanny insight into what went on in the minds of others. Hegre had an unshakable trust in Melchior's words of wisdom.

"Where are Karpov's men now?" Lise asked.

"Our backup team caught their man watching the approach to the estate," Melchior said. "They caught him, and he admitted our people were being held in the garage. They got the drop on Karpov's men. We dealt with them and headed back to the house. We heard the shots as we came inside."

"How many Karpov men are there?" Lise asked.

"Four," Melchior said.

Watching Lise, he saw the cold gleam in her eyes. Her expression was without a trace of emotion. She reached for the Desert Eagle and picked it up. She stared at Hegre for a time, then turned to where the bodyguard stood.

"All four of them," she said. "I want them buried with Karpov. See to it our people are taken care of properly."

The bodyguard glanced at Hegre.

"Do what she says," Hegre said. "Make it quick. Have the place cleaned up and get everything back to normal. Tell everyone from now on Miss Delaware speaks for me."

From that day on Lise Delaware became Hegre's near-constant companion. She proved more adept at the task than anyone previously. She took control of Hegre's security and within three months he had promoted her to his second in command.

At first there was resentment from within the ranks, but Lise commanded respect by proving that she was far better than any of them. In time she was accepted by them and Hegre himself, though he would never admit it openly. She was physically challenged by a member of the group who viewed her as merely a favored upstart. When he disrespected her in a room full of people, Lise put him down with two moves. The moaning guy was dragged away by two of Lise's personal team. He was never seen again.

The incident confirmed Lise's skill at her job. She was given more responsibility with the group, Hegre trusting her with more and more important tasks. He kept the fact to himself, never voicing that he felt safer than he had for some time. He had become aware of her true dedication, coupled with a natural affinity with the needs of the group. There was, as well, a standoffish trait to her character that suited her position in life, a detachment he put down to her early life with an uncaring father and a depressive mother. Lise had learned at an early age not to put much trust in others. She had developed a hardness to protect herself from the harshness of life. Not to become too dependent on those around her. It gave her an aura of aloofness that only Julius Hegre himself could penetrate. No matter what happened around her, Lise held Hegre in the highest regard.

Her true worth was demonstrated when she picked up on his unease over a deal being brokered through the Sicilian Union Corse. Hegre had expanded from the U.S.A. over a number of years, making deals in Europe and Asia where they offered assistance to other criminal groups, to the mutual benefit of all concerned. As always, the acquisition of additional wealth was one of the prime motivators in any business deal. The Sicilian criminal institution had entered into a deal with Hegre that involved money laundering on a large scale.

When the deal was almost complete Hegre's accountants had discovered that the local Union Corse group had been skimming money from the operation. When Hegre had asked for an accounting, the local head man had simply turned aside the challenge, accusing Hegre of being little more than foreign crooks trying to fleece the honorable Sicilian clan. It was an insult to Julius Hegre. In all his dealings, criminal though they may have been, he had never treated a business partner badly, had never cheated on a deal. Hegre felt strongly about his reputation, and the Union Corse insult hurt him.

Without any outward show of concern over the matter, Lise had begged off her responsibilities for a few days, and because of her tireless efforts over the past few years Hegre had granted her request. Lise had made sure a team of her best security people were assigned to stay at Hegre's side. Lise had used her authority to commandeer one of the group's aircraft and take a flight to France. Once there she had used her Hegre influence to recruit help and had traveled to Marseilles where the Union Corse chapter was based.

Two days after her arrival in the French city the two top Union Corse men were killed. Each man died from a shot to the head from a high-powered rifle: one on the street, the second while he stood at the window of his office overlooking the Marseilles waterfront.

The shooter was never identified, the weapon never found. The assassinations were put down to intergang rivalry. The French police ran an investigation that petered out quickly. The killing of local criminals was not an entirely original occurrence, and if the truth was known, the deaths were not going to cause many cops any loss of sleep.

The intergang scenario was true to a point, though it was in fact less rivalry and more a matter of honor.

Lise Delaware left France as quietly as she had arrived. On the flight back to the U.S. she slept comfortably, emerging from the plane refreshed and in no way affected by what she had done.

The killing of two Sicilian gangsters in France was not

big news in the States. It received some reporting in newspapers but not enough to garner much reaction.

Except from Julius Hegre.

He read of the incidents and quickly associated the location of the killings and the Union Corse with his own fallout with the crime association. That and Lise Delaware going AWOL for a few days made him come to a conclusion.

He had a quiet talk with Melchior and found the man was of the same mind.

"Let's face it, Julius, she decides something needs to be done and goes ahead and does it."

"But this?"

"Could be."

"Why?"

"For you, Julius. The young woman is your greatest admirer. Since day one she has had your back. Always. She treats any slight against you as personal."

"You really think so?"

Melchior nodded. "The Sicilians insulted you. That would stick at the back of her throat. So Lise made it right."

Hegre decided a large glass of whiskey was called for. He poured one for Melchior, and they sat quietly drinking and reviewing the situation.

"We both know she is devoted to you," Melchior explained. "That young woman will do anything you ask."

Hegre managed a smile. "And now it seems she will also do things on her own."

"I have been watching her, Julius, over the past few years. She is smart and understands more than she lets on. She realized what we do here long ago. She watches. She learns. She has total control of herself and of her abilities. Enough to make her a valuable asset."

"She is family," Hegre said. "The only family I have

left. But is it right that I should allow her to immerse herself in what we do?"

"That has already happened. There's nothing you can do about it. Except embrace what she can offer."

"And what is that?" Hegre asked, already knowing Melchior's answer.

His close friend simply told him in words Hegre would have used himself, confirming that Lise Delaware, of his blood, had already integrated herself into the family business. Given the opportunity, she would become even more a part of the group. It was a natural progression, a way of keeping control of the organization through family strength.

"She has found her calling, Julius. To be part of the group. You want my honest opinion? Embrace her. Bring her fully in. She will serve you well."

Hegre had to admit the feeling was growing on him. Bringing Lise into the fold would hold his dream together. It would fulfill a dream he had held close for a long time: that a blood member if the family would emerge as his eventual successor.

And now it appeared that heir had emerged.

Lise Delaware.

The next in line.

"One more thing, Julius. Keeping her at your side allows you to watch over her. If she is with you, that is a way of protecting her. Let her devote her energies to the organization. It is what she wants." Melchior saw the change in Hegre's expression. The softness in his voice when he spoke about Lise. Hegre was a hard man, with little time for sentiment, but his attitude had changed where the young woman was concerned. One of Melchior's talents was being able to judge people and the way they reacted.

"Do not underestimate her. Give her the chance and she will be the best."

Melchior's prediction bore fruit.

Lise Delaware proved her worth quickly. Without show, without any flamboyant displays, Hegre drew her deeper into the daily workings of the group, explaining the how and the why.

He instructed her in the various enterprises Hegre undertook, from straight criminal acts to the more complex financial deals that were far off the books. Lise had a sharp intellect and she quickly grasped the complexities of the myriad operations. Hegre gave her projects to manage, allowing her the opportunity, though always keeping an eye on what she was doing. She grasped the intricacies quickly.

One of her skills was her ability to interact with people. Her beauty drew the attention of male counterparts. They were lured by her quiet sensuality, and it was easy for her to draw out information they might be reluctant to impart to other men. Lise used her sexuality to its best advantage. It was a weapon none of Hegre's men could employ.

Lise, despite her growing responsibilities toward the group, never let her protectiveness where Hegre was concerned waver. She was always at his side when he moved outside the house. She drove him personally. She accompanied him to meetings. It became the norm. Others became used to seeing her beside him. Lise was always silent until Hegre asked her a question, and he valued her opinion, trusted her judgment.

Hegre's organization flourished. Whatever enterprise they went into, success became the watchword. It was almost too easy to make money. The world was in constant turmoil, so it followed that clients, new and old, wanted the professionalism Hegre offered. He had global contacts, people in many lofty positions. Hegre understood human nature, the vices that controlled people's emotions. He sourced those vices and used them to bring people under his control.

Manipulation went hand in hand with the corrupting lure of money. Hegre always paid well when he was seeking to control someone. It was, he realized, so easy to entice some people with the promise of money. A briefcase full of untraceable cash offered for a favor still had the power to turn an individual. That was proved on more than one occasion. It applied to all manner of individuals. Bribery covered the spectrum. Police, people in a position of power—they were all there for the taking. Businessmen, financiers, Hegre sought them out and used them.

CHAPTER ELEVEN

Julius Hegre prided himself on the professional attitude conveyed by his organization, the stream of successes that showed those he dealt with the level of skill he offered. The only black mark on Hegre's otherwise unblemished record was the recent failure to deliver the promised virus to the North Koreans. Interference from an American undercover agent, then further involvement by an unknown, persistent and highly dangerous individual had resulted in the entire venture being terminated. Hegre had lost good people, the North Koreans had suffered losses and the virus itself, which would have netted the organization a great deal of money, had been taken from them.

Lise, who had been overseeing the operation, had only just survived. In the final confrontation she had managed to escape at the last moment, losing the valuable virus consignment and suffering a minor bullet wound that had left a scar on one arm.

Months down the line, the memory of that confrontation stayed with her. It was her only failure. The scar on her arm, which she refused to have removed, was a reminder of that incident. She kept it as a way of recalling what had happened.

She also remembered the man who had given her that scar. *A tall, black-haired man with intense blue eyes.*

Although he had been taken captive by Hegre, drugged and put under pressure, he had escaped and lived to inflict casualties on the group. In the end he had destroyed the deal with the Koreans and wiped out the Hegre team.

After the event, when Hegre had regrouped, they had attempted to find out about the man. They had come up empty. The man, Cooper, appeared to be some kind of independent operative. He was skilled, uncompromising, and Lise was left with a grudging respect for his abilities—but also a hunger for retribution.

Hegre had its own anonymity, keeping a low profile that enabled it to stay one step ahead of anyone trying to get inside its setup. That took money, coercion and a continuing effort to stay below the radar.

Cooper seemed to operate under an independent cloak. Hegre was unable to tie him in with any of the known agencies, and it was this fact that both intrigued and angered Lise Delaware.

She used every resource available. Hegre had its own information sources, but none of that had any effect on the attempt to trace Cooper.

Lise disliked unresolved issues. The fact that she could not trace Cooper stayed with her. Hegre himself knew that until she brought the matter to an end she was going to let it fester. He advised her to let it go, but even as he did he knew she wouldn't. She could not. But she did not allow it to cloud her judgment on other matters and was able to set it aside when she was working on something.

There were the lucrative deals to be made, especially for the procurement and sale of military hardware. Much of this was done overseas, where Hegre had his foreign agents making deals. His reach was far and wide. It covered Europe, South America, Asia and Africa, which was proving to be extremely profitable at the present time. With various unstable regimes at each other's throats, having a regular supply of weapons on tap meant Hegre was seldom without a fresh contracts.

They were all markets open for someone with an eye for business. Julius Hegre was that man. He dealt with every business venture on a strictly confidential basis. Deals were done in behind closed doors, no different from legitimate business. Julius Hegre had high standards and expected anyone who dealt with him to have the same. He applied swift and non-negotiable penalties to anyone who broke contract demands. There were no exceptions. A deal with Hegre was similar to a blood bond. There was no margin for errors. No allowance for reneging. Punishment was always final. A mistake was never allowed to be repeated.

The high standards Hegre kept hurt him personally when the North Korean deal was blown wide open and the client had been denied what he had been paying so highly for. Hegre repaid every cent of the advanced fee and added a sizable amount to cover the North Korean's loss. It was the first time the Hegre organization had failed. Hegre himself accepted the defeat because he felt there was no profit in brooding over it. He simply put the matter behind him and concentrated on future business. The hardest part was the loss of a substantial amount of money after returning the North Korean cash and the goodwill payment. It had left a sizable hole in the Hegre coffers.

Hegre knew Lise had not fully accepted the defeat. For her, the loss of face became a personal thing. She covered it as much as she was able. Yet Hegre was able to see beyond her outer calm. Inside she was angrier than she had ever been. Occasionally her restraint crumbled and she would exhibit irritation toward anyone around her. She was a hard taskmaster at the best of times, but following the North Korea loss she became even harder to please.

The only people she held herself together for were Hegre himself and Dominic Melchior.

Second to Hegre, she had great respect for Melchior. She understood his position within the organization. He was intelligent, aware. Listened a great deal and gave out unfailing advice. Lise trusted him. For Lise he was the voice of wisdom, a sounding board for any doubts she might have. They often sat in the peaceful surroundings of his office with his tasteful decorations and the shelves of books. It was a quiet place where she could gather her thoughts and engage in conversations with her uncle's trusted adviser.

For his part Melchior enjoyed her company. He accepted that behind the youthful facade lay a strong-willed leader with a capacity for ruthless violence. It came with the territory. The Hegre organization was, and it had long become an accepted matter of fact, a criminal fraternity. It practiced criminality, ran a business that thrived on lawlessness. The money it made came from illegal practices, and on many occasions it indulged in murder and brutality. Melchior had taken that on board many years ago. It did not cause him any sleepless nights.

So the presence of this attractive young woman unafraid to use deadly force did not trouble him. She was as smart as she was beautiful. She exuded an aura of contained sexuality. She was capable of flirting, never overtly, but with a hint of a smile on her lips, as she worked her magic.

It intrigued Melchior. If, privately, he might have harbored a sense of attraction toward her, he kept that hidden. No matter his personal feelings, he would never reveal them. It would have been a betrayal of his loyalty toward Hegre, and Melchior would never consider risking that loyalty.

Instead he maintained his composure and acted as her

adviser, staying as close to her as he could and offering sage advice when she came to him.

They had many quiet sessions when Delaware expressed her feelings over various matters, and Melchior, in his unhurried manner would advise and suggest. With his skill as a lawyer and mediator, his way with words, he was always able to offer solutions to her problems. She, in turn, found him a willing listener, one who never judged her, but who always offered solutions to her questions. Their relationship was harmonious, always moving along the same lines and always providing satisfaction.

CHAPTER TWELVE

The flight touched down at Hong Kong International Airport. Bolan and Mitchell picked up their bags and made their way through the crowded terminal to the exit an hour later, after customs had played the delaying game.

"That was not fun," Mitchell said.

Bolan shrugged. He'd been through the same thing in too many airports around the globe to ever allow himself to become ruffled.

They emerged into the light of a warm day, letting the tide of people surge around them. Bolan was looking for their local contact. He spotted him quickly and they crossed to meet him.

Andy Chen nodded in recognition. He was a lean man with a worn, lined face. His black hair was worn close to his collar. He wore a light-colored suit and an open-necked white shirt.

Chen was a freelance, long-term intelligence man who had served in Hong Kong for a number of years. He operated for the U.S., monitoring what was going on and reporting to his control in Washington. Mack Bolan had met Chen a few years back and had been impressed by the man's quiet confidence.

"Mr. and Mrs. Hamilton, welcome to Hong Kong."

Chen was standing beside a meticulously maintained ten-year-old Mercedes sedan. The paintwork gleamed. He ran the car as his cover, providing a vehicle chauffeuring service. It had proved to be a handy way of overhearing conversations. He took Bolan's and Mitchell's luggage and placed it in the trunk, then opened a rear door for them to enter the car. Once behind the wheel, he eased the car away from the terminal and picked up the road that would take them to the North Lantau Highway and Kowloon.

"I have you booked into the Holiday Inn hotel on Nathan Road," Chen said by way of opening the conversation. "Very nice room."

"Before you launch into the guided tour," Bolan said, "what's the situation?"

Chen's face was creased by a wide grin at Bolan's segue.

"This man wastes little time on niceties," he said. "Always down to business."

"Really," Mitchell replied. "I hadn't noticed."

Chen laughed. "I think the lady knows you well enough, Cooper."

The car cruised along the highway, water glinting on either side of them as they approached Kowloon.

"Who are we liable to be up against?"

"Everyone calls him Mr. Lau. He's a powerful man, an old-fashioned trader. Anything for anything. He likes money. Lau has many friends and few enemies. Those he might have had are most likely dead. A word of caution— do not take him lightly. Mr. Lau would cut your throat in an instant."

"Has the name Hegre ever been mentioned?"

Chen hesitated before he answered. "Only once. I heard it spoken by one of Lau's men during a mah-jongg game. He was very angry even though he said the people were dangerous. Especially a woman who is very highly placed. He said she had made him look a fool over some trivial matter."

"Did he have a name for this woman?" Bolan asked

"Dela something," Chen said. "I don't recall if that was all of it. Lau's man was upset at the way he had been treated."

"He said no more?"

"Not in my presence," Chen said. "But a few days later his body was found floating in the harbor. I learned that his throat had been cut and his tongue removed."

"Bad," Mitchell said.

"A sign to warn others," Chen said. "Step over the line and this could happen to you." He looked closely at Bolan. "So you have had previous dealings with these people?"

"In a manner of speaking."

"Nothing pleasant then?"

"No. But right now I need to get a line on what Hegre is dealing with here. So who was this dead guy?"

"Thomas Lam, one of Lau's negotiators. He had contacts all across the region and traveled a great deal, here and abroad. I was his chauffeur whenever he was in town."

"And you were watching him?"

Chen nodded. "I kept an eye on him. As one of Lau's employees, he met a wide range of people. Persons of interest. And I had many of them ride in my car. Ran them all over town."

"Not all criminal types?" Mitchell asked.

"No. He mixed with all kinds. People who could open doors, offer protection for the right price." Chen spread his hands. "Money placed correctly can work wonders, and Lam always seemed to have plenty of it."

"Criminal organizations work that way. Spread the seed money to pull in the big payoff," Mitchell said.

"Is that in the Bureau's manual?" Bolan asked.

The question got him a thump on his shoulder.

"Mr. Chen, anything you can give us will be helpful," Mitchell said.

"From what I have picked up recently, Lam had been concentrating his efforts around the Golden Shark Cannery at the harbor. He was seen visiting there a number of times before his death."

"What do we know about the company?" Bolan asked.

"Visitors are not welcome. Contracts are given to local fishing boats for their catch. The cannery refrigerates fish and has its own fleet to move the product up and down the coast. That's handy for distributing other items."

"Contraband?" Bolan suggested.

"Suspected but never proved. Like I said, getting near the place is difficult."

Bolan didn't answer. When Chen glanced in the rearview mirror and saw the expression on the American's face, he knew something was about to happen. From past experience with the man, Chen could imagine the thoughts floating around in the his brain.

"Anything on the *Echo Rose?*"

"It is close," Chen said. "My friend in the shipping office will update me later."

Chen eventually drove them to the hotel, where they checked in, Chen playing the chauffer role to the hilt, carrying the luggage up to the room.

Mitchell sat on the edge of the king-size bed, a gentle smile on her face.

"Hey, partner, you prefer the left or right side?" she asked.

"You want me to step out while you make your domestic arrangements?" Chen asked.

"Only if you embarrass easily," Bolan said. "Chen, we need some hardware. We came in empty-handed. Can you fix that?"

"No problem. Tell me what you want and I'll get it."

Bolan made a quick list and handed it to the man. Chen

scanned it, smiling, then folded the note and slipped it into a pocket.

"It will take me a few hours to pull it all together. I'll bring it by later." He said goodbye and left the room.

"Do you mind if I take the first shower?" Mitchell said. "That was the longest flight I've been on in a few years. I need to unwind."

"Go ahead. I need to make a call."

Bolan placed a call to Stony Man via an established secure line and spoke to Hal Brognola.

"Hey, Striker, how's Hong Kong?"

"Bustling, as usual," Bolan said.

"Chen looking after you?"

"Yeah. Right now he's out hunting down merchandise for us."

Brognola didn't need elaboration on that remark. Bolan and Mitchell had gone into the zone without any kind of ordnance.

"You guys take care," Brognola said. "If any information comes up, I'll pass it along. To be honest, right now the team isn't getting very far on the Hegre front."

"Chen has given us a possible way in. We'll be taking a look later."

"Talking of *we,* how's Mitchell doing?"

"She's good. Doesn't have to prove anything to me."

"I'll pass that along to SAC Duncan. He's concerned."

"Tell him she'll be in line for promotion after this is over."

"He'll love that."

"I'll call you with an update."

Bolan used the room phone and called down for room service, asking for cold drinks to be delivered. The service proved to be faster than Bolan expected. The order arrived just as Mitchell, wrapped in a white bathrobe, emerged from the shower, toweling her hair dry. When she saw the drinks, she grinned approvingly.

"I could really get to like being in your company, Cooper."

Bolan poured her a glass of chilled orange juice, adding a touch of vodka and mixing it with the plastic stir stick.

"I hope this is appropriate for an FBI agent?" he asked, handing her the tall glass.

"The rule book doesn't apply in this part of the world," Mitchell said. She tasted the drink and nodded. "Just enough."

"Of which?"

"Why, orange juice, of course. The correct proportions for a federally approved alcoholic beverage."

"We wouldn't want to exceed the FBI limits," Bolan said. He drained his glass of juice and headed for the bathroom. "No sneaking a refill while I shower. We have things to do."

"Mr. Cooper, what kind of a girl do you think I am."

"That's something I still need to find out…"

CHEN HAD FULFILLED Bolan's request to the letter. He brought a carryall with him when he returned to the room a couple of hours later. He placed the bag on the table, unzipped it, then stepped back as Bolan examined its contents.

Chen had purchased a pair of Glock Model 22 pistols. Each weapon held a thirteen-round magazine. The bag also contained six loaded magazines, spring-clip belt holsters, two sheathed steel tanto combat knives, black combat-style shirts and trousers, as well as rubber-soled lace-up boots. The last item was a state-of-the-art sat phone.

"Is this going to be enough?" Chen asked.

Bolan was checking one of the Glocks. He dropped

the magazine and cleared the breech so he could work the action. He had already noted the pistol was clean, barely used. The action was smooth, the trigger pull easy. Mitchell was following his lead, checking her pistol. She nodded her approval to Chen.

"Nice piece," she said.

"It should be," Chen said. "Comes from a reliable source."

Bolan passed a set of the black clothing to Mitchell.

"Looks about your size."

Mitchell caught the bundle. "My color, too."

"My friend in the shipping office came through," Chen said. "The *Echo Rose* is due to dock this evening."

Chen waited in reception while Bolan and Mitchell changed clothes. In the bag were two long, lightweight overcoats they slipped on to cover the black outfits and their weapons.

It was almost dark when Chen drove them to the Kowloon docks. The parking lot that served the harbor area was barely half full. Chen pulled in between a pair of old shipping containers perched on thick railroad ties. He had told Bolan they were used to store equipment no longer in use. He reversed in so he would be able to exit quickly. In the distance they could hear the night sounds as fishing crews went about their business.

"Fishing boats don't start coming in until dawn, but there is always work going on preparing for the day's catches."

He had a layout of the harbor area on a rolled sheet of paper and spread it across the hood of the Mercedes.

"This is our position." His finger traced a route for Bolan and Mitchell. "Through this fence brings you into the Golden Shark's yard. The main building is here."

Bolan checked out the site. The cannery faced the harbor where fresh catches would be landed and taken directly inside the building.

"We are on thin ice here," Chen said. "Not a lot to go on. Do you believe it's worth going in on the information you have?"

"We're following a thin trail here, Andy," Bolan said. "We believe diamonds will be traded so that Hegre has the money to pay for the delivery of uranium stolen in Kazakhstan. Iran is looking to be the end buyer. If we can prevent the diamond deal and pick up more detail on the uranium trafficking, it might give us the chance to stop it."

Bolan let the rest of his words trail off, allowing Chen to make his own assessment. The man processed the statement, his face giving nothing away.

"The amount of processed uranium Iran would be able to produce goes way beyond what they'd need for conventional use. They seem to be in a desperate rush to get things moving, despite international diplomacy. The last thing we need is an escalation in tension, so stopping that uranium is a must."

"Okay, you sort of convinced me."

"Let's go take a look at this setup," Bolan said.

CHAPTER THIRTEEN

An hour passed and then they saw the *Echo Rose* enter the harbor. It was being guided by a tug and was approaching the jetty. Powerful lights were situated along the jetty, and they had a clear image of what was happening.

Bolan reached out and placed a hand against Mitchell's shoulder. To her credit the woman remained silent, her gaze following the finger pointing along the jetty.

They watched as the tug eased the ship into position, nosing the freighter against the hanging rubber tires that absorbed the slow momentum of the ship as it made contact. The docking maneuver was carried out with precision by whoever handled the tug. Once the freighter was in position, lines were thrown and hauled to the capstans at the fore and aft. The heavy pulse coming from the *Echo Rose*'s engines wound down as the power was reduced and finally cut. The tug powered itself away from the freighter and vanished across the harbor, leaving behind a white wake.

"That's what I call good timing," Mitchell whispered.

"Get comfortable. We could be in for a long wait."

"Just my luck. All the way to the exotic east and I end up on a backwater jetty staring at a rusty freighter."

"Think of it as an educational trip."

Mitchell muttered something unintelligible as she settled in for what might turn into a long wait. Surveillance was part of FBI procedure, watching and waiting for something to happen. Often the effort was fruitless, with the expected result failing to occur. Frustration could be the outcome after long hours of inactivity. It was tedious, but necessary. Mitchell would admit to disliking the process. It came with the job and she put up with it.

More lights had come on across the harbor. Reflections showed on the oily water. Bolan maintained his watch on the ship. A side hatch was opened level with the jetty, and a short gangway pushed out to make contact with the dock. The berthed ship moved gently with the swells of the water. From somewhere within the vessel music from a crackly radio floated on the air. Bilge water was ejected from the outlet pipes. The *Echo Rose* was at rest.

Half an hour later several members of the crew emerged, clattering across the gangway onto the dock. Gradually they drifted away from the ship, vanishing in the shadows. Over the next few minutes more men emerged and wandered along the jetty, heading for a few hours' relaxation. Figures moved about on the deck. Lights gleamed from portholes.

Bolan had just glanced at his watch. It was almost nine o'clock.

A stocky figure clad in denim jeans and a gray shirt stood in an open hatch, pausing to light a cigarette. He didn't seem in any hurry as he walked the gangway down to the jetty. He paused to adjust a bulky leather satchel hanging from his left shoulder. The guy walked slowly away from the ship, turning in the opposite direction to the one used by the rest of the crew members. He was making a failed attempt to appear casual. Bolan leaned forward, watching the man move along the jetty in the direction of the Golden Shark Cannery. He stopped to drop his half-smoked cigarette, grinding it out under the sole of his shoe.

"Mitchell," Bolan said softly.

"I see him. He's not a great actor. Top marks for appearing suspicious."

They watched the man reach the Judas gate set in the cannery's main door. He worked the latch, pulled the door and stepped inside.

"Let's go," Bolan said.

They discarded their overcoats.

Chen slipped out of sight without a word. It had been decided earlier that he would check out the rear of the cannery as a precaution.

Bolan and Mitchell eased away from their place of concealment and headed for the cannery, keeping tight to the front wall. Bolan had his Glock in his right hand. Close behind him Mitchell eased her own weapon out.

At the Judas gate Bolan gently raised the latch and eased the door open. He took a long, studied look inside and saw that the main area of the cannery building was in shadow. Machinery stood silent. Stacks of boxes and wire crates filled much of the space. He breathed in the strong odor of fish.

At the far end of the large building he saw a pool of light and picked up the sound of men talking, a mix of English and Cantonese.

"Let's get inside," he said.

He widened the gap so he and Mitchell could slip through. Bolan closed the access behind him and they stood for a moment while their vision adjusted to the gloom. They moved through the hulking machinery, closing the gap until they were within twenty feet of the seven men grouped around a long trestle table. The delivery guy was there, smoking again as he watched a man with a jeweler's loupe to his eye. The man was bent over the mass of diamonds that had been tipped out of the satchel, onto a spread of what looked like black velvet. The spread of uncut stones caught light from the overhead fluorescent tubes. Bolan had rarely seen such a large number of diamonds in one place and could understand how they were worth the $80 million Kurtzman had quoted.

The guy with the loupe said something to a man standing next to him. Of the seven three were Caucasian. The rest were East Asian and on guard duty. Three of them were armed with H&K MP-5s. The fourth, more finely dressed, man stood apart. *Lau?* Bolan wondered.

Mitchell was close to Bolan. He could hear her soft breathing, feel the press of her shoulder against his.

"When we go," he said quietly, "there won't be time for hesitation. Those shooters will try to take us the minute they see us."

"I get the message," Mitchell said. "Shooters first…"

Raised voices speaking Cantonese came from the far end of the cannery. The shouts grew closer. Louder.

Something warned Bolan this interruption was not going to be good. He held Mitchell back.

Figures stepped into the pool of light around the trestle table holding the diamonds.

Two armed men pushing a third man in front of them. He had his hands bound in front of him as he stumbled forward, his head down until one of his captors reached out to take a handful of hair and jerk it back.

He had been beaten hard. His face was bloody and badly swollen. Blood had spilled down his white shirt and the jacket of his suit. Bolan recognized him instantly. It was Andy Chen.

"What the fuck is going on, Lau?" one of the Caucasian men asked in an American accent. "What gives?" This must be the Hegre group, Bolan realized.

"We found this man sneaking around the back of the

building, Kendrick," one of Chen's captors said. He spoke in English for the benefit of the American.

"You know who he is?" Kendrick asked.

"Chen is an undercover agent," another of Lau's men said in English. "He works for your damn people. Maybe CIA. He buys and sells information. We were told about him by one of our informants. He met two people off a flight from the U.S., a man and a woman."

"Son of a bitch. Could be that Cooper guy and the FBI chick."

"Who is this man?" Lau asked. "This Cooper?"

"Someone our principle would love to get her hands on, Mr. Lau," responded Kendrick.

"What is so special about him?" Lau asked.

"Jesus, how long have you got?"

While the discussion went on, the man with the jeweler's loupe continued his inspection.

Kendrick's partner turned to face Chen. He considered his next move, glancing at Kendrick, who made a brief nod. Then the first man reached behind him in a fluid motion that looked as if it had been carefully rehearsed. He drew a black handgun and raised it without pause.

"Cooper, he's going…"

Bolan had already recognized the signs. He tracked with the Glock and triggered three rounds, placing the .40-caliber slugs in the would-be shooter's chest. The guy went over backward, a shocked expression on his lean face. He dropped to the floor, his finger pulling back on his weapon's trigger and sending a slug into the shoulder of one of Chen's captors.

The building echoed with the sound of gunfire, the muzzle-flashes lighting the shadows.

Mitchell had broken her motionless stance, aiming and firing her Glock in a series of steady shots. She put down two of Lau's men before the group broke apart and scattered.

Andy Chen dropped to the floor, below the gunfire, his hand reaching out to grasp the gun dropped by his attacker. He raised himself to his knees, swinging the pistol around to make a shot. He was a fraction of a second too slow as Lau drew a pistol and shot him through the back of the skull.

Bolan had seen the move and two-handed the Glock, placing three rounds into Lau's head, knocking him off his feet as blood and brains erupted from the shattered skull.

The group had broken apart, moving clear of their original position to circle Bolan and Mitchell. Only Kendrick remained close to the guy inspecting the diamonds. He said something to the jeweler. The man began to scoop up the gems and return them to the leather satchel.

"How do we get out of this, Cooper?" Mitchell asked.

It was a fair question, and Bolan didn't have a ready answer. They were facing a superior force. He had underestimated the opposition's number.

Kendrick spoke up.

"Put the guns down, Cooper. You and the FBI chick can't shoot your way out of this. I'll give you a chance to stay alive. At least until I deliver you to Delaware. It's a onetime offer. Figure the odds. Die now—or later."

Bolan understood the implication behind the guy's offer. He was about to take Bolan and Mitchell for a face-to-face with Lise Delaware. She wanted to meet Bolan before she dealt with him, and Bolan had a score to settle for her previous crimes and the current murders of Mitchell's teammates. And it also might grant him and Mitchell a chance to escape Hegre.

"Not much of a choice," Mitchell murmured.

"It'll get us a reprieve, and give us a chance at freedom."

"Play his game but don't sit back and give in?"

Bolan nodded.

"I'm in your hands," Mitchell said.

The Executioner could see Lau's gunmen converging on their position. He was no quitter. He was also no gung-ho cowboy prepared to take the fight to a superior force and die in a blaze of reckless glory. Dead meant the end of everything. Mack Bolan had too much to live for to allow that to happen right now. And he had Mitchell to consider. He had brought her into this situation and was responsible for her.

"Okay," he said.

He reversed his Glock, raising his arm to show the weapon. Mitchell followed suit and they were encircled by the armed men. Their weapons were removed, as were their cell phones. Their unsmiling captors pushed them across the floor to where Kendrick waited.

"Smart move, pal," he said. "Delaware really wants you alive."

"We wouldn't want to disappoint the lady," Bolan stated.

"When I bring you in, there'll be a bonus for me," the man said. "What the hell, Cooper, we all have to earn a living."

"This is a living?" Mitchell asked, contempt in her voice.

"They want you alive," the guy said, "but I don't think Delaware will be concerned if you're bruised in transit."

"Don't give him the satisfaction," Bolan cautioned her.

"Listen to the man, FBI. You'll stay on your feet longer." The filled satchel was passed to him. He draped it from one shoulder. "Traveling money," he said.

"Take it," Bolan said. "You could live in style with it."

"You think Delaware would let that happen? That woman would follow me to hell if I took off with her diamonds."

"Kendrick, we need to clean up here," one of Lau's men said. "We need to get these bodies moved. Time for you to leave."

Bolan and Mitchell had their pockets checked, their passports removed.

Kendrick nodded. "The plane should be ready by now." He looked across at Bolan and Mitchell. He dropped the passports and their weapons into a carry bag. "Hey, you won't need your passports for this trip. And it's all expenses paid."

CHAPTER FOURTEEN

Two of Lau's men prodded Bolan and Mitchell to move, following the two Hegre men through to the rear of the cannery. They left through a roller door. A dark colored SUV was parked next to a loading ramp, a driver already behind the wheel. Before they were forced to climb in, Bolan and Mitchell had their hands bound behind their backs with duct tape. They slid onto the wide rear seat, Kendrick watching, his right hand gripping a SIG-Sauer pistol. Kendrick's partner, Hatch, joined them, his own pistol in his hand

Kendrick had a few final words with one of Lau's men, then climbed into the passenger front seat, swiveling to cover Bolan and Mitchell.

"Delaware might want you alive and kicking," he said. "But give me any grief and I *will* shoot you dead." He patted the heavy satchel. "This is priority."

The SUV rolled smoothly across the cannery's freight yard, through a gate and onto a dark strip of road. The industrial area fell behind them as they were driven through a sparsely populated region, moving along the coastal road. The SUV's suspension had a hard time maintaining a smooth run as it bumped and rocked across the uneven road.

"Not exactly the Pacific Coast Highway," Kendrick commented. He grinned. "It'll be smoother when we get airborne."

"To where?" Bolan asked.

"Not home turf," Kendrick said. "Isn't that right, Hatch?"

The guy nodded. "Not home turf."

Mitchell made a soft sound that only Bolan picked up. It was obvious she was far from impressed by the company she and Bolan were being forced to endure.

They drove for almost two hours before the SUV turned off at a basic airstrip. Moonlight showed them a wooden cabin and a wind sock drooping on a pole. A battered panel truck was parked beside the hut, and a two men were lounging on chairs beside the hut's door. They watched the SUV arrive and park next to the hut.

A rough landing strip ran the length of the field, and a Douglas DC3 Dakota sat at one end of the strip, its engines idling. A rusting fuel bowser was just pulling away from the DC3 as the SUV arrived.

The DC3 was old and bore no markings except for the numbers painted on the rear. The scraped and gouged fuselage had long ago lost any other identification markings. Even the tires of the landing gear were worn almost smooth.

"Is this the best Hegre can afford?" Mitchell asked.

Kendrick gave a short laugh. "This plane is so well known in the area nobody pays attention to it. You'd be surprised at the cargo it's carried."

"What's the inflight movie today?" Bolan asked as he climbed out of the SUV.

"If there is one," Mitchell said, "it'll have to be a silent classic. I can't believe we're going to fly in that thing."

The aircraft's Pratt & Whitney engines sounded smooth and even, despite the overall age of the venerable aircraft. It was a tribute to the design and build of the plane that it was still airworthy.

Kendrick pushed the muzzle of his pistol against Bolan's spine. "Let's move, hotshot, time to say goodbye to China. You made a long trip for nothing."

They made their way across the grass, Hatch falling in beside Mitchell. The side door was open, with a short aluminum ladder propped in place. Hatch climbed in first, covering Bolan and Mitchell as they joined him. Kendrick followed, hauling up the ladder and closing the door.

The interior was empty, illuminated by faint lights. It was clear the plane was not used for passengers. At the front of the fuselage Bolan saw the cockpit section, visible through the open hatch.

"You two get yourselves settled," Kendrick said. "Hatch, keep your eyes on them."

As Bolan and Mitchell sat with their backs to the fuselage, Hatch sat down across the deck from them. Kendrick ducked through the hatch and entered the cockpit. Bolan could hear him speaking to the pilot. Kendrick sat in the empty copilot seat.

The engines began to build up, the roar penetrating the aircraft. They felt the slight jerk as the DC3 began to move over the rough strip. Vibrations rippled along the aircraft as it picked up speed.

Hatch turned to stare out one of the side windows, watching the dark landscape slide by.

Mitchell glanced across at Bolan. He shook his head, a subtle motion that told her not to make any sudden moves. Having to remain still was frustrating. She complied with her partner's signal. She knew he wouldn't be prepared to simply quit and take whatever their captors had planned. As short as their acquaintance had been, she knew enough about the man to accept that he was going to react.

How or when she didn't know.

She just knew he would do *something* when the opportunity presented itself.

The DC3 lifted off the ground, climbing steadily, the sound of the engines smoothing out as it reached cruising height and settled on course. Clouds could be seen below them.

Kendrick reappeared. He moved along the body of the plane, pausing to slide the heavy satchel from his shoulder and place it on the deck. He dropped the bag holding Bolan and Mitchell's belongings next to the diamonds.

"Likely the most expensive cargo this crate has ever carried."

"Not my idea of fun," Hatch said. "Playing nursemaid to a bag of stones."

"Tell me, Hatch—have you ever been happy?"

Hatch scowled. "Go to hell."

His reaction only made Kendrick smile. Turning to Bolan he said, "Just about four hours and we'll be in the Philippines. Make yourself comfortable, Cooper. This could be your last ride."

He turned and stepped back through to the cockpit area, dropping into the empty copilot seat.

Hatch made a play of exhibiting his SMG. "I should shoot you now. Save everybody the trouble. You killed my buddy Rafer."

Bolan stayed silent. There was no point antagonizing the man. The time to act would be when they were over land. Not the South China Sea.

The moment Hatch turned to stare out the window again Bolan caught Mitchell's attention.

"Later," he mouthed. "When we hit land."

Bolan's mind had been working the permutations. Waiting until the plane touched down might have seemed the best opportunity, but on the negative side was the chance that Kendrick could have a strong force waiting for his arrival. Enough armed men to ensure that Bolan would have no opening to make a move. The alternative was for Bolan to attempt a takeover while the DC3 was still in the air. It had the promise of success. There were only three men to deal with and one of those was the pilot, which took him more or less out of the frame.

In the end Bolan had to take a calculated risk. He understood that. Since the beginning of his first campaign, risk had been factored into most every move he made. It came with the territory. And he was once again in the arena.

Flight time dragged. Compared to modern aircraft the DC3 moved slowly. At twelve thousand feet it was making approximately 230 miles per hour. An almost leisurely pace. The drone of the twin engines could be heard as the props pulled the machine on toward the Philippine Islands.

Hatch lost his concentration. The hard-eyed stare glazed over and he had to keep shaking himself out of his lethargic state.

Bolan kept a close watch on the man. He understood the position he was in. Before he could take any action he needed his hands free.

With his back against the inner curve of the aircraft fuselage, he had located one of the strengthening struts. They were flying in a cargo version of the plane, not an upholstered passenger aircraft. The strut had an exposed edge. Not razor sharp, but rough enough to provide a surface capable of tugging at the duct tape as Bolan sawed his binding against it. It was slow work. The soldier had to keep his movements measured, so that Hatch wasn't alerted. The guy was less than fully alert, but any undue movement coming from Bolan might grab his attention.

After an hour of careful, minuscule movements, Bolan felt the tape give a little. He put on pressure to weaken it, then returned to his patient sawing motion. He had also managed to scrape his left wrist against the metal edge and he could feel blood running down across his fingers.

The faint movement of his shoulders had alerted Mitchell to his attempt to free himself. She remained still, but her eyes were alternating between Bolan and Hatch.

"Hey, Hatch, you still with us?" Kendrick called from the cockpit.

Hatch's eyes snapped open and he stared across at Bolan and Mitchell.

"Yeah, we're having a ball back here." He gazed at Mitchell with undisguised lust in his eyes. "If it was just me and the woman, I'd really be having a high old time."

"You just concentrate on keeping them nice and peaceful. Only thing in your hand should be your gun."

Pale dawn light was showing as the frayed tape loosened a fraction more. Bolan increased his sawing action. He spread his wrists at the same time. The binding gave suddenly, and he pulled his wrists free. He nodded at Mitchell.

Hatch suddenly pushed upright, turning his head to check the captives. Bolan froze, simply maintaining eye contact with the man.

"I don't think this guy likes me," Hatch said, directing his comment to Kendrick. He grinned. "Jesus, he'd burn me if he had X-ray eyes."

"Quit moaning. We'll be landing soon."

Hatch turned and swayed as he made his way toward Bolan, stepping over Mitchell's prone figure.

"If I hadn't been told to deliver you alive..." he said. Then he added, "By the time the bitch queen gets done, you'll wish I'd put a bullet between your eyes."

He laughed.

Bolan flexed his hands, feeling the blood circulate now

that the tape was gone. He watched Hatch, awaiting his chance, never once forgetting the MP-5 the man carried. He was also aware of the man's restless nature. Hatch was pacing back and forth, continuously leaning forward to stare out through the plane's windows—Bolan made a guess that Hatch was not a good flyer. His thought was confirmed when the aircraft made a slight lurch to one side, riding an air pocket. Hatch threw out a hand to press it against the fuselage, muttering to himself.

As the plane tilted, Bolan caught a glimpse of greenery far below, a fragment of lush forest. It showed for a couple seconds before the aircraft righted itself and settled into steady flight again.

Bolan saw his chance coming up. When Hatch stared out of the window again, Bolan glanced at Mitchell. She gave him an acknowledgment.

"Hatch," Bolan said. "You want to check my wrists? I can't feel a damn thing."

The man swung around, looking down at the seated figure. He stepped across the deck and stood over Bolan.

"What am I, your fucking nurse?"

Behind him Mitchell drew her legs back. She swung them forward, slamming against the back of Hatch's knees. The guard's legs caved, buckling and knocking him partially off balance.

Bolan stood upright, freed arms swinging wide. He threw a full-on right punch that smashed into Hatch's face, crushing his nose, following with a left that hammered against the man's exposed jaw. Blood streamed from Hatch's nose. He gave a startled squeal, tears streaming from his eyes. Bolan launched himself at Hatch, slamming him back against the bulkhead, pinning the MP-5 against the man's chest.

Hatch had a powerful physique and the strength to go

with it. He pushed back against Bolan's attack, breath gusting from his mouth as he tried to force Bolan away. The Executioner resisted, aware that he needed to take Hatch down fast. The noise they were making would attract Kendrick, and once that happened Bolan's advantage would evaporate. He swept his left arm around in a powerful elbow smash that connected with Hatch's cheek. The blow stunned the man, and for a moment his resistance weakened.

He recovered quickly, slamming a heavy knee against Bolan's hip, the force of the blow pushing the soldier to one side, giving Hatch the chance to bring his SMG into play, finger curling against the trigger. Realizing Hatch's intention, Bolan stepped back, then swung his booted foot up in a roundhouse kick. The boot connected with Hatch's weapon, knocking it off target. Hatch's trigger pull continued, and as the MP-5 completed its swing the weapon discharged a long burst. The stream of 9 mm slugs ripped through the fuselage and stitched a ragged line across the port wing before tearing through the engine nacelle.

Within seconds the punctured holes were emitting streams of black oil from punctured lines. The oil feathered back along the curved engine cover, the volume increasing as the ruptured pipes split under the impact of misshapen bullets.

The crackle of autofire brought Kendrick out of his copilot's seat, snatching his pistol free on the move. He burst through the cockpit opening, his eyes fixed on the struggling Bolan and Hatch. He failed to notice Mitchell on her feet. As he appeared, she launched a powerful roundhouse kick that caught him low in the stomach. Kendrick doubled over and Mitchell brought her knee up, catching him in the side of the head. Kendrick fell against the bulkhead and Mitchell closed in, despite the disadvantage of having her hands secured behind her.

Kendrick swung his gun arm around in a defensive move, the pistol catching Mitchell across the cheek. The force of the blow toppled her to her knees, Kendrick bringing his pistol round to fire. Bolan had taken a double-handed grip on Hatch's weapon, tearing it from the man's hands, and he twisted around as Kendrick leveled his weapon on Mitchell. If he had thought about it, Bolan might have held back from firing the autoweapon within the confines of the plane, but his overriding concern was to stop Kendrick from firing. Bolan squeezed back on the trigger and felt the MP-5 vibrate as it unleashed a stream of 9 mm slugs. The range was close. Kendrick was kicked back as the slugs tore into and through his body. The tail end of Bolan's burst smashed into the plane's instrument panel.

Kendrick fell back inside the cockpit, slamming hard to the deck, and as he landed with his arms thrown over his head, the pistol in his hand fired off a single shot.

The wayward slug hammered into the back of the pilot's head, taking away a chunk of bone and emerged out the top of the man's skull. The pilot arched his body, toppling forward. His weight slammed against the controls and the plane fell into a steep dive.

Bolan went backward as the deck canted underfoot. He saw Hatch, blood streaming down his face, reaching for the pistol jammed behind his belt. As the bulkhead brought his backward tumble to a stop, Bolan swept the MP-5 around and hit Hatch with a ragged burst. Hatch screamed as the slugs cored into his body. He twisted half around and went down.

Bolan dropped the MP-5 and turned, stepping over Kendrick's bloody corpse and dragged himself into the copilot's seat. Once again he was grateful for the lessons Jack Grimaldi gave him when they had some downtime, but he had never practiced coming out of a death dive. He leaned across and hauled the dead pilot away from the controls. He slid onto the seat. With the pilot's weight clear of the controls Bolan was able to grasp the yoke on his side of the cockpit.

The downward spiral of the aircraft threatened to resist Bolan's attempts to regain control. He could feel the pressure and ignored the urge to quit. The aircraft seemed determined to continue its dive. Bolan maintained his grip on the yoke and gradually the nose began to lift. As the aircraft pulled out of the dive, he brought it back onto an even course and felt the flight level out. The howl of the engines subsided.

Behind Bolan, where she was leaning against the back of the seat, Mitchell said, "That's something I could have done without." She looked out the port cockpit window at the damaged engine. The oil spillage had become a ragged stream of black smoke. "And that doesn't look too promising."

Bolan checked out the smoke. He could hear the ragged beat of the damaged engine.

"Cooper, tell me you can handle this."

"I don't get the chance to fly very often. Especially not in one of these babies."

"Hey, don't spoil the illusion by telling me that. I take it you can land this thing."

"What if I tell you no, I can't?"

"Do not even go there, Cooper. My quota for so many surprises in a day is running close to the line."

"The day isn't over yet.

"Great. What else can go wrong?

"We could run out of fuel."

"Being on a date with you is such a blast."

Mitchell edged around so Bolan could work the tape free from her wrists. She rubbed the chafed flesh, watching the increasingly thick smoke streaming from the engine. Blood had run down the side of her face from the where Kendrick had hit her.

With the port power reducing, Bolan was having to compensate for the way the DC3 was trying to veer off course.

"Go check in the back. Pick up our belongings. And check for any parachutes."

Mitchell gave him a questioning look that told him that suggestion was something she did not want to hear, then left the cockpit.

Bolan took a look out the front and side windows. He was flying by instinct, with no instrumentation to inform him exactly where they were, or even their height. Bolan was flying blind for want of a better description.

He figured the plane was at around four thousand feet. Below them lay unbroken forest with occasional pale patches he figured might be water. Above them the sky was clear, showing a few banks of cloud.

The trail of smoke from the port engine caught Bolan's attention again. He saw brief flickers of flame in the dense smoke.

That, he thought, was all he needed.

"Cooper, good news and bad news," Mitchell said as she returned to the cockpit. "I found our ordnance and the satchel of diamonds. Your sat phone was in the bag." She handed it to him.

"You mentioned bad news," he said.

Mitchell had leaned forward, staring out the side window at the smoking engine. It was making unhealthy sounds now, and the amount of smoke had increased. More flames began to show inside the smoke.

"Tell me that's normal," she said.

"No. That's *my* bad news."

"What is it with you and problems, Cooper?"

"Anyone can have a quiet flight."

Mitchell cleared her throat and looked away from the engine. "Okay. So here's my bad news. I found a parachute. But just the one."

Bolan absorbed the information and made a swift decision.

He took the Glock Mitchell passed to him and holstered it. Braced against the copilot seat, Mitchell slid her own pistol into her holster, securing the quick-release strap.

She stared out the window for a few seconds, then took a breath.

"We're going to jump, aren't we?"

Bolan nodded.

"Just great. I've been shot at, abducted, stuck on a plane with a burning engine and now you want me to jump. I've never done that before. Is it always like this for you, Cooper?"

"There are days like this."

"Just my luck to choose one of them."

"Sling that satchel around your neck and make sure it's secure."

"Oh, sure, let's not lose the diamonds. We're going to die, but we'll have diamonds."

"Mitchell, we're not going to die. And I don't intend those diamonds falling back into Hegre's hands."

Bolan pushed up out of the seat and took the parachute pack from her hand. He swung it into place, securing the harness with practiced ease. He returned to his seat and steadied the aircraft again.

"Go find the exit door and wait for me there. When I get there you grab hold of me. Use the harness straps to hold on and wrap your legs around me real hard."

"Cooper, who says I'm that kind of girl? We don't know each other all that well. Even though we've shared beds a couple of times."

Her attempt at humor fell a little short this time. She was scared and Bolan understood why. Leaping out of a burning aircraft and depending on the security of a single parachute was not the most inspiring way to exit.

"Go," Bolan said.

He watched her as she left the cockpit and made her way along the plane.

"Ready," she called above the increasingly ragged pound of the damaged engine. Then added, "Ready as I'm ever going to be."

CHAPTER FIFTEEN

The smoke was increasing. So were the flames. Bolan's grip on the yoke tightened. It was becoming harder to maintain any kind of steady flight. He pushed the throttle levers hard forward, hearing the increasing whine from the clean engine. The whole body of the aircraft was shuddering.

Bolan left the seat, crossed the cockpit and moved quickly along the cargo area. Mitchell was pressed against the side of the fuselage, waiting for him. As Bolan reached her, he felt the plane sideslip. The nose began to drop, the aircraft starting to veer off course. He knew they needed to get out fast, before it became impossible to make a clear exit. They had no time for debate. Staying where they were was not an option.

"Now," he snapped and saw the bright shine of fear in her eyes. Her face was white, drained of blood. She reached out and slid her hands through the straps across his chest, gripping tightly. Her head pressed into his shoulder and she swung her long legs up, curling them around his taut body at waist height.

Bolan grabbed the door's release handle and activated it. As the slipstream caught the edge of the door it was dragged free, swinging back against the exterior fuselage. Bolan felt the powerful drag of air tearing at them. He didn't fight it, simply let his body fall free.

The slipstream caught them and hurled them around like

leaves in a high wind. They were flung clear of the plane, bodies helpless as they fell, turning over and over. The wind tore at them. Bolan heard Mitchell's scream of pure terror as they fell. He concentrated on remaining clear of the plane as it wheeled over, free from any control, and for a moment he sensed its bulk swinging overhead.

Bolan wrapped his left arm around Mitchell's slim body, hugging her tighter as his right hand reached for and pulled the chute's release ring. The white canopy was freed, billowing above them and blossoming as it filled out. Their descent was brought to a sudden halt, the impact jarring them in the instant before the chute dragged them yards back into the air. And then they were drifting, dropping in a steady arc, everything suddenly silent save for the soft flap of the canopy above their heads.

"Hey, you can look now," Bolan said.

She raised her head and looked at him.

"Are we…?"

"On our way," he said.

She chanced a look around at the open sky they were slipping through. For a moment she panicked again as she realized there was nothing between them and the ground.

"Oh my God," she said.

She became absorbed in the moment, her gaze flicking back and forth, like a child caught in the wonder of a new sensation. Bolan had gripped her with his other arm now, keeping her close. A little of her normal character returned as she gained confidence.

"Cooper, there are some big buckles digging into me," she said. "Well, I'm hoping that's what it is."

"Quick release," Bolan said. "Vital piece of equipment."

Her smooth cheek was pressed to his as she whispered, "I'm sure it is."

Glancing down, Bolan saw the treetops spreading out

all around them. They were dropping quickly, the extra weight bringing them in faster than normal.

"Use my chest to protect your face," Bolan said, "and don't let go anytime soon."

"I wouldn't think of it," Mitchell began to say.

Her words were lost as they hit the upper canopy. Branches cracked, snapping under their weight. The smooth descent became a twisting, shuddering fall as they crashed through the foliage, leaves flying and branches dragging at them as they fell. There was nothing they could do to stop their fall. The spread of the parachute canopy snagged on branches, slowed the speed of their fall, but they were bruised and battered as they slipped toward the forest floor.

It all ceased with a shock as the canopy finally caught in the branches and they were brought to a hard stop, suspended by the entwined parachute, swinging back and forth. When Bolan glanced down, he saw they were no more than a few feet above the ground.

"Cooper, that was almost fun," Mitchell said. "But let's not do it again too soon."

"Just when I was getting comfortable with you hanging off my neck. You can let go now, by the way."

She glanced down, let go of him and dropped to the ground. He hit the release button and the parachute harness opened and he landed beside her.

"You want me to take that satchel?" he asked.

"That satchel and I have been together through a great deal of empty space, Cooper." She patted the bag. "I think we've bonded. So hands off."

They both heard the plane hit the ground about a quarter mile east of their position. Soon after, the black smoke rising from the wreck could be seen against the blue of the sky.

Bolan took stock of their situation. The thick spread of forest held a humid atmosphere. They began to sweat almost immediately. The forest was dense, trees and heavy vegetation combining to create a dense undergrowth.

"Air Hegre is scratched off my list," Mitchell said. "Landing us here."

She hunched her shoulders against the drag of the heavy satchel, wondering if she had made the right decision in keeping hold of it. Mitchell was already developing a dislike of diamonds.

Bolan took out his sat phone and checked the signal. He caught a lucky break and speed-dialed the number that would connect him to Stony Man.

"Striker?" Barbra Price's familiar tones came through clearly. "We were starting to get worried. You guys okay?"

"Change of location," Bolan said.

Price took the news without expressing surprise. She was used to Bolan's swift changes of operation.

"So where are you now?"

"Somewhere in the Philippines."

"Okay. So how can we help?"

"Get Bear to use the GPS chip to pinpoint our exact location. We need to move away from here PDQ."

Price didn't waste time saying goodbye. She put Bolan on a brief hold as she transferred him through to Kurtzman and the Computer Room.

"You lost again, big guy?"

"In a manner of speaking," Bolan said.

Kurtzman laughed. "You're lost. Don't pretend you just took a wrong turn. Barb said you're in the Philippines. How did that happen?"

"We had to jump out of a crippled plane. Along with a satchel full of stolen diamonds."

Even Kurtzman had no answer to that.

"Can you locate us?"

"Doing it now. Hold on."

"You do realize we are missing something here," Mitchell spoke up.

"Such as?"

"Water. The way this heat is draining us of moisture we'll be shriveled up before you can say I need aqua."

Bolan agreed Mitchell had a point. The inhospitable climate was not going to offer them any comfort. Apart from the humidity, the air had its share of flitting insects that might start to take an interest in the humans who had dropped in so conveniently. The salty sweat they were producing would be a beacon to every flying insect within the area. The black clothing they wore might prevent too many of the insects from worrying them. Long sleeves and buttoned collars would mean only their hands and faces would be exposed.

Bolan's sat phone emitted a sound that brought him back to Kurtzman.

"We have you on screen. You're located in the province of Aurora, in the eastern part of Central Luzon. Heavy forest. You need to move east toward the coast and Baler the closest town. It's twenty-eight miles away."

"Keep tracking us," Bolan said.

"You'll get updates if and when. Keep your GPS on screen. I downloaded your location so the signal should keep you on track."

"I'm hoping you're the only one who knows our location. If we stay lucky, Hegre will figure we went down with the plane."

"There could be some kind of tracking equipment on board. In case, as has happened, the plane went down."

"You think so?"

"If I had a sackful of valuable diamonds being transported, I would want to know where it is."

"I'll keep that in mind," Bolan said.

CHAPTER SIXTEEN

Jerry Clayton was the team leader. He had three men under his command, all well armed, all experienced. He had them spread out as they followed the trail of the escapees. Clayton understood his responsibilities. He answered to Lise Delaware and that added to the gravity of the matter. Within Hegre she commanded respect and expected total obedience. The woman was hard, expected results and allowed no kind of failure. Right now Clayton understood his position.

Cooper and Agent Mitchell were targeted. Delaware wanted them captured, Cooper especially.

The tracking unit Clayton was using had picked up the signal from the small transmitter in the satchel holding the stolen diamonds. The transmitter had been planted simply as a precaution before the diamonds had arrived in Kowloon. The uncut stones were too valuable to be left unprotected. That forward thinking had proved priceless when Clayton had received a brief, panicked message from the aircraft pilot, saying that Cooper had broken free. There had been the sound of gunfire, then the radio signal had ceased.

Along with Mitchell, the man had brought down Hegre's aircraft, killing the crew and bailing out to freedom. Clayton admired the man's persistence, his way of engineering his escape and taking the woman with him, along with the diamonds. He respected Cooper's ability to think on his feet, to take whatever slim chance presented itself and use that chance to pull himself clear. Clayton reminded himself to keep that in mind as he pursued his quarry. Cooper would be on alert now, ready to fight back, and he was not a man to take lightly.

The team had witnessed the plane going down some miles from the planned landing site. At first Clayton had believed Cooper and the woman had gone down with the aircraft, but his checking of the signal had shown the diamond satchel was on the move.

Clayton impressed on his team that the man they were chasing was not to be considered an easy mark. He warned them and left it at that. They were all professionals. If they hadn't been, they would not have been working for Hegre. That said, when information was presented to them Clayton expected his people to use it. He was not in the habit of holding their hands once they were in the field.

He felt his cell phone vibrate. It was on silent, as always when he was tracking someone. Clayton unclipped it from his belt and answered.

"Tell me something good."

It was Delaware.

No preamble.

Always direct.

"The satchel signal is moving. It definitely proves Cooper survived the crash. We have him ahead of us, and we're closing in."

"Cooper I want alive. If the women is still with him and ends up dead, I can't say I'll be concerned. It would be helpful if she was able to tell us what she knows, but your priority is Cooper. And the diamonds."

"Understood,"

"Be certain about that. And make sure your men understand, as well. If I end up viewing Cooper's dead body, someone will be sorry."

Delaware shut down her phone, dismissing Clayton.

He knew she was not making idle threats. She never did. She always made good on her promises. If he and his team fouled up, it would most likely be best if they didn't go back.

Clayton waved his arm. "Let's move. Let's get this done. Delaware wants the man alive. Remember that."

"Hell, what do we do if he takes a killing shot at us?" one of his team asked. "Delaware sitting on her butt giving orders doesn't mean Cooper will play ball."

"High bonuses don't mean shit if we're standing targets," one of the other men said.

"We take Hegre's money, we play to his rules. Or Delaware's to be exact."

"Jerry, that's just crap. Following rules doesn't stop a bullet if we have to hold back."

"Between you and me," Clayton said, "I don't figure on getting killed either. If we have to make a choice, Cooper's dead. We *try* to take him alive but not if it means putting ourselves in his sights. Wound him if you can. If not, drop the bastard. Same goes for the FBI woman. I never liked the Feds anyway."

Clayton checked the handheld tracker. He jabbed a finger in the direction it indicated.

The team moved out, following Clayton's lead as they pushed through the dense forest, minds concentrating on their target. They were moving away from the Hegre base where the plane would have landed. Clayton, seeing the direction Cooper was taking, assessed the man's line of travel. He was heading toward the coast and most likely the city of Baler. If he reached it, he would be able to get help. That couldn't be allowed to happen. Not with that satchel of diamonds. Delaware would be angry enough of they lost the man—she would go ballistic if the cache of diamonds was lost, as well.

From what he knew about this area, there was little between where they were and Baler. Nothing but forest and more forest. The guy they were pursuing was going to have to depend on nothing but his own skills. Though, from what he knew about the man, Cooper might not need anything else. The guy had broken free during the flight from China, taken down the armed crew and jumped from the plane, along with the FBI agent and a satchel of diamonds. Considering that, Clayton had revised his opinion. Cooper was no quitter. He sounded like a seasoned fighter and taking the guy might prove a hell of a task.

He failed to hold back a wry smile.

Take him alive, Delaware had ordered.

That could prove to be some job.

"Move it up," he called out. "We're not on a fucking country hike."

CHAPTER SEVENTEEN

The first shots were off target, possibly warning shots offering them the chance to surrender. They had already spotted the armed men closing in on them. Bolan saw it was time to take evasive action while there was still distance between them. He motioned for Mitchell to stay at his side as he guided them into the deepest cover he could see. Once they were hidden, he pushed the FBI agent to her knees, took the diamond satchel from her and dropped it to the ground. He had counted four armed men moving through the forest in their direction.

"These guys are moving in for the kill. I don't want them to gain any advantage. When they're in range, we hit them hard." Bolan caught Mitchell's eye. "You understand what I'm saying? Us or them. It's come to that, so we make sure we're the ones left standing."

"We go in hard. I got that."

Mitchell checked her Glock. She would have admitted to being nervous. Her hand holding the Glock showed a slight tremble.

Bolan gestured for her to move a few feet to one side, extending their field of fire.

They held their positions as the trailing group continued to shorten the distance. Bolan wanted them well inside the firing range of the Glock pistols. He raised his weapon when he saw the lead guy pause and glance at a gadget he held in his left hand. He scanned something, then raised a hand to bring his people to a stop, the motioned them back.

Bolan understood. The reason clicked into his mind even as the opposing group made their two-step retreat.

The guy had some kind of tracking device in his hand, a device that told him his prey had halted close by.

A tracking device.

And to catch a signal there had to be an activated transmitter either on Bolan or Mitchell. But no one had gotten close enough to plant anything on them that would have gone unnoticed.

Bolan's gaze dropped to the satchel on the ground at his feet. That *had* to be the source, a transmitter placed inside the bag holding the diamonds. Most likely placed there in case the satchel was removed from Hegre's possession, a safeguard so they could keep the diamonds secure. With Bolan snatching the satchel from under their noses he had allowed himself and Mitchell to be followed.

"Cooper?"

"They've got us on their radar," Bolan said. "Most likely a tracking device in the satchel. The minute we jumped from the plane, they've been able to follow us."

Mitchell snapped her Glock around.

"Incoming," she said.

Bolan saw the figure moving ahead steadily.

"When you're ready," he said.

His Glock cracked sharply, the sound loud in the confines of the forest, the shot reverberating. Bolan saw his target turn about, the .40-caliber slug taking him in the chest, left of center. There was enough impact to put the guy on his knees. He dropped his SMG and clutched at the wound seconds before Bolan's follow-up shot slammed the side of his head and laid him facedown on the forest floor.

The hit scattered the other shooters, but not fast enough

as Mitchell caught one guy as he turned aside. Her shot caught him in the left side, splintering a couple of ribs, flattening before it went in deep. The guy stumbled, gripping the trunk of a tree as he attempted to stay on his feet.

An SMG opened up, scattering tree bark and foliage as 9 mm slugs peppered the area. Now they were shooting for effect. No more warnings. A second weapon joined in, the chatter of autofire drowning out any other sounds.

"Fall back. I'll cover," Bolan called.

Mitchell immediately wriggled her way into the foliage, leaving Bolan to counter the autofire with his Glock. He held his low position, concealed by the tangled undergrowth, waited for his opening before he two-fisted the pistol and drew down on the armed figure edging into view from tree cover. Bolan's twin shots hit the guy in his left hip, puncturing flesh and shattering bone. The guy let out a groan, dropping his SMG and clutching at his ruined hip as he slipped to the forest floor.

Bolan snatched up the satchel and slung it over his left shoulder, falling back into the shadows to join up with Mitchell. She had taken up a defensive position, using the trunk of a thick hardwood tree. Her Glock was aimed back in the direction Bolan had come from.

"We're clear," he said. "Let's move on in case reinforcements show up."

CLAYTON STARED AROUND him at the remnants of his team.

One dead. The other two suffering from serious wounds.

As quick and easy as that?

His team cut to pieces.

Son of a bitch.

He pulled out his comm set and called base.

"Get through to the city. They'll be heading for Baler. They don't have anywhere else to go. Speak to Menendez.

I want his guys moving out to intercept Cooper and the woman if they go that way. Yes, dammit, they caught us and chopped us up. I got one guy dead and two needing medical assistance. You think so? Right now Delaware is the least of my worries. I got my team down, and the first rule is you look after your people, so don't tell me Delaware will be upset because I don't give a rat's ass. Just do it and send out the choppers. We need help."

Clayton ended his call. He had screwed his assignment, but he really didn't give a damn about that.

Or Hegre.

Or Delaware.

He just wanted his men to get medical attention.

And then, when that had been taken care of, he would go after that bastard Cooper.

CHAPTER EIGHTEEN

"If we find a road, maybe we can hitch a ride," Mitchell said hopefully.

They had been pushing through the forest, bodies aching and wet from sweating, for almost an hour. Bolan used his phone's GPS to maintain their line of travel. Despite the canopy of greenery formed by the uppermost tree branches, the heat hit them hard. Twice they waded across flowing streams and though they splashed water in their faces and moistened their dry lips, Bolan advised against drinking it.

"Not worth the risk," he said. "It could be contaminated."

"You really know how to give a girl a good time, Cooper. First a lightning trip to China—I've spent longer at Disneyland—a ride on a private plane that fell out of the sky and now a forest trek in the Philippines." She pushed her hands through her damp hair. "Lord, I must look like hell."

Bolan didn't answer. He was staring up through the branches, his attention on the sky. Mitchell followed his lead and picked up what had alerted him.

"Helicopter."

"And it's circling in a search pattern. There's a second one behind it."

Bolan caught her arm. He maintained their line of travel. It wouldn't help them if they broke off from the direction they were going. The cover in the forest was the same whichever way they went, and the city of Baler might offer at least some diversion.

Without warning they broke clear of the forest and into a wide natural meadow of high grass and ferns. Turning back was not an option. Veering from their designated line of travel would lead them toward the ground force they had clashed with earlier. Bolan could expect they had a backup team on the trail. Knowing the way Hegre operated, there would be additional guns on the ground. The organization had the money and resources.

Right now Hegre was making a concentrated effort to get its diamonds back. The stones represented a major investment. The criminal group was not going to give up on recovering the cache. If Lise Delaware was running the operation, she would never give up. Knowing that the man she knew as Cooper was the person who had stolen Hegre's diamonds, the young woman would pull out all the stops to retrieve them.

He put thoughts of Delaware to the back of his mind, pausing to check the Glock before he squeezed Mitchell's shoulder.

"You set?"

"To outrun a helicopter? Cooper, after everything you've put me through, I'm ready for anything. Just remind me—did I actually talk myself into teaming up with you?"

"Yeah."

"When we get back I'll volunteer for a psych evaluation."

"We head for that thick stand of brush first," Bolan said. "We'll use that cover to reassess. Make a zigzag run, and make it fast."

Mitchell understood his reasoning. An erratic course

would make it harder for a shooter in the chopper to acquire a target.

God, what am I thinking, Mitchell chided herself. *Make it harder for the shooter. Just bail and run into the open. Some choice.*

Mitchell shut down her mind and broke from cover, heading across the open stretch, because regardless of anything else, there wasn't much they could do to remove themselves from risk.

The moment she stepped into the open she felt totally exposed.

The beat of the rotors suddenly seemed that much louder. Mitchell didn't look around. The last thing she wanted was to actually *see* the damned aircraft.

She felt Bolan beside her, his easy stride keeping him in step. Mitchell was a good sprinter. Her regular gym workouts and daily jogs kept her in prime condition. The only difference was that normally she was not running for her life against hostiles in a helicopter.

Mitchell failed to hear the first burst of gunfire. She didn't miss the spurts of kicked up earth as the shots tore up gouts of dark earth and greenery. The firing was over in seconds as the helicopter swooped over her and Bolan, arcing to the right as it commenced a full turn prior to another run at them.

As they kept up their zigzag course, Bolan saw the chopper swing away. For a few seconds it was broadside to them, close enough so he could see the faces of the occupants behind the Plexiglas bubble. He came to a dead stop, raised the Glock and fired three fast shots at the aircraft. He knew his chances were slim, that hitting a moving helicopter was way off the charts. He also knew he had to do something. Yet he saw his volley land at least a couple of hits, starring the Plexiglas in the cockpit. It caused the pilot to veer away in a clumsy turn that took the aircraft clear of their position; it was not a crippling shot, but enough to force the pilot to move away.

Mitchell was at his side, her mouth opening to speak.

She had no chance.

They were still moving forward, keeping the retreating helicopter in sight, when the ground opened up beneath their feet and they tumbled into empty space.

CHAPTER NINETEEN

The chopper had swung overhead, and Jerry Clayton saw the rope snake down. It had just reached Clayton when the second helicopter appeared and dropped a couple of fast ropes. The backup team slid down and joined him. Two armed guys. The ropes were wound up, and the newcomers helped Clayton maneuver the first wounded guy into the canvas sling at the end of the first rope. They watched the man being drawn up and pulled into the chopper. They repeated the procedure with the second wounded man. The aircraft turned and headed back to base.

The second chopper swung away to make aerial recon on Cooper and the FBI woman. As it flashed out of sight overhead, Clayton spoke to the crew over his comm set.

"If you see them, lay down fire to hold them until we reach you."

He gestured to his new team. "Let's do this. Grab this pair and get back to base."

The three pushed forward through the forest, eyes alert for signs of their prey.

He wanted to get his hands on Cooper. Badly. Clayton didn't like being bested by anyone, and especially by one man and a female agent. When he got Cooper, disarmed and hogtied, there would be some personal satisfaction to be exacted. The bastard would be alive when he was handed over to Lise Delaware, but he was going to be one sore son of a bitch.

Over his years as a mercenary, Clayton had learned some nasty techniques that let prisoners suffer yet remain alive. *Why the hell should Delaware have all the damn fun?* he thought. She was sitting in comfort somewhere while he was slogging through the bad-ass Filipino jungle.

Minutes later he heard a voice coming over his comm set from the chopper.

"We spotted them ahead of us. You'll break out of the trees anytime. Big open stretch. Shit, Jerry, they've got no cover. Sittin' ducks. Hell, this is a friggin' duck shoot. I could blow them away no problem…"

"Hell, no, Sprague, do like I told you. Pin the mothers down but do not kill them. You hear? They need to be alive."

"Yes, sir," Sprague hollered. "Now here we go…"

Clayton heard the chatter of the helicopter's 7.62 mm machine gun as Sprague unleashed a burst. He could hear the chopper crew whooping and laughing.

Then the raucous yelling stopped.

There was silence, followed by gunfire and a cracking sound.

"Son of a bitch hit us!" Sprague screamed. "Hit the damned side window. Get out of range."

Clayton heard the helicopter's engine scream as it was hurled into a tight turn.

"What the fuck…" Sprague said. "Where the hell did they go? You see 'em, Pete?"

The pilot's voice came over the comm set. "No. I…they just vanished…just disappeared."

"What is he, the Invisible Man?" Clayton yelled. "He doesn't just vanish. Go around. Find him…"

"Bring her around," Sprague said to the pilot, "then set her down. Those bastards can't have gone far. Clayton isn't far behind. We'll flush 'em out. We owe 'em for shooting up the bird."

CHAPTER TWENTY

It happened too fast for them to avoid. One minute they were moving forward at a steady pace. The next the ground opened up beneath them and they dropped, falling into an empty void down a near-vertical hole that ended in a mound of tumbled dry earth. More soil cascaded around and onto them. The accidental fall into the hole had probably saved their lives, taking them out of the helicopter's fire zone.

Bolan groaned as dull aches invaded his body. The shifting soil and stones slid away as he moved, sifting down across his face. He tasted dirt in his mouth and spit it out, feeling the grit against his teeth. He drew his arms under him and pushed. More dirt slid away from him.

A muffled sound reached him.

"Mitchell? Are you hurt?"

"Why would I be hurt? I fell down a hole and was covered in a ton of dirt and rocks."

Bolan pushed himself into a sitting position, then stood, slapping at the soil clinging to him. With his eyes having become accustomed to the gloom, he could see Mitchell a few yards away, standing up herself and shaking her own covering of dirt from her clothing. He crossed to her and they stared at each other for a few seconds.

"Cooper, you look a mess."

"I feel one."

Bolan took a look around. They were in a chamber, almost circular, and to one side he could see the gleam of water where a stream ran through the area. He looked upward. Light came through the opening around fifteen feet above their heads. Dusty shafts of sunlight filtered down, lighting the chamber. A natural hole in the earth had lain across their path.

Mitchell had noticed the stream. She crossed to it, dropped to her knees and checked the flow. She found the water cool and clear. Without hesitation she bent and ducked her head into the water, scrubbing at her face and hair until she was satisfied she had cleared away the dirt. The wound on her face started to bleed again. She ignored it.

Bolan copied her actions. The water had a cool edge to it, but it *was* clear and fresh. He felt a keen stinging down one cheek where the water hit a raw scrape in the flesh. When he was refreshed, he scooped up water in his hands and took a drink. This was not the same as the water in the jungle. It was not tainted.

"Pretty good, huh?" Mitchell said, following his lead. "I never though I'd taste anything as good that didn't have a cherry in it."

Bolan looked around for his Glock. He located it not far from where he had landed. He checked it. No damage. Mitchell did the same with hers. She had managed to keep the weapon in her hand when she fell.

"You know what, Cooper, I just lost the FBI rule book. Every one of these Hegre thugs is on a new list, and it doesn't have anything on it that says arrest and detain."

"We can worry about that once we get out of here," Bolan said. "The sooner the better before the crew in that chopper figure out where we are."

Mitchell stood and took a long look at the walls of the chamber.

"I hate to say it, Cooper, but that might be a problem."

Bolan had already checked out the problem. At first glance he didn't see anything that might provide a way of climbing the chamber's sides. The soft earthen walls looked less than sound. The raw earth, with jutting crooked roots, wasn't the most solid surface to climb.

He stood at one section and studied it for a while before attempting to climb it. The soil was soft enough to dig his hands in, but the moment he followed through with his boots and put his full weight on, the hand- and footholds broke away and he was forced to step down.

"Even Spider-Man would run into problems trying to climb up there," Mitchell said.

"Let's walk all the way around," Bolan suggested. "Take opposite sides. Look for anything that might give us a chance to get out."

Mitchell nodded, and the started around the chamber, checking out the exposed sides.

It was Mitchell who spotted the yard-wide fissure in the wall. She followed the gap and saw it reached the top.

"Here," she called and waited until Bolan joined her. "What do you think?"

"We're not going to find anything better."

"If Hegre's people locate us when we're climbing out of here, it isn't about to get any easier."

"If you wanted easy, you chose the wrong profession."

"Mmm."

"Ladies first?"

Mitchell put her Glock away and tackled the climb without hesitation. She pushed into the fissure, bracing her back against one side, using her feet on the other. In this position she was able to maneuver herself up the gap a foot or so at a time. It was slow, muscle straining. The soft earth clung to her, adding its own weight as she eased her way toward the top of the chamber. Loosened dirt crumbled away from her as she moved, and more than once she slid down a foot or so until she was able to stabilize herself.

Bolan positioned himself so he could see the rim of the chamber, his Glock held two-fisted as he watched for any movement above her.

The fissure widened a foot or so from the top. Mitchell was able to drag herself into this wider ledge, spreading herself so she could peer over the rim. She drew her weapon.

Bolan holstered his Glock, slung the satchel across his back and eased into the fissure, ignoring the cold, clinging soil. They would have to deal with the transmitter later. His back against the earth, his boots wedged in the side facing him, Bolan began his ascent. He used every ounce of strength in him, conscious of his vulnerability during the climb. His muscles begged for relief, but Bolan pushed the discomfort to the back of his mind. If any of Hegre's crew showed up now, his aches and pains would be the least of his worries when the opposition opened fire. He and Mitchell would be clear targets.

"The helicopter has landed," Mitchell called. "Thirty feet away. The crew's climbing out. Both armed."

He was close to the rim now. Mitchell crouched in the hollowed out top section. Bolan reached out to drag himself clear.

The earth at the rim exploded under autofire, the shots loud in the silence. Gouts of soil blew into the air. Bolan heard Mitchell's yell. She pushed the Glock over the rim and fired twice.

Bolan rolled into position beside her. His eyes scanned the rim, watching for any movement.

"They took cover when I shot back," Mitchell said.

Bolan pressed in close to Mitchell. Her head turned, eyes bright.

"How do we get out of this one, Grasshopper?"

Bolan eased to the edge of the rim and peered over, staying within the fringe of thick grasses that grew in abundance. His scan showed the spread of empty terrain he and Mitchell had been crossing before they fell into the hole. The flatness of the land offered little deep cover.

He could see the helicopter, rotors still moving as they wound down.

So where was the crew? Bolan wondered.

"Anything?" Mitchell asked.

"They're being cautious. Once they show themselves, they're the targets."

Bolan saw a flicker of movement almost directly ahead of him. Nothing much, just a dark patch in among the thick grass. He focused in and saw the movement again.

Someone was belly down in the grass, scoping the hole.

Bolan built up the image of the prone figure, let his eyes filter through the tangle of grass hiding the guy. Now he found the curve of a shoulder, the neck, the cheek nestled tightly against the stock of the weapon being used. Bolan made out the configuration of an FN P-90. He had used the weapon himself and knew it had single shot and full-auto capabilities.

"You see him?"

"I see part of him. We need to divert his attention so I can take my shot."

"Let's remember there are two of them."

"We catch them before they can react."

"Do I have a sign on my forehead that flashes decoy?"

"Only a small one," Bolan said.

Mitchell sighed. "How do we do this?"

"Draw him out. I need him to raise himself."

"Cooper, tell me you can hit him."

She stared into the blue eyes as Bolan looked at her. It was enough to convince her. She knew he could do it. Her trust in him was complete.

"Let's do it," she said.

CHAPTER TWENTY-ONE

Bolan gripped the Glock two-handed, fixing the muzzle on the indistinct target.

Mitchell's move came suddenly, almost catching Bolan by surprise.

She pushed up off the ground, clearing the rim and darting to the left a couple of steps, then just as quickly changed direction and veered right.

Bolan saw the concealed shooter swing the P-90 toward her, rising from his low position to track her as she changed direction.

It was a slow-motion moment.

Mitchell's lithe figure a blur.

The P-90 moving to catch its target.

The shooter caught off guard by Mitchell's sudden move.

And Bolan following the shooter as he rose from concealment.

He cleared his mind of everything except making the shot, blanking out Mitchell and her vulnerable position. All that mattered at that moment was taking his shot.

The muzzle of the P-90 stopped moving.

The guy was going to fire.

Bolan held the Glock motionless and stroked the trigger.

The two shots came so fast they sounded as one.

The target reacted as the .40-caliber slugs struck. The dark form jerked away.

The P-90 fired as the guy's finger reflexed against the trigger.

There was movement to the right of the first guy. His partner rose in a sudden jerk. He carried an identical weapon to his partner. The weapon spit out a couple of 5.7 mm slugs.

Out the corner of his eye, Bolan saw Mitchell pause in midstride, then stumble, going down on one knee.

He centered the Glock on the guy and took his shots, firing three times, and the man flew backward from the force of the .40-caliber slugs. The P-90 curved through the air as it was loosened from the shooter's grip.

Bolan crossed to where the first shooter lay. The guy stared up at him, eyes wide and sightless. The slugs had cored through his chest directly over his heart. Bolan picked up the P-90 the guy had dropped and made a quick search of the body. There was a spare 50-round magazine in the harness under his jacket. Bolan dropped it into one of his pants pockets.

As Bolan approached the second man, he saw the guy was moving, one hand groping for the P-90, inches away. His eyes met Bolan's a split second before the soldier hit him with a head shot that slammed his shattered skull to the ground. The Glock locked back, the magazine empty.

The Executioner went to where Mitchell was crouching. He reached out to grip her right arm and keep her upright.

"Mitchell, were you hit?"

She turned, face taut, lips pulled back in a grimace.

"My side," she whispered. Her right hand pressed her body above the hip. Blood oozed between her fingers. "Damn, it stings."

Bolan pushed her hand aside and saw the bloody three-inch tear in her shirt.

"Let me see."

She remained motionless as Bolan lifted the shirt to expose her torso. There was a seared furrow in the firm flesh. Heat from the slug had partially sealed the edges of the wound. It was bleeding slightly.

"We need to get that dealt with soon," Bolan said. "The good news is, it isn't life threatening."

"That's okay then," Mitchell said drily.

"Let's get out of here before any more of Hegre's gunners come looking for us."

"I don't think that was a wise thing to say," Mitchell said, putting a hand to Bolan's shoulder and turning him about.

The three men breaking from tree cover were angling in their direction.

"Stand or run?"

Bolan checked the P-90. It was locked and loaded.

"I'm done with running from this bunch," he said.

"Me, too.".

Mitchell moved into a shooter's stance, gripping the Glock double fisted. The weapon moved in a short arc as she fired twice, and Bolan saw one of the shooters drop to the ground.

The surviving gunners were frozen briefly by the suddenness of Mitchell's response. Bolan didn't give them much time for reflection as he stepped forward, the P-90 at his shoulder. He raked the pair with concentrated fire from the SMG, the stream of slugs punching into them and spinning them off their feet. Bolan hurried forward. One of his targets was dead, the other wounded, face twisted as he clawed for his discarded weapon. The P-90 stuttered briefly, the guy arching his body in a final spasm.

The last guy to die was Jerry Clayton.

Bolan crossed to where Mitchell was checking out the guy she had shot. Her slugs had struck his heart.

"FBI training?" he asked.

Mitchell gave a slight shrug. "My instructors said I had a natural instinct for shooting. They refined it. In my line of work I guess that's a handy thing. It's not something I'm particularly proud of. Being good at killing people."

"Yeah. Just remember not to use that *instinct* if we ever get into an argument."

"Which way do we go?" Mitchell asked.

Bolan thumbed in the direction of the helicopter.

"I'm finished with walking," he said. "Let's ride the rest of the way."

"You can fly that thing?"

"Are you forgetting the plane?"

"Cooper, it crashed."

"We can't have that happen again in the same day. Defies probability."

Mitchell sighed. "I have to admit there's a kind of twisted logic in there somewhere."

"I always believed the FBI had *some* smart agents on their payroll."

"Don't let SAC Duncan hear you say that. He believes every agent is as smart as they come."

"There should be some kind of first-aid kit on board."

"Something positive at last."

Bolan recovered the other P-90 and handed it to Mitchell.

"No time to be queasy when it comes to arming yourself."

"Cooper, when it comes to self-protection, I'm downright greedy."

Mitchell glanced back the way they had come.

"Do you think they'll have sent more men out to look for us?" Mitchell asked as they took a break.

"If there are any more, I would," was his terse reply.

"*You* wouldn't have let us get away to start with."

Bolan glanced at her. "Praise indeed from the hotshot agent."

"Hotshot? Right now all I feel is filthy."

Bolan pushed drooping hair back from her face. "Are we feeling a tad fragile, Agent Mitchell?"

"Cooper, I don't do fragile."

"I knew you were going to say that."

She accepted his arm as they crossed to where the helicopter stood. It was a Bell 206 JetRanger.

Bolan saw the registration marks on the boom of the machine. There were no other identification marks on the helicopter. The dark blue, silver and gold paint job was in immaculate condition. He swung open one of the rear doors and helped Mitchell inside.

Bolan dumped the heavy satchel on the closest seat.

"Does this come with the standard model?" Mitchell asked, indicating the 7.62 mm machine gun lying on the cabin deck.

Bolan, searching for and locating the first-aid box, shook his head.

"I'm guessing that's a Hegre refinement."

With Mitchell keeping an eye on their surroundings in case there were more shooters in the area, Bolan used the medications in the first-aid box to tend to the ragged tear in her flesh. He had pulled on a pair of thin, sterile gloves from the pack before touching her. Taking a moment to watch his actions, Mitchell realized that for all his size, his powerful hands were gentle as he cleaned the wound, applied salve and finally a dressing. Mitchell closed her shirt and slumped back in the seat

"How do you feel?" he asked, packing away the first-aid box.

"Grateful to be sitting down," she said.

"You want to take a look inside that satchel for a tracking device?" He handed her the pair of surgical scissors from the first-aid kit. Mitchell dragged the satchel onto her lap, opened the flap and started to check out the leather bag.

Bolan secured the doors, then climbed over to sit in the pilot's seat. He spent a little time studying the layout and controls, then pulled a map from a side pocket.

"Cooper, where are we heading?"

"We can fly directly to Manila. There's a U.S. Embassy there. We can get help to fly home."

"And then?"

"Move to the next stage of putting Hegre out of business."

"Couldn't we just fly to somewhere sunny with blue water off a white beach? These diamonds should buy us a nice, quiet island."

"Okay, you're on. Let's go."

Bolan fired up the Bell. With the power on, the instrument panel became active. Bolan scanned the readouts. The fuel gauge showed full. He had received helicopter training from both Jack Grimaldi, Stony Man's ace pilot, and from David McCarter, the British leader of Phoenix Force, one of the Farm's top-notch antiterrorist squads. Both were excellent fliers.

He could hear Mitchell murmuring to herself as she inspected the interior of the satchel.

"I just hope they haven't simply dropped the damn thing in among the diamonds." She fell silent for a time, then gave a soft cry of victory. "Got it. It had been worked into the leather behind the lock mechanism."

She leaned forward and showed Bolan the dime sized disc resting in the palm of her hand, a compact, but powerful mini transmitter capable of sending a constant electronic signal for pickup by a handheld receiver.

"You know what to do with it," Bolan said.

Mitchell opened the door and dropped the transmitter outside. She closed the satchel and secured the straps, then placed it on the cabin deck.

"Buckle up," Bolan said.

"We in for a rough ride? Hey, I'm only kidding. Just thinking about our last flight."

Mitchell worked her way forward and into the seat next to Bolan's. She pulled the seat belt into position and stared out through the canopy. Bolan powered the engine, watching the readouts. He gently worked the controls, increasing the power from the collective and raising the column to angle the rotors. He felt the aircraft respond as he moved the controls in conjunction with each other. As soon as he had achieved the height he wanted, Bolan used the cyclic to turn the Bell in the direction he wanted. He powered up, feeling the engine drive the helicopter forward. With the aircraft on a steady course, he leaned forward and tapped coordinates into the GPS unit, corresponding to their destination—Manila. The city lay some 146 miles from their present position.

"We should reach Manila in a couple of hours," he said.

Mitchell had been gazing out through the bubble.

"It'll be dark by then," she pointed out.

"We'll be fine."

"Cooper, there don't appear to be any parachutes in sight."

"There are no parachutes in helicopters."

"Comforting piece of information."

Bolan took out his sat phone and tapped in the speed dial for Stony Man. This time it was Hal Brognola who picked up.

"Striker, what's happening? All we know is you're in the Philippines."

"I've been a little busy," Bolan said.

"You and Mitchell okay?"

"At the moment. Right now we're flying to Manila in a helicopter we acquired from Hegre."

"You need any backup?"

"Contact Mitchell's boss, SAC Duncan. He needs to speak to the U.S. Embassy in Manila to arrange to have someone meet and escort us in. We have the cache of diamonds hijacked in Australia. That is going to hurt Hegre. Get Mitchell and me on a flight back home. There's more to this than just a diamond heist."

"It'll be done, Striker."

"We're a couple of hours out of Manila. Ask Duncan to find out where we can land safely."

CHAPTER TWENTY-TWO

"He was there," Lise Delaware raged, her fury a palpable thing. "With that damned FBI agent. They crashed the aircraft from Hong Kong and walked out alive with the diamonds. Clayton and his team went after them. They were all killed. Last report had Cooper and the FBI woman in one of our helicopters, most likely heading for Manila. They'll make contact with the U.S. Embassy. I know it."

Melchior, as ever, listened in silence, sitting motionless in the leather wing chair, his face impassive.

As always he said nothing until the flow of words ceased and Delaware sank back in her own office seat, her anger dissipated.

Melchior waited a few heartbeats before he spoke, fingers pressed together.

"Even as a child you were passionate about matters that involved you personally, Lise. I recall instances where minor incidents caused an outburst."

"Children can be extremely volatile when they are faced with such matters."

"But as we grow we can control those instances, Lise. We must if we are to grow into capable adults."

"Dom, are you suggesting I am not a mature person?"

Melchior saw the faintest of mocking smiles on her lips.

"I would never consider you anything but, my dear, yet you do have a capacity for the occasional lapse."

Delaware's shoulders relaxed as she leaned forward and

said, "This man. Cooper. Each time he appears it is to cause me—*us*—more upset. There is an elusive quality about him. He appears, creates havoc, then walks away leaving chaos behind."

"And it is like an itch you are unable to scratch. A drift of smoke just beyond your reach."

"Yes. Always out of reach."

"Out of your control?"

"Oh, yes."

"Which is the source of your irritation. Your stumbling block, Lise."

"My fault?"

"I hesitate to call it that. But you want to be in control of every facet of life. Control is your definitive line. Never less. Which makes life difficult for you if something goes beyond your grasp."

Her unflinching gaze settled on Melchior. The way she stared at him made him feel uncomfortable. The moment passed quickly and she sat back.

"So, should I take up needlepoint? Something to make me relax? Maybe painting soothing water colors."

"I wouldn't go that far."

"I know you're right, Dom. I just get uptight when I feel I've let Julius down. I owe him so much. I owe him my life. Everything. Just the thought that I might be disappointing him makes me want to curl up in a dark room. Is that wrong?"

"Just get it into your head that you will never disappoint Julius. Push that aside and keep on doing what you do best. Accept in life there will be times when it doesn't go the way you want it to. We all have to take second best sometimes. It's no crime and certainly no reason for feeling inadequate. Just take a step back and look at what you are achieving. The Cooper matter will be resolved in time. Don't allow it to dominate your thoughts and actions."

"Easy to say. Not so easy to make the problem go away."

"You've had a bad run, Lise. There are too many negative thoughts in your head right now. You need to clear them out."

Delaware smiled. "Dom, I have the solution to do that. Kill that son of a bitch Cooper. When I do that, all my problems will go away."

CHAPTER TWENTY-THREE

The arrangements had been made, and after a brief stay at the U.S. Embassy, Bolan and Mitchell hitched a ride to the States with the U.S. military. Once back in Washington, Mitchell had headed to FBI headquarters to be debriefed by Duncan and to have her wound attended to. Bolan continued on to Stony Man Farm.

Hal Brognola pushed the slim file across the War Room table in Mack Bolan's direction. He sat back and waited while the soldier read through the intel. The Executioner's face gave nothing away as he fully scanned the text, only his eyes moving across the pages. He took his time, knowing that every detail in the document had been painstakingly gathered by Stony Man's cyberteam and deserved his full attention. Bolan had the greatest respect for Aaron Kurtzman's people. As far as he was concerned they were, bar none, the best around.

"Since your earlier involvement with Hegre, Aaron and the team have been devoting a lot of time to the matter. The little that we and the FBI had on these people, the deeper the digging went. A lot was researched on free time, too. I think Aaron especially was determined to hook on to something."

"That guy hates to come up empty."

Brognola smiled. "He's not the only one."

His remark was aimed at Bolan.

The Executioner refused to accept defeat.

It would have been easy to admit he fought a war that

never ended, a war that couldn't be won. But Bolan didn't see it that way. He fought his battles one by one, took on his enemies as they made their presence known and cut them down. He would never quit. He could not quit. He neither sought, nor wallowed in glory. That was not his reward. The satisfaction came from seeing the opposition fall back, no matter how small the steps were. And he would keep doing that as long as he was able.

THE WAR ROOM door slid open to admit Aaron Kurtzman and the tall figure of Dr. Huntington Wethers. Kurtzman was the top man of the Stony Man cyberteam, and Wethers one of his most dedicated people. Kurtzman rolled his wheelchair into position at the conference table and Wethers took a chair across from him. A telephone conferencing unit sat on the table.

Kurtzman had been confined to the wheelchair since a covert strike against Stony Man, some years back. The wounds he had received during the attack had left him paralyzed from the waist down, but hadn't diminished his dedication to his profession. Kurtzman was a cybergenius. The generous black-bag funding diverted to Farm operations had allowed him to equip the cybersection with the most up-to-date computing systems around. He was constantly adding to the hardware. It gave him the ability to gather whatever intel was needed.

Kurtzman had assembled a small, but dedicated team of cybertroops. Their combined skills and ability to seek out the information needed by Bolan and the Stony Man action teams were legendary—though what they achieved was never broadcast beyond the walls of the Farm.

"Okay, Aaron, this is your call, so go ahead," Brognola said.

"I have to tell you this is all down to Hunt," Kurtzman

said, glancing at the man facing him across the table. "If he hadn't picked up the initial trace and dug into it, we wouldn't be having this conversation. He should give the briefing."

"I got lucky," Wethers said quietly.

He was a modest man, who never took much credit for his own successes. He was a team player. Always neatly dressed, the African-American looked more like a conservative banker than a former professor of cybernetics.

Barbara Price entered the War Room and quickly took a seat.

"Okay, people," Brognola said. "You'll have me in tears if this goes on. Hunt, run it by us."

"From the intel Striker passed to us after his first run-in with Hegre, I ran every computation I could on what we had, which wasn't a great deal. All we really had was the name Hegre and the dead from the final shootout. I ran identity checks on the facials the FBI took, reached out to every database we had a way into."

"Some even the FBI haven't got," Kurtzman added quickly.

"I picked up on this guy Greg Rackham. Ex-military. From his ID I cross-checked and we came up with three more names. All were associates of Rackham. It seems they were all on the fringe of criminal activity until they vanished from sight. This must have been when they became involved with the Hegre organization. We've learned that Hegre is an extremely reclusive setup and stays out of the spotlight. But it exists and because it exists, it *can* be tracked."

"We couldn't figure out the origin of the name," Bolan said. "You have any more data on that?"

Hunt Wethers allowed himself a brief smile. "I think I have a lead on that. I ran some in-depth searches on Rackham's facial identity. Anything and everything. I put his picture on a continuous search and simply let it run. Nothing for a few weeks in fact. Came up with a number of images worldwide. Traffic cams. Security footage. To be honest I was getting tired of seeing his image coming up. Then the money shot. A shot of Rackham with a young woman. Her description fit the one you gave us of the woman you came across at the viral bust, Lise Delaware. I isolated the image, enhanced it. Came up with a pretty sharp shot."

The photo materialized on one of the wall-mounted screens. Bolan took a quick look and confirmed the identity.

"That's her," he said. "Great work, Hunt."

"I used the image to generate a further search. Came up with a number of correlations. Had to backtrack between social security databases. Passports. Then birth certificates."

While Wethers spoke, Kurtzman activated one of the other wall screens and brought up a number of images. He used a laser pointer to highlight them.

"Lise Delaware," Wethers said, "is in her early thirties, which ties in with the data we've gained. Her mother, married name Delaware, died when the girl was fourteen. Rose Delaware was a longtime depressive. She had struggled with it for years and from medical reports she was pushed over the edge by the divorce proceedings from Lise's father.

"Police reports indicate the girl came home from school and found her mother dead in the bathroom. She had cut her wrists and bled out. Now this is where it gets really interesting," Wethers said. "Lise was basically abandoned by her father. A benefactor stepped in and took Lise to his home and raised her. Lise's mother was his sister. So the new man in Lise's life was her uncle, Julius Hegre."

"What do we know about this Julius Hegre?" Bolan asked.

"Not much more than the information on the screens," Wethers said. "The guy is pretty secretive about himself and his criminal business dealings. Outwardly he runs a group of highly successful financial enterprises. The group invests, trades, has connections in multifaceted dealings. Hegre is a distant figure. His criminal activities are camouflaged by his legitimate businesses. Hegre stays out of the headlines. He knows a lot of powerful people, but no one knows much about him. He communicates through his subordinates. Quite a shadowy figure. He moves around a great deal. Even has his own aircraft. Has homes in New York. A mansion in the Hamptons. Other locations. I haven't learned very much more about him but I would guess he's a clever man."

"Anything from other agencies?" Bolan asked.

"The FBI hasn't broken through the barriers Hegre has put up."

"But Stony Man has?" Bolan suggested.

Kurtzman chuckled. "Don't spoil the surprise," he said.

"I decided to go for any weak spots in the Hegre chain," Wethers said. "The lower I went the cracks started to show. But the icing on the cake was when I came up with a trace from Mossad."

Wethers nodded in Price's direction. She leaned across and tapped in a number to one of the phones on the table. As it dialed out they could all hear as it was transmitted through the conference unit sitting on the table. It was picked up after a couple of rings.

"Agent Sharon?" Price said.

"Shalom."

Bolan said, "Ben, this is Cooper."

"How are you, my friend?"

"Good. Last I heard you were suffering from some war wounds."

"Thanks to your people, I was pulled out of that terrorist camp."

Phoenix Force had come across Sharon being held captive during a mission in the Middle East. He had been flown to a U.S. Navy ship and treated before being returned to Israel, badly dehydrated and having lost weight. He had also suffered a fractured arm while in the hands of the enemy.

"They have good medical treatment back home."

"And very pretty nurses, I hear," Price said.

"We must never forget the nurses," Sharon stated. "Now, it seems we have mutual interests in a currently developing matter."

"An intermediary group we suspect of brokering deals for Iran," Bolan said.

"Hegre? An organization you had contact with some time back. A deal with the North Koreans?"

"It was our first involvement with Hegre. Even though the deal didn't go through, our information on the group was thin. Our people have only recently pulled out information about Hegre. The name of the man running it is Julius Hegre, and a woman named—"

"Delaware?"

Bolan smiled. He could always depend on Mossad to have a handle on any situation. The Israeli security force had excellent intel.

"Lise Delaware. We only recently found out she is related to Julius Hegre. He's her uncle. Our cyberteam discovered that he took her under wing when she was young, and it looks like he recruited her into the family business. From my dealings she runs interference for Hegre, and does it well."

"That we hadn't uncovered yet," Sharon admitted.

"We'll send you what we have," Brognola promised.

"There has been a rumor the Iranians have been looking to increase their supply of uranium to process," Sharon said. "Their range of centrifuges has been increased at their biggest enrichment plant."

"I believe the centrifuges at Nantaz have been upgraded to the IR-2m," Wethers said.

"Yes. The IR-2m has improved performance," Sharon said. "It can process enrichment much faster. Reports say Iran will soon have enough enriched uranium to create a nuclear device, despite what they are telling world leaders. The more centrifuges they have, the more product they can process."

"More, bigger, this gets crazier," Price said.

"My exact feelings," Sharon told her. "But we can't escape the facts. And facts tell us a consignment of uranium yellowcake has been stolen from a rail shipment in Kazakhstan."

Yellowcake was the term used to refer to the uranium powder, packed in barrels for delivery to processing facilities.

"This only came to light in the past couple of days," Sharon added. "Duplicate barrels were found at the port of departure after storage in a warehouse. A dozen. It wouldn't have come to the attention of the warehouse staff if a forklift hadn't hit a stack and brought the barrels down. Couple of them burst open and spilled the contents. No uranium. Just salt."

"Any suspects?" Bolan asked.

"Local authorities are investigating but nothing so far."

"For our part we have come up with a single name. An individual known to arrange deals involving contraband.

This man has contacts in the Middle East, Asia and even Russia. Henrick DeJong. Originally from South Africa—"

Kurtzman interrupted. "Sorry, Ben, but that name is one we recently came across ourselves. A cell phone that Cooper brought back from China. DeJong was on the call list." Kurtzman spread his big hands. "It was on my list to bring up during this meeting."

"If DeJong has contacts within Hegre, does contract work for them," Bolan said, "it could be a way in for us. Find DeJong, and we might find Hegre."

"The cell contact?" Brognola said.

"Let me find out," Kurtzman said and made an internal call.

"Have you made that phone number from the cell Cooper brought in? The one with DeJong's name against it?"

Akira Tokaido's voice came over the conference unit. "I was just going to call you," he said. "It's a Moscow number. A night club in the city, Babushka, which is run by a guy called Sergei Lubinski. I ran a make on him through the criminal files of the Moscow police. Pretty unsavory. He has a finger in a number of rackets in the city. And he has a reputation as a transporter. He can move anything for a price. Moscow cops have him down as being part of a bigger organization, but they've never been able to make a solid connection."

"Thanks," Kurtzman said. "Keep working on that link."

"Could that connection be our reclusive Hegre?" Price said. "Their way of having an active conduit in the city?"

"One more thing," Sharon said. "Ayatollah Fikri. He's extremely radical and spends a lot of his time delivering statements about the evil of the West and the need for true Muslims to wage war against it. He's no friend of Israel either. We made a connection between Fikri and a money trace funneling a research program looking at uranium enhancement. One that hasn't been publicized."

"Ben," Bolan said, "thanks for your input. We'll keep you updated."

"Sounds like a departure is imminent," Sharon said. "Take care, my friend. Goodbye." The connection was broken.

"Open a file on Henrick DeJong, Akira," Brognola said. He turned to Bolan. "What's your make on this?"

"Hegre losing the diamonds is going to leave them having to make alternative arrangements. If they want that uranium for their client, they'll need to negotiate with DeJong."

"Which will give DeJong an advantage," Price said. "He might decide to up the price."

"From what I've learned about this Delaware woman, that isn't going to be an easy thing to do," Kurtzman said.

"Who said life had to be easy?" Bolan said.

CHAPTER TWENTY-FOUR

For Commander Valentine Seminov the day stretching ahead looked like just one more round of administration, forms to fill in and monthly assessment charts to compile. For the past week the Moscow Organized Crime Department had been so quiet Seminov could have believed the city's criminals had taken a mass vacation. He knew that was far from the truth. Crime did not take a holiday. Seminov had a bad feeling that something would happen without warning, and his department would be once again flooded with problems. He pushed his chair away from his paper-strewed desk and stood, crossing to stare out the rain-streaked window. The street below was almost deserted, with just a few hardy Muscovites braving the cold and wet.

Seminov heard the door click behind him and then the smell of freshly brewed coffee assailed his nostrils. When he turned he saw his assistant, Officer Nikolai Dimitri, entering the office. Dimitri had a small tray in his hands. He pushed the door shut with his foot and crossed to place the tray on his own desk.

"I'm sure you are ready for this."

Seminov's broad face showed a genuine smile.

"Nikolai, I must be training you well. Coffee, exactly on time to rescue me from that damned paperwork."

Dimitri handed his superior a steaming mug.

"I never realized this job could be so boring," he said.

"If I never see another form to fill in I will be a happy man."

Seminov swallowed hot coffee. At least, he decided, the coffee was better since the OCD had moved to their new premises. The building was no more than a couple of years old, modern, reasonably well equipped and located in central Moscow.

The building that had originally housed the OCD had been destroyed by a bomb blast, and Seminov's department had been relocated to an old warehouse on a deserted industrial site. They had struggled in the creaky old structure, having to operate with poor equipment, and for a while it looked as if they would be staying permanently. Unbeknown to the department, Seminov's boss, the district commissioner, had been working tirelessly to have the OCD relocated to better premises. In the end his persistent campaign won over the authorities and a replacement headquarters was granted.

For Valentine Seminov it meant having his own office again, a large room where he could spread out and gain a little privacy. Through the glass that made up the office's front wall, he could look out over the main section of the department, where his team was working tirelessly. Seminov took pride in his people. Despite the overwhelming flood of cases that just kept coming, the OCD had its fair share of successes.

Which made the recent lull in new cases a mystery in itself. Seminov didn't believe for one moment that the Russian criminal fraternity had taken time off. Fresh cases would arrive, Seminov would assign a team, and they would step onto the old familiar carousel once again.

He slumped into his big swivel office chair, mug in hand, and watched as Dimitri sat staring at his computer monitor, slowly shaking his head.

"It's never ending," the young officer said. "I go home at night with these figures rolling around in my head."

Seminov's booming laugh filled the office.

"No, young Dimitri, the only thing rolling around at night is you and that beautiful young lady in your bed. Irina. Do not try to deny it, Sergeant Nikolai Dimitri. Remember who you work for. Me. Nothing escapes my attention."

Dimitri reddened. He should have known his friendship with the stunning young woman from the OCD's filing section would not stay a secret for long.

"Nikolai, I applaud your good taste. If I was a younger man you would have competition."

Dimitri's phone rang at that moment and he snatched up the receiver, grateful for the distraction. He listened, then caught Seminov's attention.

"A call for you, Commander."

Seminov picked up and listened for a moment. A wide grin cross his face.

"Good to hear your voice, my friend."

"I will be flying in tomorrow, Valentine," Mack Bolan said. "Can you meet me at Sheremetyevo? My flight lands at 9:30 a.m." He gave Seminov the flight number.

"Of course, my friend. I look forward to seeing you."

"*Do svidaniya,* Valentine."

The call was ended. Seminov stared at the silent phone in his hand.

"Is everything all right?" Dimitri asked.

"I'm not sure," Seminov answered.

The American he knew as Cooper was certainly not one for long conversations if a few words would suffice. In this instance he had been even briefer than usual. The one thing Seminov had deduced from the call was that

Cooper had something important on his mind. Something that required a face-to-face meet.

"Commander?"

"Clear your calendar for tomorrow, Nikolai. Give anything you are working on to one of the other officers. Make sure we have a vehicle available. Tomorrow morning we have to pick someone up from Sheremetyevo." Seminov tapped his fingers on the desk. "And, Nikolai, this stays between you and me. Understand? No one else needs to know where we will be going. The less that is broadcast to potentially unfriendly ears, the better."

"Of course, Commander."

"Tell no one. Not even the beautiful Irina."

Dimitri sighed, knowing Seminov's teasing might turn into something regular. Not that he really minded. He considered himself a lucky guy to have the affections of such a gorgeous and loving young woman. A little ribbing from Commander Seminov was a small price to pay.

THE FOLLOWING MORNING Seminov and Dimitri drove the eighteen miles to the airport. Sheremetyevo International Airport lay to the southeast of Moscow. Dimitri, driving the dark colored SUV he had been assigned by the OCD's motor pool, didn't ask any questions. He could see that Seminov was occupied with his thoughts. Whoever the man was they were meeting, he was important to his boss.

The day was wet, constant cold rain issuing from a clouded sky. Streams of spray flew up from the tires of vehicles on the highway, and Dimitri had to keep the windshield wipers on permanently. Dimitri glanced at the clock on the dash. They were in plenty of time to meet the plane coming in from the U.S.

"When we meet this man," Seminov said abruptly, "I

want you to listen rather than talk. If he has made this journey, there must be something urgent to attend to."

"Yes, Commander."

"Don't get me wrong, Nikolai, Cooper has been a good friend to me. We have worked together before, and he puts himself at great risk when matters call for it." Seminov smiled. "A very dedicated man. One who will not step away from trouble if it occurs, and when Cooper is around, things do happen."

"Does he work for the American government? CIA? One of their agencies?"

"This is where things become a little gray around the edges, Nikolai. Cooper has what is considered his own— what is the word—yes, *agenda*. From what I have been able to understand he is not officially part of any American organization as such, but he sometimes undertakes special missions that have high clearance. He does what he needs to do to bring down those who work against society. The worst kind."

Dimitri considered that for a while. "He is a vigilante? He takes the law into his own hands?"

"Words, Nikolai, that cannot do justice to what Cooper does. He is a special man. And take my word for it, young Dimitri, he's deserving of our respect."

Dimitri concentrated on driving, digesting Seminov's words. His superior was a special man himself, a dedicated police officer who had spent his working life combatting crime and criminals. There were, Dimitri understood, cops and then there was Commander Valentine Seminov. Viewed from that standpoint there was nothing else to say. If Seminov vouched for this American, that was more than enough for Nikolai Dimitri.

At Seminov's request Dimitri parked the SUV in a restricted zone close to the terminal building's exit doors. An airport security guard confronted them, ready to make his presence felt. Seminov simply produced his OCD badge and held it up where the man could see it.

"Let us not make this an issue—" Seminov checked the man's label badge "—Officer Trenshka. I'm here on OCD business. If you wish to take this further, call your supervising officer and we can discuss the matter. On the other hand, I would appreciate your cooperation by making sure my vehicle is looked after while we are here."

The airport cop nodded, managing a brief smile. One look at Seminov's imposing figure in his leather coat and the OCD credentials, made him realize he was skating on thin ice. He was aware of the OCD's reputation. OCD handled the toughest crime cases around. Commander Valentine Seminov was a name he had heard before, a legend even in his own department. Not a man to cross.

"Yes, Commander Seminov. Your vehicle will be safe here."

"Much appreciated."

The airport cop almost saluted as Seminov and Dimitri walked away.

"I think he was ready to wet his pants." Dimitri grinned as they went inside the terminal building.

"You think so?" Seminov growled. "Then my work out there is done."

They made their way through the crowded terminal, heading for the arrivals lounge. Seminov scanned the overhead, electronic board, looking for Cooper's flight information. When he found it he saw the flight was on time and would land within the next few minutes. He led the way to the arrival gate.

When the passengers from the flight began to emerge from the gate, Seminov had no trouble spotting the American. Cooper stood head and shoulders above most of the other passengers, his imposing figure instantly recognizable. He was dressed in dark, casual clothing, and carried a small flight bag. When he saw Seminov, the American acknowledged him with a brief nod.

As Cooper cleared the crowd, Seminov saw he was not alone.

The young woman walking beside Cooper immediately drew attention. Tall, athletic and confident in her stride, she wore a dark business suit, a white shirt and black low-heeled shoes. Seminov found it hard to ignore the dark hair framing a beautiful face and bright eyes that were taking in everything around her. She gave off an air of being in control of herself and seemed fully at ease beside Cooper.

Seminov stepped forward, spreading his big hands as he confronted Cooper. He threw his powerful arms around the American, hugging him. Bolan reciprocated, with none of the stiffness Seminov had found in many Westerners.

"Good to see you, old friend. Always good to see you."

They broke apart after a few moments and Bolan put his hand on the woman's shoulder.

"Commander Valentine Seminov," he said. "Moscow OCD. Valentine, this is Sarah Mitchell, an FBI agent. We're working together.

Seminov beamed at the young woman. He was an open individual, and his natural exuberance would not allow him to merely shake her hand. He offered her his outstretched arms. Seminov was pleasantly surprised when Mitchell stepped forward and embraced him, her grip firm and confident.

"I've heard so much about you, Commander," she said.

As they stepped back from each other, Seminov gave

an amused laugh. "Whatever Cooper said about me...is most likely true."

"Who is this?" Bolan asked as he glanced at Dimitri.

Seminov gestured for Dimitri to step forward. "Sergeant Nikolai Dimitri. He is my partner. Almost my shadow." Seminov lowered his voice to a conspiratorial whisper. "I have to teach him how to be a policeman. Believe me it is hard work."

Mitchell was the first to take Dimitri's hand.

"I'm sure that is not the case, Commander Seminov," she said. "Good to meet you, Nikolai Dimitri."

"And you," Dimitri said in his best English.

"If Valentine is teaching you, Sergeant, try not to pick up his bad habits," Bolan said.

"Come," Seminov said. "We have transport outside. While we travel you can tell me what this is all about."

"Don't we need to go through customs?" Mitchell asked.

"Pah," Seminov said. "Not a problem, young lady. OCD has special privileges. You stay with me and I will show you."

He folded Mitchell's arm in his own and led the way. She caught Bolan's eye, but all he did was incline his head.

"On your own, Agent Mitchell."

Minutes later they emerged, after an unchallenged walk through customs following Seminov's quick word with the officers, from the terminal and went straight to the parked SUV. The airport cop was standing close by. He acknowledged Seminov with a smile.

As they all climbed in, Seminov patted the cop on the shoulder.

"Well done, young Trenshka. Cooperation is important. I will remember you."

With Dimitri behind the wheel, the SUV pulled away

from the terminal and picked up the road that led to the main highway. Bolan and Mitchell sat in the rear.

"Your first trip to Russia, Sarah Mitchell?" Seminov asked.

"Yes, Commander."

"Not Commander. Valentine. Please." Seminov gestured through the rain-streaked windshield. "Not at her best today, Russia. In more ways than one if you understand my meaning."

"America is having her problems, too," Mitchell said. "It's difficult times for us all."

Seminov nodded. "So, Cooper, what is this all about, this very secretive visit? And be assured anything you have to tell me can be for Dimitri's ears, as well. He can be trusted. I vouch for that. I know his secrets."

Bolan ran through the details, bringing Seminov up to speed on what had already taken place. He left nothing out, finishing by giving the names of DeJong and Lubinski.

"If I had heard that story from anyone else," Seminov said, "I would not have believed it. You crash a plane and walk away with only a few scratches. Do battle with the enemy and survive." Seminov shook his head. "Only you, Cooper. But shame on you dragging this beautiful young woman along with you."

"There was no choice, Valentine," Mitchell said. "These things happen. It was forced on us. And it *is* my job."

"So you believe this contraband uranium may be helped on its way by Lubinski?"

"Intel from my source and Mossad would suggest that. I'd say Hegre is trying to keep this low-key. Iran is on too many watch lists to make a buy with too much fanfare. You know the situation. They'll go whatever route they can to get what they want into the country."

Seminov rubbed his forehead. "Not the first time this

has happened. Those people are determined to gain their membership in the nuclear club."

"I won't let that happen," Bolan said.

Seminov understood. And he also knew that if it was humanly possible, Cooper would put a stop to the scheme.

CHAPTER TWENTY-FIVE

Julius Hegre closed the cell phone. He went over the conversation he had just ended with Henrick DeJong. It had not been the kind of conversation he enjoyed. Less than pleasant. He was about to call Delaware when the door of his office opened and she walked in.

"Not so good news?"

"I've just spoken with DeJong," Hegre said. "He has problems with Lubinski over the delay in paying the man."

"Damn. This is getting ridiculous. Surely Lubinski knows he will be paid."

"The deal was on delivery. He has delivered. We haven't paid." Hegre spread his hands. "One of the first times we have failed to honor our debt."

"Do you believe in bad luck?" Delaware asked. "Because if it does exist, we are experiencing one hell of a long run."

Delaware paced the office, hands braced against her hips. Hegre watched her, understanding her frustration. She was going through a bad time personally. Her meticulous planning was way off track. Nothing like this had happened before. Under Hegre's guidance Delaware and the organization had mounted successful operations that ran smoothly and ended successfully. Until now. The collapse of the diamond venture had gone against them and Hegre himself had to admit it had been a disaster.

The planning of the operation, the actual heist, had

worked well. The diamond cache was intended to prop up Hegre's finances and assist them over the upcoming operational period. The loss of the diamonds had left Hegre with a deficit that demanded they break into their reserves to finance the uranium deal for the Iranians.

Ayatollah Fikri, the man behind the contract, was difficult to deal with. He was a cold and arrogant individual. He did not conceal his disdain for the people he was employing; he had from the start made it clear he considered Hegre beneath him, that the Hegre organization was an example of Western degeneracy. In Fikri's eyes Hegre was low on the human scale, but he had to use them because he had no other choice. The embargo on importing uranium into Iran was strictly enforced. There was no other way so Fikri had to go the illegal route. It was a means to an end, an end Fikri felt was totally justified by his ambition to present Iran with the means to build its own nuclear capability.

Hegre had obtained the required uranium. As with the diamond theft, it had taken a great deal of planning and executing. Such an enterprise had cost money. If successful, it would have allowed Hegre to recoup the outlay. The diamonds had been intended to pay Hegre's way without having to divert other funds.

Stepping back to assess the current situation, Hegre realized that was not running the way he expected. The large amounts of up-front money needed to be forthcoming if Hegre was to avoid the unpleasant experience of disappointing the people he had involved in the operation. In his business it was not advisable to let his suppliers down. The people who worked on Hegre's behalf in numerous capacities had to be kept happy. The word that Hegre was becoming less than dependable would soon be passed around. That would affect future business, and that was something Julius Hegre did not appreciate.

"Lise, we will come through this," he said, hoping he sounded confident.

"The last thing we need right now is for this uranium deal to collapse on us. The Iranians are not known for their tolerance. Upset them and we could have a lot of grief coming our way. These people do not smile and say *fine, you screwed up, let's forget it*. They come after you. One way or another, they come after you. So we had better make sure Fikri gets his hands on his uranium."

Hegre understood her concern. The Iranians *were* a worry. He didn't enjoy the fact, but he took it on board.

"Then, Lise, my dear, we had better be sure to make a satisfactory delivery to our impatient client. Make sure we can maintain our chain of supply. The last thing we need is a fatwa being issued with *our* name on it. Avoiding that is our overriding concern."

"Julius, is there something you are not telling me?"

Hegre avoided her direct gaze. He touched the neat line of pens on his desk, moving one to bring it back in line. It was something he did in moments of stress. When he had something on his mind.

Watching him, Delaware experienced a twinge of concern. He not a young man any longer. The ever present strain of running the two Hegre divisions was putting great pressure on him. He put on a brave face, but she had noticed the way it was affecting him. Times when she caught him lost in thought, the weariness in his face. Hegre would have denied how much it all was wearing him down if she had spoken up. All she could do was try to shield him as much as she could and carry some of the burden.

"No secrets, Julius. We always tell each other the truth."

Hegre found her intense stare intimidating. She had the

unerring ability to see through any kind of deception. And with Hegre her assessment of his moods was unavoidable. He could not hold out for long. She knew him too well.

Finally Hegre said, "It's Dolf Stabler. He still owes us a great deal for earlier operations. A very great deal. I think he realizes we are struggling with finances. I have spoken to him twice, and he keeps stalling. With everything else going on I did not want to bother you, Lise."

"I thought the Bellarus organization had released that money."

Hegre shook his head. "No. I spoke to Stabler again yesterday. He's enjoying our difficulties. Since he stepped in to take over Kempress's position, the atmosphere at Bellarus has changed. Stabler is nothing but—excuse my hypocrisy—a crook. He is out to consolidate his grip. Bellarus brings in a great deal of business—and money."

"Yes, and we need our owed share of that money, Julius. We need it now."

Delaware picked up one of the desk phones and punched in an internal number. She spoke briefly as she gave her orders.

"This ends today," she said.

DELAWARE VISITED MELCHIOR in his office. He looked up from his work as she strode in.

"Tell me about Stabler," she said.

"I presume Julius has explained the situation?"

"You knew, as well? Damn it, Dominic, this is important."

When she called him by his full name, Melchior knew she was angry.

"With everything you are dealing with, Julius did not want you burdened with this."

"Don't treat me like a child. I don't need shielding from the big, bad world, Dom. Now explain."

"The Bellarus group has always been a hard business competitor. Hard but fair. Things have changed. Stabler has taken over because Lewis Kempress has been forced to step back because of ill health. The man has cancer. He's lost his influence. Stabler is making his play for a better position. I believe he wants to take the chair away from Kempress."

Lise considered what Melchior had just told her.

"He's not using us as a stepping stone," she said. "The man is nothing but a wannabe. He throws his weight around with his own people because no one has the backbone to stand up to him, and now he's practically blackmailing us because we are having a financial crisis. Right now we need the money Stabler owes so we can meet *our* current obligations."

"You do not have to convince me, Lise. But forcing Stabler's hand could be difficult."

Delaware smiled. "I don't accept failure," she said. "Let *me* handle Stabler."

"But of course, my dear. I wouldn't expect less."

Delaware was informed her car was ready along with her two-man backup team. She slipped on her black coat, checked the holstered Desert Eagle and the lock knife in her side pocket. She noticed Melchior watching her.

"Just making sure I have my negotiating equipment in place," she said. "I'll be back in a couple of hours. Our Stabler problem will have gone away by then."

Melchior understood.

Delaware's vehicle was waiting outside when she emerged. As she climbed into the passenger seat, she glanced briefly at the two Hegre men accompanying her.

"When we make the meeting, just follow my lead. Understood?" Both men nodded. "This won't take long."

Delaware sat and gazed out the windshield, oblivious to what was going on around her. Nothing seemed to faze her. The screech of tires, the blaring of horns. She was unmoved by it all. She was concentrating on what lay ahead: a confrontation with someone pushing hard to intimidate Hegre. Though the man in question, Stabler, considered himself up to the task, he had yet to experience a face-to-face with Lise Delaware.

They rolled out of New York, across the Hudson, to New Jersey. A half hour later the SUV turned off the main highway and picked up a quiet feeder road that wound its way through a commercial-industrial park. It cruised the commercial strip and then turned in between open metal gates and stopped outside the office building of the Bellarus company.

Delaware stepped out and made for the entrance doors, pushing through to a reception area. Her two-man team flanked her as she walked to the desk. A young woman glanced up at Delaware.

"May I help you?" she asked.

"I am here to see to see Dolf Stabler."

"Do you have an appointment to see him?"

Delaware smiled. "Just tell him I represent Julius Hegre. He *will* see me."

The woman caught the expression in Delaware's eyes and picked up her phone, speaking quickly when it was answered. The receptionist nodded at the answer she received and pointed along the corridor leading off from the reception area.

"Fourth door on the left," she said. "Mr. Stabler is expecting you."

Delaware turned away without another word.

At the appropriate office door she paused, then rapped on the panel. The door was opened quickly and Delaware strode into the large, well-appointed office. A large, curving desk dominated the far corner, with a window looking out across the site.

Dolf Stabler rose from his seat as Delaware and her team entered. The door was closed behind them by the bodyguard Stabler had with him.

Stabler was tall and solidly built. His square, broad face was topped by close cropped dark hair. He wore a suit that screamed money. The cream shirt under the jacket was hand stitched and the leather shoes could have kept a family in food for months.

"Doesn't Julius Hegre make house calls any longer?" Stabler asked.

Delaware paused at his desk, looking him over.

Behind her the Hegre team had placed themselves where they could easily cover Stabler's man.

"My uncle only deals with important clients," Delaware said quietly. "As Mr. Kempress has temporarily stepped down, he felt this meeting was necessary in order to correct certain imbalances. To put it clearly, you are screwing with us, Stabler."

The impact on Stabler was immediate. His face flushed with righteous anger and he leaned forward to slam his heavy hands down on the desk.

"No one speaks to me that way," he yelled.

"But I just did," Delaware answered. "We need to clear something up right now. Hegre has been dealing with Bellarus for some time. A satisfactory arrangement for both parties. Contracts have always been honored. Until now."

Stabler, comfortable within his own surroundings, allowed a slow smile to edge his lips. "Let's say things change. As in fees for services provided. I have looked at the figures and decided they were not in our favor. So I have changed them."

"Nothing like a little self-promotion to give you delusions," Delaware said. "The trouble with delusions is they make you believe you can't be touched."

Delaware's right hand had slipped into her coat pocket, gloved fingers closing around the handle of the lock knife. Her gaze never faltered, eyes fixed on Stabler's. In a smooth, controlled move she drew the knife from her pocket, thumb flicking the stud that opened the blade. Light caught the tempered steel as it locked into position. Delaware's arm swept up, reached its apex, then descended.

Her action was too fast for anyone in the office to react. Her aim was true, the six-inch blade a blur. Perhaps, in the microsecond before it happened, Stabler realized her intention. His awareness came too late. The blade entered through the back of his right hand, cutting easily through flesh and tendon and bone with a moist crunching sound. Delaware had put all of her considerable muscle power into the down stroke and the knife sliced its way through Stabler's hand and buried itself deeply in the desktop. Well over three-quarters of its length lodged tightly in the wood.

Blood began to spread out from beneath Stabler's pinned hand even as he began to scream. His cry stopped abruptly when Delaware pulled her Desert Eagle and slammed it across the side of his head. Stabler slumped to his knees behind the desk, held in position by his pinned hand, dazed. The man's bodyguard responded too slowly, his attention on his boss's hand. By the time he had reached for the pistol under his coat, one of Delaware's team was at his side, the muzzle of his own weapon pushed into the side of the man's skull. He took the guard's weapon and slipped it under his belt.

The other Hegre man stepped out of the office and moved back along the corridor to confront the startled receptionist. He showed her his own pistol, slowly shaking his head. His unspoken threat was enough to persuade her not to make any kind of fuss.

In his office Stabler pushed slowly upright, reaching out with his free hand to draw his chair close so he could sit. He hunched over the desk, his left hand gripping his other wrist. Blood had pooled on the desk top, soaking into papers spread across it.

"So, Mr. Stabler, do we understand each other now?" Delaware asked.

Stabler raised his head and stared up at her.

"I won't forget this...."

Delaware smiled. "I hope not, because that was my intention. That you realize how serious I am. I could easily have cut your throat. As it is, I have simply made my point. To show you Hegre does not appreciate your kind of behavior. I do not care about your attempt to climb the ladder within Bellarus. Ambition is fine. But not at Hegre's expense. Stabler, understand who you are dealing with. Hegre is too powerful, too influential to be intimidated by someone like you. You continue with the agreed arrangements, and this goes no further. If you attempt to continue with your little exercise, I may be forced to take this higher. I leave that for you to consider."

Stabler, face oozing sweat, held her gaze for a few seconds before he gave a slight nod.

"Don't imagine that after I leave you can suddenly revert to your previous stance. Hegre has too many contacts for you to influence matters. It would surprise you to know just how many. Close attention will be kept from now on. We have an understanding. Yes?"

"Yeah," Stabler said hoarsely.

"Fine. So all we need now is for you to get on your computer and transfer the very large amount of money you have been withholding from us. Money that belongs to Hegre. Are we agreed?"

Stabler nodded. Using his left hand, he worked on his keyboard, Delaware watching every move until he tapped Enter.

Delaware took out her cell phone and called Melchior.

"Dom, go online and check the main account. No time for questions, just do it."

She heard the muted sound of keys as Melchior accessed the account. A minute or so passed, the only sound Stabler's low moaning.

There was a soft gasp over the phone as Melchior read the figures showing in Hegre's account.

"Make the necessary arrangements," Delaware said.

Melchior would move the large amount to other Hegre accounts to avoid any chance of it being recovered. And, most important, the money needed to pay off Lubinski would be transferred to the Russian's Moscow account.

"Doing it now."

"Talk to you later," Delaware said. She looked down at Stabler. "This was all so unnecessary. All it's done is left you with an unexpected problem."

Stabler frowned through his pain. "What problem?"

"How you're going to get that blade out of the desk without tearing your hand apart."

She turned to her backup and said, "Time to go."

They picked up their man at the reception desk and left the building, encountering no resistance.

CHAPTER TWENTY-SIX

Bolan and the others drove directly to OCD headquarters where Seminov ushered his visitors to his office. Dimitri was dispatched to get coffee. Bolan and Mitchell were offered seats in front of Seminov's desk. The Russian commander threw off his overcoat and sat facing them.

"Better surroundings than the last time," Bolan said.

"Yes," Seminov agreed, grinning. "Someone realized that OCD deserves the best. Here we deal with the worst criminals running around Russia. So we should have the facilities to match that."

They waited until Dimitri arrived with hot coffee for them all. The sergeant drew up a chair and joined them.

"This information you have from the Israelis," Dimitri asked. "You believe it is reliable?"

"My source is a Mossad operative I've worked with before, and his people are good. The suggestion that Sergei Lubinski is involved is sound."

"Lubinski is a sharp operator," Seminov said. "He can provide just what a client requires. And we suspect he uses the club, Babushka, for cover."

"Contraband is one thing," Mitchell said. "If Lubinski is helping transport uranium to Iran, it takes him to a different level."

"For what gain?" Dimitri asked. "Apart from physical damage, nuclear explosions would simply spread radiation over large areas. Wind could carry the poison, even as far as the country that launched the devices. Where is the sense in that?"

"We're talking about individuals steeped in religious fervor," Bolan said. "Individuals who have convinced themselves that Israel is their sworn enemy. A purveyor of hatred for Islam. The intel from Mossad suggests it's what Iran is doing. Iran is a wild card. It has too much invested to pull out now. Fikri has the backing of a number of extreme ayatollahs. They're against any kind of appeasement with the West or Israel. They would pull the nuclear trigger if they had the hardware, regardless of the consequences. In Fikri's mind it's his duty to strike at the enemies of Islam. Any damage done to Israel would be a blessed event. He has a lot of supporters in Iran and abroad. Mossad has identified Fikri as being behind recent issues firing up young followers to strike against Western targets. It doesn't need to be explained how risky that kind of thinking is. He may not have a battle plan, but his policies are more than just bluster. The man has openly declared his resentment of American and Israeli involvement and promises reciprocal action if Israel doesn't back off from what they call defensive strikes."

"Do you believe this man would use nuclear weapons if he had them?" Dimitri asked.

"Feasibility studies back home have put Fikri at the top of the list," Mitchell replied. "The man is an unrepentant advocate of extreme action against what he considers the true enemies of Islam. The only thing holding him back is a lack of the nuclear material required to produce WMDs. Reports from inside Iran passed to U.S. intelligence confirm the man's willingness to use nuclear devices if he can gain enough material to construct the weapons."

"Do these people believe setting off nuclear devices is

going to bring about an Islamic victory?" Dimitri asked. "That they would come off without harm?"

"Nikolai," Bolan said, "we are talking religious fanatics here. People who see and hear only what they want. No amount of talk, persuasion, will take them off the path. They have judged us and condemned us. Everything we stand for is blasphemy to them. And it justifies the bombings. The killings. The endless vilification of our very existence. They refuse to even sit down and talk. How do we deal with that kind of thinking?"

Dimitri shook his head. "Then we have learned nothing from all the years spent waving nuclear weapons at each other."

"The cold war was a different time," Seminov said. "Now we are into blackmail by zealots. Crazy men who have nothing but utter hatred in their hearts."

"Criminals I can handle," Dimitri said. "But this madness could kill us all."

"So we stand up and face it," Bolan said. "If we stand back and let it go on we deserve the results."

"So, my friend, what do we do?"

"Lubinski. DeJong. We take the war to them."

Dimitri handed over a file.

"Photographs," he said. "Lubinski and his local employees. Just so you will recognize them."

"Okay," Bolan said.

SEMINOV NODDED.

"Then first we get you dressed for a visit to Babushka."

As well as clothing, Seminov provided Bolan and Mitchell with side arms, aware they would not have been able to carry on the flight. The OCD armory held a wide selection of ordnance. Knowing Bolan's preference for Berettas, the Russian cop handed him a 92FS pistol. The weapon was in excellent condition and came with walnut grips. The pistol had a 15-round magazine, and Seminov handed over an additional magazine.

"Fires true," Seminov said. "Every weapon in here has been checked and test fired."

"Pleased to hear that."

"For the lady, a Glock," Seminov said.

Mitchell took the Glock 26 he passed to her. She ejected the magazine, lost the 9 mm round in the breech and dry fired the weapon a couple of times.

"It feels good, Valentine."

Seminov smiled as she reloaded the Glock. "It will not let you down."

He handed them both holsters for the guns, a shoulder rig for Bolan and a belt holster for Mitchell. His final gift to them was a pair of compact comm sets.

"Tuned to my frequency. If you need help you just call."

"We may do that," Bolan said.

"Now," Seminov said, "you are ready for Babushka."

CHAPTER TWENTY-SEVEN

The afternoon rain had gone, leaving a cool, clear night. Seminov's SUV was parked on the far side of the broad street. Dimitri had pulled it into a gap in the line of cars.

"We'll wait here," Seminov had said. "Across from the club. My face is known to Lubinski and his crew. You make the play inside. However you want. But I will be on the end of the comm set. Close. I can bring OCD in force if you discover anything. Cooper, don't hesitate. I would hate to have to attend your funeral."

They had no problem getting inside the club. There were two guys on the door who seemed more interested in the young women making their entrance. They paid no attention to Bolan and Mitchell as they sauntered through. It may have been that Bolan's clothing—the casual but quality suit, handmade shirt and gold wristwatch—marked him as a potential big spender. The loose cut of the suit jacket concealed the Beretta in the shoulder rig. If the door guy was there to stall any unwanted guests, he failed miserably to spot Mack Bolan as anything but another customer. He paid more attention to Mitchell as she smiled at him. Babushka, as Seminov had explained was a popular venue with the tourist crowd, a place that attracted not just Russians, but an international clientele.

Once Bolan was through the door, Mitchell left him to drop off her coat at the coat-check booth. Bolan made his way to the long chrome-and-black bar that occupied one wall of the club, slid onto a stool that allowed him an un-restricted view of the interior, and ordered a drink. The drink came with a price that was more than double its actual value, which the soldier knew was normal for a club like this. He paid for his drink and took a long look around.

The mingling languages ran through English, French, Italian and Russian. Babushka had an international clientele. It offered good music and plentiful drink and food. Watching from the bar Bolan thought, *welcome to the new Russia.* He could have been in a club in New York, or London, a dozen places where money broke all the barriers.

On a small raised stage a combo played some solid jazz. Bolan didn't have a lot of spare time to indulge in listening to music, but he could appreciate the excellent music from the four musicians.

At the far end of the club, to one side of the stage, was a plain door that showed *private* directly beneath Cyrillic lettering on a metal plate. Bolan was still sipping his first drink when he saw three guys go through the door, one after the other.

He recognized two of them from the photos Seminov had shown him: they were a pair of Lubinski's enforcers, Krigor and Baba.

The third guy, tall and lean with dark skin and wearing a trimmed beard, was a stranger to Bolan. Middle East? Someone from Fikri's camp? The client come to arrange delivery details?

The voice in Bolan's ear was not from a stranger. Mitchell kept it low and intimate as she eased onto the stool just behind Bolan.

"Hope I haven't kept you waiting, love," she said.

Bolan turned to face her and had to control his expression when he took in her strictly non-FBI dress for the evening. He hadn't seen what Seminov had provided her with before they left the OCD building as it had been covered by the coat.

She had on a simple, classic black dress. It accentuated her supple curves and the hem, ending well above her knees, showed a pair of toned and shapely legs. As Bolan ordered her a drink, he found himself trying to work out where she might be concealing her ordnance as she was not wearing her holster. As if reading his mind, Mitchell placed the plain black shoulder bag she carried on the bar and tapped it with a long finger.

"Concealed weapon. For special occasions."

"Works for me," Bolan said.

"Valentine has good contacts. And good taste."

"Yes he has."

"*So?*"

Bolan waited until the bartender placed Mitchell's glass in front of her.

"Check out the door just beyond the band. Marked private."

"I see it."

"Two of Lubinski's guys, Krigor and Baba, went through just before you showed. A third guy I haven't seen before, too. Appeared Middle Eastern."

"Mossad's intel is panning out."

Mitchell tasted her drink, nodding in appreciation.

"We need to find out what Lubinski and company are up to," Bolan said.

He had been checking out the dimensions of the club. The private door had to lead into the depths of the building. He guessed there would be offices. Storage areas. And there had to be other means of access.

Mitchell had plainly been thinking along the same lines as she swiveled her stool to scope out the rear of the club.

"You have your transceiver switched on?" she asked.

Bolan nodded and she said, "We should split up and work our way outside and circle the place. See if we can find an alternate way in."

"Going our separate ways already? It's going to be a early night."

Mitchell smiled at him. "The night isn't over yet...."

She slid off the stool and smoothed down the risen hem of her skirt. A warm hand touched Bolan's cheek as she turned away. He noted that she was wearing low-heeled shoes that would allow her to move quickly if the occasion arose. No spiky high heels that might let her down in an emergency.

"I'll take the left side of the building," she said.

Bolan watched her merge with the crowd, making her way to the exit and slipping between the customers just entering. He stayed where he was, taking his time finishing his drink before easing away from the bar and crossing the dance floor until he walked by the coat-check booth and exited the building.

Clear of the crowd heading for the entrance, Bolan moved across the parking lot. By now his presence had been forgotten by the doormen. He moved and paused, moved again, easing around to his left so that he eventually found himself at the corner of the building.

The light had not faded enough to hide him completely. Bolan couldn't worry about that. The surveillance he and Mitchell were hoping to carry out needed to be carried out sooner, rather than later. The meeting taking place at the rear of the club might break up at any time.

The soldier turned quickly, moving along the bare wall, away from the busy entrance to the club.

Bolan spotted a couple of security lights attached to the side of the building. They were high up and angled to cover the area away from the wall, not up close to the building. If he stayed close in to the wall, he would be able to move in the shadows. He came to a chain-link fence that prevented further access to the rear of the building. There was a section formed into a gate that ran on a wheeled track. It was locked.

Pausing at the fence, Bolan saw a couple of cars parked in the delivery area behind the club. He checked out the fence. There were no indications of alarms or cameras. Close inspection told him the fence was not electrified, or fitted with sensors. He stood close to the wall, in a shadow, and ran through his options. If he wanted to get over the fence, the only viable way was to climb.

Bolan made his choice and acted on it without further thought. He buttoned his suit jacket to prevent it flapping open. Reaching up, he curled his fingers through the links and clambered up the fence, reaching the top and pulling himself over the links, letting his body swing clear. He hung for seconds before letting himself drop. He flexed his knees as he landed, taking the impact. Bolan flattened himself against the wall. He moved his fingers to ease the ache left behind from gripping the wire links.

The comm set in his jacket inside pocket buzzed gently. Bolan took it out and activated the button.

"Cooper? Can you hear me?"

"Got you, Mitchell."

"What's your position?"

"Inside the perimeter fence. Going to check the layout. You?"

"The same." She paused. "And don't even ask how I managed it wearing a dress."

"Now that you mention it…"

"Let's just accept it didn't do a thing for my dignity."

"For the job, Mitchell, for the job."

"I have a couple of vehicles back here. They look like delivery vans."

"I spotted them, as well."

"No movement. I can see the back wall of the building from my position," Mitchell said. "There's a small loading dock with a roller door."

"I'll be in position in a few seconds."

Bolan traversed the length of the building and peered around the corner. He saw exactly what Mitchell had described: the empty rear area and the two parked vans with the Babushka logo painted on the sides. To his left was the loading dock and the entry points.

"I'm in place," he said into his transceiver.

The FBI agent's dark head rose from behind the loading dock. Bolan made his way to her side.

He dropped the comm set into his pocket and took out the Beretta 92FS. He ran a quick check.

Mitchell had discarded her bag after removing her weapon. The Glock 26, a smaller model, with a reduced butt, held ten 9 mm rounds in its double-stack magazine. The FBI agent's comm set was now suspended from her neck by a thin nylon cord.

"Let's do this," she said.

They stepped up onto the loading dock and Bolan checked the door to one side of the loading dock. It opened without a sound. Mitchell checked the interior then slipped inside. Bolan followed, closing the door behind him.

The freight area was no more than twenty feet square and empty save for a few stacks of cardboard boxes and crates holding empty bottles. Scuff marks on the concrete floor showed where goods had been moved around. On the wall across from them was a set of double doors. The faint sound of music filtered through from the club area.

Bolan led the way to the set of doors. They were mounted on two-way hinges that allowed the doors to swing either way. Bolan eased open one of the doors and checked the other side. Now he could hear the murmur of voices. He edged through the door, Mitchell close behind.

A group of people was gathered around a long metal trestle table in a small storage area. A couple of attaché cases sat on the trestle table, and a thick stack of banded currency was in view.

Bolan saw Krigor and Baba standing back a few feet. Both armed now, with H&K MP-5 KAs hanging from their shoulders by black straps.

Sergei Lubinski was transferring the cash to one of the attaché cases.

DeJong was in deep conversation with the Middle Eastern contact. DeJong had a file in his hands, passing it to the man.

As silently as Bolan and Mitchell had entered, some fragment of movement had registered in Baba's peripheral vision. His shaved head snapped around, and he locked in on the newcomers. His warning yell alerted everyone, including his partner, Krigor. They both reached for the SMGs hanging at waist height.

Bolan sensed Mitchell moving to one side, away from him, and he knew he didn't need to give her any instructions.

Baba had gripped his MP-5, starting to raise it. As Krigor moved he had to step back to clear DeJong and his contact.

The moment Baba made his offensive move, Bolan brought the Beretta on line, easing the muzzle into target acquisition. Baba's stocky body offered a good target. Bolan eased back on the trigger and felt the 92FS recoil as it fired. He triggered a second and third shot, the cracks echoing in the building. Baba took a step back, eyes widening in shock as the trio of 9 mm slugs punched in through his chest and lodged in his heart. He buckled at the knees and fell facedown on the concrete floor.

The last of Bolan's shell casings had barely hit the floor before Krigor ran off a long burst from his MP-5. The volley was high as the muzzle rose, tearing through the door behind Bolan and Mitchell. Mitchell, crouched, pushed forward her weapon in a two-handed grip. It cracked twice. Krigor was half turned as her shots ripped into his left shoulder, one exiting through his back in a bloody spurt. The Russian attempted to steady his sagging SMG with his right hand. Mitchell's pistol rose, held, then fired, putting a third shot through his left eye. Krigor gave a shrill cry, dropping to the floor.

In the scant seconds the shooting took, Lubinski and DeJong broke away from the table, ignoring what lay on its surface. Their contact followed on DeJong's heels, clutching the file he had snatched from the South African's hand. All three were heading for the far door that would take them back into the club and the crowd of customers.

Bolan clicked his transceiver.

"Valentine, we have three hostiles heading through to the club. Likely to be coming out through the main entrance. Lubinski, DeJong and an unknown man of Middle Eastern appearance."

"I hear you."

Mitchell was moving after the escaping three.

"Hold it," she yelled.

It was a waste of breath.

Bolan and Mitchell converged on the men.

Lubinski, in the rear, hauled himself to a stop, his right hand producing a handgun from under his coat. He turned, mouthing something in Russian as he raised the pistol. Bolan fired on the move, the Beretta dispatching a pair of 9 mm slugs that tore into Lubinski's gun arm; the rounds ripped flesh from the limb and shattered bone. The Russian lost his grip on his weapon, stumbled and slumped back against the wall, gripping his limb and moaning loudly. Blood was spurting from the torn material of his shirt.

DeJong and his companion disappeared through the door and merged with the crowd in the main part of the club. Bolan and Mitchell saw them swallowed by the mass of customers, quickly losing sight as the pair kept moving.

An arm appeared above the crowd clutching a handgun. A number of shots rang out, directed at the ceiling.

Panic followed. The crowd turned toward the exit en masse and tried to get out at the same time, a throng of alarmed people pushing and shoving. There were casualties as self-preservation took over. People stumbled and fell and were stepped on by those around them.

Bolan spoke into his comm set again.

"Lubinski is down, Valentine. DeJong and the third guy are in the crowd somewhere. On their way out."

"So we can see. You stay where you are in case they try to double back."

"Go and secure that rear door," Bolan said to Mitchell.

She acknowledged and headed to the door they had entered by, leaving Bolan to cross to where Lubinski lay semiconscious. He picked up the pistol the Russian had dropped, ejected the magazine and the round in the breech.

Lubinski stared at Bolan. His face was fish-belly white, glistening with sweat. The fingers wrapped around his arm were dripping blood. White bone gleamed through the lacerated flesh under his hand. He was curled up at the base of the wall, showing no interest in moving.

"You understand English?"

The Russian nodded. "I understand. Who are you? Ah, *American?* Yes, American. You are the one Delaware is looking for. I have heard about you."

"Word gets around. How much *am* I worth to her?"

"For anyone who gives her what she wants—a half million dollars."

"Only half?" Mitchell said as she came across the storage area. "Obviously she doesn't like you as much as I imagined."

"Delaware must be running out of ready cash."

"Diamonds are not her best friend at the moment," Mitchell said.

Bolan turned and checked out the table where the abandoned attaché cases and the money sat. One had some of the stacked money in it. The other was empty except for a cell phone. Bolan checked it out. The text on screen showed as Arabic script. He showed it to Mitchell.

"The Iranian contact's phone? Makes me wish I'd taken those language courses at college."

Bolan tapped in the number that would connect him with Stony Man. When Price came on he asked for the Bear. Kurtzman listened to Bolan's request, then told him he would download the cell phone's message contents and pass the results to Erika Dukas, the Farm's top language expert.

Dukas had skills in an ever growing list of foreign tongues. Her natural ability to master languages, to translate, and her ability to understand dialects had proved her worth to Stony Man. Since joining the Sensitive Operations Group, Dukas had helped out on a number of operations.

Bolan knew that the translator would come back with a full breakdown of the cell phone's contents. With Kurtzman's promise Bolan finished the call.

"These people you can call on," Mitchell said. "They seem capable of handling pretty much everything you ask."

"Pretty much."

"Any chance they could help me with my tax return?"

The door to the club crashed open, and Seminov stomped in. From the look on the Russian cop's face Bolan knew things had not gone well. Seminov was muttering to himself as he stood over Lubinski. Nikolai Dimitri, his pistol still clasped in his hand, eased around his commander and faced Bolan.

"We missed them," he announced. His dismay was obvious as he looked around and saw the results of Bolan and Mitchell's encounter. "At least you got a result."

"DeJong and the other guy got away from us, too," Mitchell said. "It would have been hard to locate anyone in the general panic out there. Nikolai, don't beat yourself up over it."

"She's right," Bolan said. "You and Valentine caught the bad end of the deal."

"I don't like to let my friends down," Seminov grumbled as he turned away from the groaning Lubinski. He sighed. "Still, at least we have Lubinski. OCD has been after that piece of shit for a long time." He caught himself and glanced at Mitchell. "Forgive my language."

"Agent Mitchell has her own choice phrase when she gets mad," Bolan said lightly.

Mitchell smiled. "Valentine, I sympathize with you, so pay no attention to Mr. Perfect Cooper."

Dimitri was on his cell phone, calling for OCD backup and requesting medical help for Sergei Lubinski. When he had finished, he crossed to the metal table and stood looking at the stacked money. He was like a child viewing presents in a Christmas store.

"How much do you think there is?" he asked.

Mitchell picked up a wad of the cash, flicking through the bills.

"These are hundred dollar bills," she said. "Not new.

I'd say each wad is around five grand. So we have a lot of money here. A lot."

"The question is," Bolan said, "who was paying whom?"

Seminov stood over the moaning figure of Lubinski.

"Who was giving the party, Sergei? DeJong? Or the man with no name?" He nudged Lubinski's leg. "Don't waste my time. Who was the paymaster?"

Lubinski realized he was not going to win in this situation.

"DeJong," he said bitterly. "He brought the money for me. He works for Hegre."

Lubinski passed out before Bolan could ask him any more questions.

Russian efficiency was working well and they picked up the shrill sound of sirens within a few minutes. A pair of medics appeared, a wheeled gurney ready to take Lubinski. They bent over the man and worked to stem the blood flow from his arm before they loaded him on the gurney, strapping him securely.

"Valentine, we need answers," Bolan said.

Seminov nodded. He spoke rapidly with the medics, then to Bolan.

"They can bring him around for a while. You can talk with him in the ambulance before it leaves. Ask your questions."

"Thanks."

The club area was empty as Bolan and Mitchell followed the gurney outside. Seminov was staying behind to handle the removal of the money and the bodies. When they emerged from the club, the parking area had already been cleared, leaving only the ambulance and the OCD vehicles. A number of Seminov's men, all armed, were patrolling the front of the club. The area was crisscrossed by the flashing lights from police and medical vehicles. A group of local journalists was gathering, cameras flashing as they recorded the scene.

Mitchell found herself scanning the immediate area, checking rooftops on the opposite side of the street. It was normal practice, drilled into her by the FBI training she had been given. Bolan was doing the same, and it was only their vigilance that prevented the sudden attack from being successful.

Bolan saw the movement on the adjoining roof—a dark outline of head and shoulders rising above the parapet. The long outline of a rifle was angled at the gurney as it rolled toward the ambulance.

"Mitchell…" Bolan warned.

She had seen the threat and her reaction was identical to Bolan's.

They shouldered aside the medical assistants and grabbed the rails of the gurney.

The distant rifle snapped out a shot, the slug hitting the concrete in the wake of the gurney. More shots followed, the hard crack of the rifle sending a stream of shots that chipped at the concrete as Bolan and Mitchell hauled the gurney into the cover of the parked ambulance. A couple of shots hit the opposite side of the vehicle as the gurney was shielded by the gunfire.

One of the medics was down, clutching at his hip where a ricochet had hit.

Bolan moved to the rear of the ambulance, his Beretta in his hand, rising to track the figure across the street. Behind him Mitchell stayed by Lubinski's side, covering him with her own weapon.

The shooter was still visible when Bolan stepped out from behind the ambulance. He raised the Beretta and ran forward, heading across the street. Behind him Seminov and Dimitri emerged from the club, weapons in their hands. Seminov bellowed orders to the OCD cops and they began to move, rushing across the street, stopping traffic as they fanned out to cover both sides of the building.

Realizing he was about to be surrounded, the shooter emptied his magazine and laid down a hard volley, firing more for effect than gaining target acquisition. There were a few seconds when the firing ceased as the guy ejected the empty magazine and reloaded, then started to fire again. This time he took his time and two OCD cops went down.

Bolan put away his Beretta and crouched in the middle of the street, scooping up a weapon dropped by one of the shot OCD officers, a 7.62 mm Molot VEPR semiauto rifle. In the seconds he had as he took a grip on the rifle, Bolan noticed the 10-round magazine. He looped his arm through the webbing strap to stabilize his aim. Still on one knee, he shouldered the Russian rifle and held the target in his sights, ignoring the slugs peppering the street around him. His finger caressed the trigger.

The rifle cracked, once, twice.

The rooftop shooter jerked upright, his weapon flipping skyward.

In the split second he was exposed Bolan fired again and his slug slammed into the shooter's head, just over his left eye. The guy's head snapped back, a splash of blood spurting from the rear of his skull as he toppled out of sight.

Seminov appeared at Bolan's side, issuing more orders.

"I have never seen such shooting, my friend. And in such poor light. That was impressive."

Bolan tapped the rifle in his hand. "Good weapon," he said.

"Something we still can make," Seminov replied.

Dimitri was helping the medic to load Lubinski into the ambulance. The medic pulled a med kit from the vehicle and went to his shot partner. The wail of sirens grew louder as additional emergency vehicles raced to the scene.

Mitchell stood by, waiting for Bolan. He jerked his head at the ambulance and they stepped inside. Lubinski had his eyes open again, a look on his face that indicated he had no clear idea what was happening.

"Some friends you have out there," Bolan said.

"They were trying to kill me?"

"Looks like your partner DeJong made a call," Mitchell said.

"They're worried what you might say about them," Bolan added. "That you'll give away their plans."

Lubinski tensed as a surge of pain rose.

"They are…" Lubinski said.

"Don't kid yourself," Bolan said. "Those shots were meant for you."

"You still want to protect them?" Mitchell asked quietly. "The people who abandoned you. Hegre?"

Lubinski stared at them, nodded, as the truth hit home. "A bad association on my part."

"What *was* your part in this?" Bolan asked.

"I can tell you that," Seminov said from the open door of the ambulance. "This dumb wit is a transporter. He provides trucks and the like to move goods. Any kind of contraband goods."

"If I am a 'dumb wit,'" Lubinski said in a moment of defiance, "I have stayed out of your reach, Seminov. OCD has been trying to catch me for years. Who is the dumb one now?"

"This time you have gone too far," Dimitri snapped. "The material being transported is illegal uranium."

"Stolen from a mine in Kazakhstan," Bolan said. "To be transported from Kazakhstan to Iran where it will be refined to be used in nuclear weapons. But then you would know that, Lubinski."

"No. Not that. Only the part about transportation."

"That makes it a pretty serious hole you've got yourself in," Mitchell said.

"You provided the vehicle," Bolan said, "which means you're in this up to your neck."

Lubinski shook his head. "My deal was to give them what they wanted, a specially adapted fuel tanker with a hidden compartment underneath the main tank. They paid far more than the job was worth. A lot more. With the money I would be able to buy more trucks. It was a good deal."

"What else?"

"All I know is what they wanted. The completed vehicle was to be shipped by regular rail freight to Aktau, Kazakhstan. I know nothing else. The tanker would be picked up from the rail depot."

"Hegre has this pretty well worked out," Bolan said.

"We need to find out what happened to it," Seminov stated. "Then stop it."

"Not until the uranium is loaded," Bolan said.

"I helped," Lubinski pleaded. "You'll remember this. You have to."

"The less you say, the better," Dimitri warned him. "Don't forget OCD officers have been shot during this incident, and one of the medics tending to you. That will be hard to ignore."

"Let us not forget the money you were receiving for this venture," Seminov reminded Lubinski. "I have a feeling it will come under illegal payments during a criminal act. That should warrant more charges. And confiscation of that money."

"No. You can't do that. It would be stealing."

"Hearing that from you," Seminov said, "gives me a warm feeling inside.

"Go with him to the hospital, Dimitri," Seminov told his sergeant, "in case his conscience begins to bother him."

"One thing, Lubinski," Bolan said. "The Middle Eastern contact. Who is he?"

"His name is Raz Malik."

The ambulance pulled away. An OCD cop approached Seminov and spoke to him.

"They have identified the shooter from the roof," the Russian said. "Taras Buleva. What you would call a gun for hire. He's nothing but a low-class assassin, one who would work for anyone if they offered him enough money."

"A free agent?"

"*Da*. Buleva might have been a killer for hire, but the man had a way of staying clear of convictions. For some time he is reported to have worked for Soviet security. Maybe even KGB. And, of course, they protected him. After the breakup he started working for the criminal fraternity. Buleva had no religion where business was concerned. He took everyone's money. He slipped through our fingers because he had *friends* to keep him untouchable." Seminov managed a slow chuckle. "Of course, no one told *you* he was under protection."

"Does that mean you've upset someone else?" Mitchell asked.

"It won't be the first time," Bolan said.

"He was pretty sharp off the mark," Mitchell pointed out.

"On a situation watch," Bolan said, "hired to be around to back up the meeting. If Hegre had him installed on that roof, he would have been able to see what happened. It would only take a quick call from DeJong to alert him. Buleva was attempting to cut Lubinski out of the picture."

"This Hegre," Seminov said. "Very organized. Nothing is left to chance."

"It's why they've been around a long time," Mitchell said. "But I think we're starting to get to know them. Since Cooper's first involvement and now that we took their diamonds away from them, I think we've cracked the wall they built to protect themselves."

"Making a crack isn't enough," Bolan said. "We need to bring that wall down to the ground, taking Julius Hegre and Lise Delaware with it."

NONE OF THEM noticed the slight figure some distance away, in with the other media figures taking photographs of the scene. The guy dressed in an ill-fitting suit was using a camera fitted with a powerful telephoto lens that enabled sharp close ups, even from a distance. He concentrated on taking a number of shots of Bolan and Mitchell, before he backed away from the busy scene and eased into the shadows.

He walked to a car parked a couple of streets away, slipped behind the wheel, took out a cell phone and made a call.

"I have photos you'll be interested in. Of the scene around Babushka and the main players. Yes, the American and the woman with him. I can send the photos to you within the hour. The usual email address? No problem. Excellent. I look forward to checking my account in the morning. Always good doing business with you. Goodbye."

"LUBINSKI DIDN'T GIVE ANY more away on the ride to the hospital," Dimitri said when he rejoined them in Seminov's office on their return to the OCD.

"Maybe because he doesn't know anything more to tell

us," Bolan said. "He was paid to construct the tanker and deliver it to Kazakhstan. The theft of a substantial load of uranium is going to have the Kazakh cops running searches. Hegre will keep it undercover and wait until the panic dies down before they attempt to ship it out."

Seminov was scanning a map pinned to the wall. He ran a finger across the sheet.

"From Aktau there is a direct route to Iran," he said.

"By commercial ferry across the Caspian Sea," Bolan stated.

"Goods are moved that way all the time. If this special tanker is loaded with the uranium in a concealed base…"

"With a conventional load in the main tank," Mitchell said. "Do you think they could carry it off?"

"Possibly," Bolan said. He studied the map. "It's there. What we need to know is where."

CHAPTER TWENTY-EIGHT

"Now he shows up in Moscow. With that damned FBI agent. They broke up the meeting between DeJong and Malik. Lubinski was wounded and taken prisoner. De-Jong had someone waiting on a roof across the street from the club as backup. DeJong called him to take out Lubinski if he had the chance. He has not had any feedback. So we don't know what happened after he and Malik left. Time is at a premium, Dom. The theft of those Australian diamonds was supposed to be a means of recouping most of the loss we suffered when we lost the virus. Until Cooper dealt himself into the deal and took the diamonds away from us. The uranium is our current operation. If we satisfy the Iranians, our standing will rise. We have to succeed to restore our credibility. Eyes are on us. Future clients. Customers we already have. But now Cooper has shown up in Moscow and has already interfered. And wherever he goes the FBI agent goes."

"The deaths of those FBI agents has involved the Bureau. Killing them has made you *their* target, as well. Don't brush Cooper off, Lise. Or Agent Mitchell."

"Do you need to mention that woman?"

"She is proving to be a capable agent."

Delaware shrugged. Her attempt to brush off the FBI agent did not convince Melchior. He was aware of her dislike of failure. She did not take it lightly. Up until her initial clash with Cooper, Lise Delaware's record had been spotless. Now that she had been proved human, her reaction was expected by Melchior. He understood the human condition; unbroken success created a false sense of invulnerability. When that confidence was broken, it left the recipient shaken and it was that uncertainty that could easily lead the individual to make mistakes.

When he glanced at her again he saw, not Lise Delaware, the driving force behind Hegre, but the girl she had once been. Some part of her commanding presence had deserted her. She sat in the seat, staring at some point over Melchior's shoulder. Her thoughts were elsewhere for that moment, and Melchior knew he had to bring back the Delaware he knew and respected.

"Lise, listen to me. Take the next step. Accept the setbacks. Give your orders. Activate the team. Contact DeJong. It's vital to get the consignment moving in Kazakhstan. Have a second team out looking for Cooper and the woman. They need to prevent him from going after the uranium."

Delaware absorbed his words. Eye contact was made, and Melchior recognized the familiar expression in her eyes as she snapped out of her dark moment. She picked up the phone on her desk and hit a speed-dial number.

"Find out where DeJong is," she said when her call was answered. "I need to know what's happening in Moscow. Then get me Becker. Have him report to me on our assets in Russia. No, he will report to me now, not when he has a *moment*. Remind him who runs things around here."

She slammed the phone down and gave Melchior a tight smile.

"I want Lubinski's club checked out in case he left anything behind that might incriminate us. He was wounded and taken to the hospital. He wouldn't have had any chance to get rid of anything that might point the finger."

"You see," Melchior said. "Now you are thinking straight again. Feeling a little better?"

"Getting there."

CHAPTER TWENTY-NINE

"Babushka is deserted," Seminov announced the following morning. "The place is closed down. Everyone has gone, scattered to the four winds. I have been trying to get that club closed for months. You show up in town and manage it in one day. How do you do it, Cooper?" The OCD cop held up a big hand. "Yes, I know, it's a gift."

Bolan and Mitchell, along with Seminov and Dimitri, were at a table in a café along the street from the OCD building. Seminov had arranged for his American guests to have a room at a local hotel, giving them the chance to shower and change clothing before they met the next day.

Seminov had put out the word for DeJong and Malik.

Lubinski was under armed watch in his hospital room. He had undergone an operation on his badly damaged arm. The Russian had lost a great deal of blood from the wound and had not responded well to the surgery. The Russian medical team was maintaining a close watch over the man and were still debating the possibility Lubinski might need more surgery.

"So, Cooper, what are your thoughts?"

"Hegre has to get that uranium to Iran. They must know the authorities are going to be on the lookout for it. Trying for a fast transport would be asking for trouble."

"Good thought," Seminov said.

Mitchell topped up her cup from the coffeepot on the table. Her gaze wandered across the café and settled on a young couple. The woman was bending over her laptop, busily working the keyboard as she talked to her male partner.

Something clicked in Mitchell's brain.

Computer.

Stored information.

"Did you assign anyone to keep watch at Babushka, Valentine?" she asked.

"Local cops, yes."

"What is it?" Bolan said.

"I can't help thinking maybe we missed something," Mitchell said. "When we busted Lubinski and his guests, did anyone notice a computer? Laptop or otherwise?"

"Things were happening a little fast," Seminov said. "But it was a stupid mistake not to order a full check of the building before now. You make me look an amateur, Sarah Mitchell."

"You had things to do. People hurt. That was your priority, Valentine."

"Cooper, your partner knows how to ease the pain."

"Valentine," Mitchell stated, "you said Lubinski was a sharp operator. Don't you think he would keep a record of his deals? Perhaps Lubinski had information written down. With an operation the size he was running, there had to be records somewhere."

They trooped outside and climbed into the SUV. Dimitri handled the big vehicle well, swerving in and out of the Moscow traffic without a pause.

Seminov took out his comm set and made a call. There was no response. He tried a second time. Still nothing.

"Now that I do not like," he said. "Foot down, young Nikolai. And turn on everything."

The screech of the siren accompanied the flashing lights on the SUV. The heavy vehicle slid around the final street corner, tires protesting at the misuse. The Babushka parking lot was empty except for a single Moscow Police Department patrol car, the vehicle empty. Dimitri swung the SUV around the deserted car and brought it to a stop facing the club's entrance.

Bolan was the first out, his Beretta in his hand, Seminov close behind. Mitchell moved to the right and checked out the chain-link fence. The gate was open.

"We might have visitors back here," she said.

"Go check it out," Bolan instructed her. "Valentine, with me."

"Dimitri, go with the lady," Seminov said.

Bolan moved toward the club's entrance. Seminov was at his rear, clutching his pistol.

The main doors were partway open.

Bolan edged closer and used the toe of his boot to push the door wider. Low wattage security lights had been turned on. The illumination was dim, but there was enough to show the huddled form on the floor a few feet ahead of them. Seminov recognized the MPD uniform. He crouched beside the still body, checking for a pulse. He shook his head in Bolan's direction, holding up his hand to show the dark gleam of blood.

"Throat has been cut."

"Valentine, are there living quarters above the club?"

"*Da*. Access from behind the bar."

Bolan moved quickly across the empty dance floor and spotted the door set in the wall next to the bar. The plain door was ajar. Bolan used his left hand to widen the gap, checking the short corridor and the staircase. He took out his comm set and keyed the button.

"Door behind the bar," he said quietly. "Valentine and I are going up to the next floor. And we found one dead cop."

"One back here, as well."

"Watch your backs." Bolan clicked off, glanced in Seminov's direction. "They found the other cop."

Seminov swore vehemently in Russian.

Bolan scanned the stairs in front of him. They were not the open kind. Both sides were boxed in, which was not an ideal situation if an enemy appeared. It was, however, the only way to reach the upper floor.

Seminov touched him on the shoulder. "I will cover you, Cooper. You can trust me." The pistol in Seminov's hand was a 9 mm all-steel Yarygin PYa/MP-443, a Russian-made pistol with a 17-round magazine and an additional load in the chamber. "Russian gun. Like real vodka. Hell of a kick."

"Let's move," Bolan said.

He could see light on the ceiling and moving shadows.

Bolan moved fast, keeping his body low, so his head and shoulders remained out of sight as he powered up the stairs. Despite his solid bulk, Seminov moved equally as quickly and made virtually no sound as he stayed close to Bolan.

The room was large and well furnished. At the far end an office had been set up with a desk and swivel chairs and filing cabinets.

Three dark-clad figures were searching the room, making no attempt to do it quietly—or tidily. They were all armed with slung MP-5s.

Bolan tracked in with the Beretta as the closest guy moved away from a standing wooden cabinet he had emptied by dragging its contents to the floor. Turning aside, he now faced Bolan. His empty expression changed in the instant he saw Bolan. He yelled a warning and grabbed for his SMG.

The Executioner barely needed to alter his aim. He squeezed the 92FS, felt the pistol kick back and fired a second time. His shots were on target, slamming into the guy's chest and pushing him back against the wooden cabinet.

As Seminov reached the head of the stairs, moving to one side so he was not blocked by Bolan, he leveled his weapon and fired on the move, his slugs catching one of the intruders as he turned. The guy pitched facedown across the office desk.

The third guy brought his MP-5 into play, opening up with a volley that peppered the walls above Bolan and Seminov. Plaster showered them as the 9 mm slugs ripped the wall open. The sound of autofire was deafening in the enclosed room.

Bolan and Seminov fired in tandem, flame spouting from muzzles as they hit the gunner and dropped him to the floor, his chest spouting blood from a number of 9 mm hits.

"Here," Bolan said as he crossed the room.

On the desk, next to the man Bolan had shot, was a laptop.

"You think this will help?"

"We'll find out soon enough."

Bolan closed the laptop and picked it up. "We need to get this back to your department. Does OCD have any computer geniuses available? We're going to need one."

"Then you are in luck. I have an extremely clever young woman by the name of Timoshenko who deals with that kind of thing."

"It wouldn't be a bad idea to have some of your people go through this place, Valentine, to see if Lubinski has any other secrets stashed away."

The sound of footsteps on the stairs alerted them both. Then Mitchell's voice reached them, the tone edged with concern.

"Cooper?"

"We're clear," Bolan said.

Mitchell appeared at the head of the stairs, Dimitri close behind.

"You okay?" she said.

Bolan showed her the laptop. "Someone was interested in this," he said.

Dimitri spotted the three bodies. "So I see."

Seminov was already on his cell phone, giving the instructions that would bring an OCD team to Babushka.

"Any trouble down there?" Bolan asked.

"One man on guard duty," she said. "Nikolai has him cuffed to a water pipe."

"Backup is on the way," Seminov announced, "and I have called for someone to remove our dead police officers. Cooper, these Hegre people have a lot to answer for."

"And they will," Bolan said. "I'll make certain of that."

CHAPTER THIRTY

The President of the United States was seated on one of the Oval Office couches, across from Hal Brognola. They were both holding cups of coffee as they discussed the matter at hand. Brognola had arrived at the White House twenty minutes earlier, responding to a summons from the commander in chief. He had been ushered directly into the meeting, and the President had gotten straight to the point.

"My advisers and I are in agreement that this possible purchase of uranium by Ayatollah Fikri is disturbing, Hal."

"I couldn't agree more, sir, which is why I'm glad to be able to let you know that Striker is already involved."

"How involved?"

"His last communication said he was following a lead that says the uranium is somewhere in Kazakhstan. He's ready to move from Moscow to follow up that lead."

"How does Moscow fit into this?"

Brognola managed a weary smile. "It's a long story, Mr. President, that put Striker on the trail in the continental U.S.A., then Hong Kong and the Philippines, following a cache of hijacked diamonds a criminal organization was going to use to pay for the uranium. That led him to Moscow…"

The President drained his cup, stood and crossed to refill it.

"When does that guy ever sleep?"

"I've given up trying to work that one out."

"Is this another of his lone-wolf missions?"

"Not exactly."

"How not exactly?"

"An FBI agent is partnering him. The Bureau is involved because they are actively investigating the murder of two of their agents, both killed while looking into the Hegre organization. SA Mitchell was running the team the two dead agents were part of."

"I take it this is a sanctioned endeavor?"

"SAC Duncan gave his blessing."

The President wondered just what that meant, but accepted it was as close to an explanation he was likely to receive.

"Drake Duncan?"

"Yes, Mr. President."

"This Agent Mitchell. Is he a good man?"

Brognola paused for a heartbeat. "From what I've heard Sarah Mitchell is one of Duncan's best."

"Sarah Mitchell? As in ex-FBI Jonathon Mitchell's daughter?"

"One of the FBI's legends. Sarah Mitchell is following in her father's footsteps. Best in her class. She worked her way up to be one of Duncan's top SAs."

The President had a smile on his face when Brognola looked.

"That is some young woman," he said. "I've met her. She'll give Striker a run for his money."

"Sounds as if you believe we have a top team out there."

"No question, Hal. No question at all." The President cleared his throat. "You keep me fully appraised. Now, what about Fikri?"

"He's a strict radical. Mossad has a dossier on him. Director Isaac Tauber emailed a copy of his file, and it makes grim reading. The man makes some of the other radical ayatollahs look positively benevolent. The man preaches hatred for Israel and the U.S., and condemns us all the way down the line. His life is one round of agitation. Even though other ayatollahs have modified their stance regarding Israel and the West, this guy threats to burn us to the ground. Destroy everything we represent. As far as Mossad can work out, the man has never set foot outside Iran. He pulls in young believers and gives them what they want to hear. He has some wealthy patrons, too."

The President sighed, a resigned sound that expressed the feeling he held. Brognola understood. No matter what the Man said, or offered to someone like Fikri, it would be ignored. There was no ground for negotiation. Period.

"Hal, I've tried everything to get through to the man. His people won't even grant a hearing. The word comes back that he will not speak to the man he considers an abomination against all that Islam stands for. We are and I quote, 'lower than the worms who crawl beneath the earth and he will not soil his ears by even listening to our words.'"

"That kind of lays it on the line," Brognola said.

"Fikri has supporters in the region. He'll push the line until he gets what he wants."

"Director Tauber is losing patience. He sees Israel being backed to the wall. If he believes the Iranians are willing to go head-to-head, he will strike. If that happens, the region could go critical."

"Then we have to hope Striker contains the threat and cuts the head off the snake. Hal, give him whatever help he needs."

"It won't be much, sir. The way he operates, he's on his own. Most likely on risky ground. We can't advertise our presence to back him in a foreign nation or we risk being accused of...whatever the offending party throws at us.

That would just give the opposition free publicity to accuse the U.S. of reckless actions."

"You don't need to quote the book at me, Hal. Damned if we do, damned if we don't. I hate having to say it, but your guy is out there on his own. Not for the first time. And that goes for Sarah Mitchell, too. If anything happens to her, Jonathon Mitchell will not be pleased."

"If anyone can pull this off, sir, it's Striker."

Outside the Oval Office windows, dark clouds heralded a stormy day. Rain was already streaking the glass. The weather suited Hal Brognola's mood. The comparative comfort of his surroundings made him feel slightly uncomfortable. His thoughts were with his friend.

"Stay safe, pal. Come home alive and well."

CHAPTER THIRTY-ONE

The OCD technician was introduced as Ludmilla Timoshenko, a slim woman, with short blond hair above an elfin face. Her dark eyes were made larger by the glasses she wore. She made no concessions to her femininity, dressing in plain slacks and shirt that concealed her body. When she entered Seminov's office, carrying the laptop from Lubinski's apartment, she walked directly across to his desk and placed the computer down.

"I take it you have conquered the machine?" Seminov said. "And please speak English for our guests from America."

Timoshenko peered over her glasses at Mitchell, then Bolan. A slight frown of irritation creased her forehead.

"No Russian?" she said.

"I speak Russian," he said, "but my partner doesn't, and we would appreciate your help, Officer Timoshenko. Any information you may have found is important to our operation. Commander Seminov tells us we are fortunate to have you assist us."

Timoshenko cleared her throat, glancing at Seminov as if to question this unexpected praise. Seminov nodded for her to continue.

"Sergei Lubinski kept records of his transactions in an encrypted file. I think he was confident it could not be broken," she said. "Actually it was a simple code to break. Like most others of his criminal type, he did not fully trust those he worked with, and the hidden files were a form of insurance for himself in case anything went wrong. Once I broke through his barrier it was easy to run through the lists of past deals he has made."

"How far back do they go, Timoshenko?" Seminov asked.

"A number of years. Is that important?"

"It could help us uncover other criminal deals he has made. But for the moment we concentrate on his current activities. Namely anything on the lists that involve his dealings with Hegre, Henrick DeJong and Raz Malik."

"Those names occur a few times," Timoshenko said. "They go back no more than a few months. In the last few weeks Lubinski has added notes about the contract he undertook for DeJong. It mentions the construction of a specialist tanker."

The OCD officer tapped keys and brought up a schematic of a long-bodied liquid-carrying vehicle. The side view showed where a false lower section would be constructed. Above this was the expected section where fuel would be pumped inside.

"These are the work plans for the construction of the altered tanker. As you can see, where the filler hatches are situated, the interior has tubes that go down through the false floor to the actual bottom of the tank. If someone used measure gauges to check the load, the gauge sticks would show the correct level of liquid. To anyone inspecting the tank it would appear to have the correct capacity."

"Clever," Mitchell said. "The drums of uranium would go into the lower section out of sight."

"Is there information on where the tanker might be going?" Bolan asked.

Timoshenko returned to the main text, pointing her finger at a few lines.

"A rented property in the city of Aktau, Kazakhstan."

"Hegre needed a location where they could load the tanker with the uranium and top up the remaining space with a genuine load," Bolan said. "All very neat and smoothly worked out."

"Lubinski kept an itemized list of all construction materials and how long his craftsmen worked," Timoshenko said. "Even the cost of the rail transfer from his workshop to the Aktau depot."

"Hegre earns its fees," Seminov said. "All very professional."

"We're hoping to change all that," Bolan said.

His sat phone rang. It was Aaron Kurtzman.

"Your guy Raz Malik is one of Fikri's faithful henchmen."

"There's a word you don't hear much these days. *Henchman.*"

"I'm attempting to increase my word power," Kurtzman said.

"I'm impressed."

"You want to keep on insulting me or hear my information?"

"I'm all ears, Bear."

"Malik is in a number of databases. Some of ours. Mossad, of course. He's a cool son of a bitch, a sharp negotiator, and he can be a hard hitter when the need arises. He has a rap sheet of around eight kills. Known but never made to stick, which tends to be the norm for these guys. Malik moves around a great deal, working for the cause, which is anything that benefits his ayatollah. According to his sheet, he's an arrogant character with not a shred of remorse in his body, and he always seems to wriggle out of tricky situations."

"He did that in Moscow," Bolan said. "Okay. Any idea where he might be right now?"

"Thanks to Erica I might have an answer for you. She translated the messages in the cell phone he left behind. Nice list of numbers we're tracing as we speak. But the data you'll be interested in was in a couple of messages left for him that would tie in time-wise to when you had that set-to in Babushka."

"You're starting to interest me."

"Two short messages he wouldn't have been able to reply to, asking where he was and telling him to call back ASAP. Erica passed us the caller's ID and we backtracked. The calls came from a landline in the Kazakhstan city of Aktau on the coast of the Caspian Sea."

"That's the best news I've had today," Bolan said. "You just confirmed what we've been working out."

"We'll keep checking. I'll let you have any other goodies that show up."

"It'll be hard to top the one you just handed me." Bolan said goodbye and ended the call.

"Good news?" Mitchell asked.

Bolan related the information Kurtzman had given him.

"Wonderful news," Seminov said. "Now I suspect you will want to go to Aktau."

He beckoned to Dimitri. "Arrange a flight from Domodedovo, Nikolai, for our two friends to Aktau."

"Pity we're not collecting frequent flyer miles," Mitchell said. "With all the points we'd be getting, we could buy our own plane."

"When you reach Aktau," Seminov said, "be careful. My advice would be trust no one except the man I will put you in contact with. Local loyalties in Aktau can favor Fikri. There is a large Muslim population in Kazakhstan. Christian, as well, but it will be difficult to recognize friend from enemy. Be extremely cautious, Cooper. This time you will be stepping into the unknown. Watch each other's backs and sleep with your eyes open."

"Officer Timoshenko," Bolan said, "thanks for your input. You've been a great help. Much appreciated."

Timoshenko blushed at the praise and offered a smile.

"I hope the rest of your mission is successful."

After she had left the room Seminov gave one of his wide smiles.

"You see, Sarah, what a charmer he is. I cannot remember the last time Timoshenko smiled the way she did just now."

"Oh, I know how persuasive he is, Valentine. Do you know another man who could get a girl to leap out of a falling plane while hanging around his neck?"

Seminov laughed. "There I believe you have created a new record, Sarah Mitchell."

"Cooper, you're a record breaker," Mitchell said. "What do you have to say to that?"

Mack Bolan said nothing.

CHAPTER THIRTY-TWO

Hamid was shaking with rage when he slammed down the phone. He crossed to stare out the window, across the dusty landscape, as dust devils skittered across the dry land. The hot air touched his skin, and he felt himself yearning for something cool to reduce his anger.

"What is it, brother?" Kasim asked. "Is there a problem?"

"The uranium is ready to be moved out of Kazakhstan," he said, "but the American has been recognized in Russia. No doubt he is searching for the shipment. I have been told he almost caught Malik in Moscow. There was shooting and DeJong and Malik were lucky to escape with their lives. Malik says DeJong sent a team back to the Russian's club to search for his computer and the American and his female accomplice returned and killed them. The Russian police were also involved. We can be assured the computer will be in their hands now."

"Should this concern us, Hamid? We are tasked only to take charge of the shipment when it has landed on Iranian soil."

"You must understand. This American—Cooper—he has been interfering too much, attempting to prevent the uranium from reaching us. If he has information that might bring him to Kazakhstan, then the shipment could be at risk. Now that it has reached this far, we cannot allow it to be taken away from us."

"We could arrange for our people in the city to intercept and stop this American."

Hamid grasped the suggestion immediately. "Do it, Kasim. Use whatever assets we have in the country. There are believers in Kazakhstan who would be willing to work in God's cause. If we can prevent this American murderer and his agent from sabotaging the operation, then we will have done a great service to the cause."

"I will call Yussef and order him to gather his people and search for this Cooper."

"Make him understand the man cannot be allowed to step in our way."

MINUTES LATER THE phone rang in a coffeehouse in the city. The man behind the counter answered the call, spoke, then lowered the handset.

"Yussef, there is a call for you."

A tall, wild haired man seated at a table stood and walked to the counter. He took the phone thrust at him.

"Yes?"

"Yussef, I have something for you to do. Meet me in twenty minutes at the Shevchenko Monument. Have your people ready to work. I will explain when we meet. Twenty minutes, Yussef. Do not be late."

Yussef returned to his table and spoke with the men there. They left the café and stepped into the busy street. On Yussef's orders the men with him departed to carry out the orders he had given.

Yussef began to walk to the monument for his meeting. His lean figure moved effortlessly through the thronged street, and he was at his destination well before the appointed time. He stood close to the monument, lighting a thin, dark cigar. He drew in the bitter smoke, enjoying the taste.

He had barely smoked half the cigar when he saw Kasim walking toward him. The well-dressed figure, lean and gray haired, had the calm of a college professor; that was not far from the truth. In his time Kasim had been a student of politics and had given lectures. Now he was second in command of the team operating in Kazakhstan, his life dedicated to God. He followed Ayatollah Fikri, reborn as a soldier.

"As salaam alaikum," Kasim said.

"Wa alaikum salaam," Yussef responded.

The traditional greeting between two seemingly old friends held suggestions of harmony that were nonetheless a precursor to the planning of death and violence.

The two men walked slowly side by side, in deep conversation. When they parted, Yussef had his orders to hunt down and kill the American named Cooper and the woman who worked with him. The sentence had been extended to include anyone considered to be assisting Cooper.

In Yussef's pocket was an envelope that contained photographs of Cooper and Sarah Mitchell. They had been taken in Moscow by one of Hegre's people and passed along to Hamid.

Yussef took a cab that dropped him outside a workshop on the west side of town. He pushed in through the bleached wooden door and made his way through a quiet courtyard leading to a shadowed, former woodworking shop. His men were already gathered, playing cards and smoking.

"We have orders that come directly from Ayatollah Fikri. A hit against this man and woman," Yussef said, laying the photographs of Cooper and Mitchell on the tabletop. "Americans threatening the delivery of the shipment of uranium. We have orders to seek out this pair and execute them in God's name. They have already interfered with our brother in Russia. Now it is our privilege to stop them."

"Do we know where they are at this time?" one of the men asked.

"They were in Moscow, but I suspect they will not be there much longer. When Malik was forced to flee from Lubinski's club, he unfortunately left behind his cell. If it was recovered, which is likely, and analyzed, I am certain the Americans would have deciphered his messages. There were calls made from here to Malik. The Americans would have been able to trace where the messages came from and this man Cooper will no doubt follow up the source."

"You think he will come here?"

"He has followed the trail of the uranium this far. He will not give up now. Cooper will attempt to get here as quickly as possible, before we can move the uranium out of the country. Unfortunately for us, security has been heightened since we took the cargo and we have been forced to hide it until the police searches die down. They are watching ports and vessels. Have the photographs of Cooper and the woman copied and handed to all our informants and our own people. Bad enough the police are on alert, we now have this damned American on a personal mission to prevent delivery of the uranium to Iran."

Bashir, the man Yussef was talking to, said, "The airport will be his best choice. A flight directly from Moscow will bring him to Aktau in a few hours."

"Yes. My thoughts, too. Cover the airport well. If he is spotted, he must be apprehended and taken from the city."

"And?"

"Both he and the woman are to be executed. Kill them and bury them in some isolated spot."

"The woman from Hegre wants the American delivered to her alive."

"That does not interest me, Bashir. Since when do I consider what a woman wants? Especially an American whore. She is of no consequence to me. Our responsibility is to complete our mission. We answer to Ayatollah Fikri and no one else. At present the uranium is secure. We must hold it until it is safe to move it to the docks. And in the meantime we concentrate on finding these Americans."

CHAPTER THIRTY-THREE

The plane was a SCAT Airlines YAK-42, and not the most comfortable Bolan had flown in. The triple-engined, swept-wing, Russian-built aircraft rose smoothly enough from Domodedovo International Airport, Moscow, as late-afternoon light glanced through the plane's windows. The flight time was announced as two and a half hours. From his window seat Bolan saw the landscape fade as they rose through the clouds. Ahead lay Aktau, in Kazakhstan's Mangystau Province. At that moment it was all Bolan and Mitchell had, apart from the contact Valentine Seminov had provided.

The Russian cop, with his unerring skill, had arranged for Bolan to be met at the airport by Arkady Greshenko, a covert Russian operative who had been based in Kazakhstan for a number of years. Greshenko was a veteran of a number of undercover missions in and around Aktau, where he kept an eye on the comings and goings in the city. Aktau's position on the Caspian Sea, with direct access to Iran, had generated enough interest for the Russians that they kept a presence in the area. Greshenko represented Russian interests. His cover was a small travel agency, allowing him to maintain a presence in the city of Aktau. He arranged matters for Russians making visits to the area where the coastal city drew a small but steady flow of visitors.

Seminov, with a wide sweep of contacts in Russia and

elsewhere, had known Greshenko for many years. They
had worked together on criminal cases many times and
had a good relationship. Seminov's call to Greshenko had
resulted in Bolan and Mitchell gaining an ally in the Kazakhstan city.

"Arkady will be of great help," Seminov said. "He
knows the city and the surrounding countryside. Trust
him as you trust me. That is, of course, if you do trust me."

"Valentine, if you're looking for a compliment, you've
got one," Bolan said. "If this Greshenko is half as good as
you, then we have nothing to worry about."

Seminov grinned at Mitchell. "You see how he can flat-
ter me, as well, Sarah."

Mitchell shook her head. "If you two would like a private moment, I'll leave the room."

Seminov frowned, not immediately catching her meaning, then burst into laughter.

Dimitri came into the office, clutching a folder. He held
it out to Bolan.

"Travel visas. Documentation that customs will require
on your arrival," he said. "Courtesy of the OCD. They are
made out in your passport identities. You will not be able
to take your weapons with you, but Arkady will furnish
you with what you need. He will meet you outside the airport. We have emailed him your pictures so he will recognize you."

"Valentine, thanks for the assist," Bolan said.

"Thank me by finding that uranium and stopping this
madness Fikri wants to spread. That will be enough, my
good friend. You take care of yourself—and this beautiful young woman. If she comes to harm, I will be a sad-
dened man."

Dimitri drove them to Moscow's Domodedovo airport.
He followed them inside and said his farewells quickly.

"Be careful," he said. "We will be waiting to hear of your success."

He hugged them both, turned and left.

"I believe that young man will miss us," Mitchell said.

"Me, no. But he will miss Sarah Mitchell."

"No."

"I think he enjoyed working with the lady FBI agent."

Mitchell grinned. "Aw, shucks, boss."

"VALENTINE IS A good man," Mitchell had said as the jet eased up off the runway. "A good friend."

She had then settled back in her seat and slept the entire flight, leaving Bolan to his own thoughts.

Hegre.

Lise Delaware.

Delaware was a vengeful woman, orchestrating a cycle of death and organized crime that had pulled Mack Bolan across the miles to China and the Philippines, to close escapes and threats in Russia. And it was far from over as the chase continued, drawing the Executioner to Kazakhstan. There he would pick up the threads leading him to the stolen uranium and then remove it from the plans of Ayatollah Fikri, Iran and its seemingly insatiable desire to create yet more nuclear weapons to add to the list of the global threats. Removing Iran's current scheme to add to the worldwide arsenal would not be an end to the nuclear horror, but it would hopefully take away that nation's current hope to become a nuclear power. Bolan understood that, even if he succeeded, Iran would not end its search. The date of nuclear acquisition would be extended and, as long as that day stayed in the future, the possibility of some kind of peace might be resolved.

No guarantees, Bolan understood, *but any bit of hope had to be fought for.*

That end was no different from his own personal fight against the forces of evil, in whatever form they took. Bolan had long accepted that his War Everlasting was just that. A relentless fight against enemies who outnumbered him, who fell away on one battlefront only to be replenished by others. The numbers were against him, overwhelming if he sat down to count them. But that thought never occurred to Bolan. He fought because he had no other choice. However small his victories against darkness, they *were* victories. And for Mack Bolan it was enough. He would come through, maybe bloodied and battered, but never for an instant, bowed. It was not in his nature to accept defeat, or even to allow the thought to form in his mind.

He glanced at the young woman next to him, marveling at her dedication. Since he had met Sarah Mitchell, his respect for her had grown. Out of her determination to take down Hegre and her loyalty to her fellow FBI agents who had sacrificed their lives, Mitchell had proved herself more than once. He had no doubt she would add to that distinction in whatever lay ahead of them. As courageous as she was beautiful, the FBI agent was a genuine example of the Bureau's motto.

FBI.

Fidelity, Bravery, Integrity.

Bolan could find no better way to describe her.

THEY MADE THEIR descent in bright sunlight, only a half hour beyond the stated arrival time. Bolan felt the aircraft bank as the pilot lined up on their runway, the plane trembling as the flaps were lowered. He caught a blurred glimpse of the strip as the plane completed its descent, heard the squeal as the wheels touched. The heavy bulk of the aircraft settled. The pilot reversed the jet's thrust and deceleration pressed them into their seats. The plane slowed, trundling along the runway and finally turning onto the side strip where it came to a stop.

Aktau's Shevchenko Airport was medium-sized. It would have been dwarfed in the shadow of any of the major international American or Russian hubs. The terminal building was not particularly impressive, but it served its purpose.

Passing through customs was fast and without problems. Mr. and Mrs. Hamilton, arriving in Kazakhstan for a private visit, were stamped and passed through with a minimum of delay.

As they emerged on the other side of the checkpoint, Mitchell said, "That went well. Maybe *too* well."

Bolan took her arm and steered her across the arrivals hall. "Enjoy the moment," he said.

"Am I starting to show signs of paranoia?"

"Just a mild attack."

They stepped outside, felt the heat. It was the kind Bolan could take. He placed his flight bag on the concrete, glancing around without making too much of a show.

The parking lot, across from the terminal building, was only half full. A pair of buses were waiting to take passengers away and a few taxis hovered in the hope of picking up fares.

"Mr. and Mrs. Hamilton?"

The man who approached them was of average height, his graying hair brushing the collar of his shirt. The shirt was striped blue-and-peach, the Chinos he wore, light colored and slightly creased. His weathered face wore a neutral expression but his brown eyes were sharp and clear.

"Arkady Greshenko," he said. His English bore a strong Russian accent. He smiled at Mitchell. "Your picture does not do you justice. You are beautiful." Greshenko took Mitchell's bag. "I have my car over there."

He led the way across to a dusty, large and angular Volvo, an older model that purred into life when Greshenko turned the key. He swung the vehicle around and drove out of the airport parking lot, heading for the road to Aktau.

"It is only twenty-five kilometers to the city. Sixteen miles, if you prefer. It will not take long. So, how is Seminov? I have not seen him for a few years. Is he still as ugly as ever?"

"I'm sure he likes you, too," Mitchell said from the rear seat.

"So, it seems we have a problem here in Aktau. One that Valentine believes I may be able to assist you to solve."

"Did he explain the problem?" Bolan said.

Greshenko nodded. "In his usually direct way. Uranium. Iran. A cell of operators working on behalf of this Ayatollah Fikri. More problems with these damned Islamic dissidents. Being here on the edge of the Caspian means we get these people playing their dangerous games all the time. The trouble is these people are more dangerous than anyone can imagine. Unpredictable. They have single line of thought. If you are not, as they see it, of their faith then you must be an enemy. It is very narrow-minded. It makes me glad I have no religious leanings."

"Did Valentine tell you about the location we have uncovered?" Bolan asked.

"Yes. But first we might do well to pay attention to the vehicle that has tailed us since we left the airport," Greshenko said.

"Dark SUV," Bolan replied. "I've been watching."

Mitchell didn't turn. She looked into the rearview mirror.

The vehicle was fifty feet back. Though the road was

quiet, with nothing to hold it back, the SUV was keeping pace with them, able to maintain clear observation without committing.

"I don't recognize the plate number," Greshenko said. "Or the vehicle. Most probably a rental."

"Hegre?" Mitchell asked, directing her question at Bolan.

"Could be."

"Please, what is this Hegre?" Greshenko asked.

"A criminal organization we have been tracking," Bolan said. "They act as go-betweens on illegal deals. It's a large organization with a lot of contacts. This time they're acting for Ayatollah Fikri. They set up the theft of the uranium and worked a deal with a man in Moscow who provided the special truck to carry the uranium across to Iran. Fikri isn't able to buy uranium on the open market because of sanctions. So he's trying to smuggle it in by the back door. Hegre offers its services and gets paid for doing that."

"People like Fikri make it difficult for us all," Greshenko said. "They have no conscience about building and spreading nuclear poison."

"And they are persistent," Mitchell added.

"Hegre? Or Fikri's people?" Greshenko asked.

"Both. Somebody has been butting in ever since we started on this," Bolan said. "Why should it be any different here in Kazakhstan?"

"Should I stay on the main highway, or take a side road?" the Russian asked.

"We don't know what they want," Bolan said. "If anything happens, I'd rather we were away from civilians."

"Cooper, we're not armed," Mitchell warned.

"Look in the glove box," Greshenko said. "I think you will find something of interest there."

Bolan opened the flap. The glove box was large and

deep. The items of interest turned out to be a pair of Steyr Mannlicher M-A1 pistols, with synthetic polymer bodies, striker fired, and in .40 caliber. There were two extra, filled magazines, which held twelve rounds, to go with the weapons.

"I decided these would be of more use than sunblock," Greshenko said.

"You were not wrong," Bolan said.

He passed one of the pistols to Mitchell, along with a spare magazine. They quickly checked the weapons and made sure they were ready to use.

"Hold on," Greshenko said moments before he swung the Volvo off the road and onto a narrow, uneven side road that cut across country. The terrain on either side was uneven, with a scattering of trees and bushes. A thick trail of pale dust rose as Greshenko expertly guided the heavy car along the strip. Mitchell had turned now so she could watch their rear.

"Do you see them?" Greshenko asked.

"It's difficult with all the dust you're raising, but yes, they're behind us, and coming up fast. That proves one thing. They *were* following us."

"Somebody has good intelligence," Bolan said. "They were waiting for us at the airport."

"That suggests they're anxious we don't start searching for their hidden prize."

"Do you believe they will try to kill us?" Greshenko asked.

"That would be the thing to do. Deal with us now and get it over with."

"That's a comforting thought," Mitchell said. "Déjà vu, Cooper. Haven't we been here before?"

"This has happened already?" Greshenko said.

Mitchell patted him on the shoulder. "Only all the time," she said.

The Volvo hit a bump in the trail, rose into the air then slammed back down. Greshenko wrestled with the wheel for a few seconds to bring the car back in line.

"Not the best road I could have chosen," he murmured. "But the Swedes build very tough cars."

"Our guy is closing in," Mitchell said. "His gas pedal must be flat to the boards."

With its larger wheels and better suspension, the SUV was closing the gap. The power under the hood was also making a difference. The heavy vehicle surged forward and even through the dust billowing up from beneath the Volvo's tires, Mitchell saw a man lean out from the passenger door. The subdued crackle of autofire reached her. An SMG. Flames spit from the muzzle. Mitchell felt the thump as slugs hit the Volvo's rear below the trunk.

Now he's got his range, she told herself.

She saw the shooter raise his arm.

"Incoming," she yelled and ducked.

The SMG fired again. The second burst of fire drove a stream of slugs into the Volvo's rear window, which disintegrated. Glass fragments showered over Mitchell as she let herself drop down onto the seat.

Greshenko jerked as a stray slug struck his right shoulder. He slumped forward, almost falling across the wheel. Making an effort, he wrenched the Volvo's wheel, sending the car off the trail. The car jolted from rut to rut as Greshenko aimed it at a clump of trees.

"They're still coming," Mitchell yelled, twisting in her seat to check out the rear window.

More autofire reached their ears. Slugs peppered the rear corner of the Volvo, the sturdy body of the vehicle absorbing the impact.

"When we reach cover, get out," Greshenko said. "Let me draw them away."

His right arm hung at his side, his shoulder pumping blood.

"We can't let him…" Mitchell protested.

"We have to. It gives us the chance to catch them from behind if we move fast," Bolan said.

The tree line was coming up fast, Greshenko swinging the Volvo at the widest gap he could see.

"Do it," he said. "Just shoot straight and don't miss."

Bolan grasped the door handle, the Steyr in his right hand.

Behind him Mitchell held herself close to the rear door, the door already freed from the catch.

The mass of timber engulfed them, the Volvo brushing a rough barked trunk. Greshenko hauled on the wheel, steering as direct a course as he could.

"Go," he shouted.

Bolan and Mitchell pushed open their respective doors, hoping they wouldn't slam them into the trees sliding by. The moment they had wide a wide enough gap, they rolled clear of the car.

Mitchell's door slammed against a tree, and it was pushed against her back as she slid clear. The impact knocked her to the ground, breath driven from her body. She sensed the Volvo disappearing into the trees as she sucked air into her lungs, struggling to stay in control.

The SUV loomed large, plowing its way forward.

As Bolan rolled to his feet, he saw the Volvo veer off course and slam into the trees.

The oncoming SUV filled his field of vision, the shooter still leaning from the window. It began to slow as the Volvo came to a hard stop.

Bolan, pushed back into the undergrowth, swung his

Steyr and acquired his target. His finger stroked back on the trigger, and he laid a double tap into the exposed head of the shooter. The .40-caliber slugs hammered in above the guy's eye, blowing out through the back of his skull. The shooter flopped over the window frame, half out of the SUV, a spray of blood misting the air.

Bolan moved out of cover, circling the SUV as it slid past him. The driver had jumped on the brake, bringing to vehicle to a slithering stop as the tires lost traction on the carpet of leaf mold.

The Executioner ducked at the rear of the SUV, catching a glimpse of movement inside. He figured the driver and one man in the rear.

The guy in the back popped up, staring around as he tried to locate a target. Bolan picked up muffled conversation from inside. The right-hand rear door was booted open and an armed man emerged, his SMG swinging back and forth as the guy looked for a target. Bolan, crouching, leaned around the rear corner and tracked the guy with his pistol. He held back only long enough to ensure he had full target acquisition before he fired. A trio of .40-caliber slugs cored into the guy's chest. He fell back against the open door, his eyes wide with shock. The expression was still there as he toppled to the ground.

The driver had scrambled free from behind the wheel, pushing open his door as he grabbed for his own weapon. He turned, seeking Bolan's elusive figure and saw Mitchell, on her knees, the Steyr in her hand swinging into firing position. The pistol exploded and the .40-caliber slug punched in under the guy's jaw, angling up to blow out through the top of his head, taking off a chunk of skull as it emerged. The guy went down without a sound.

Bolan cleared weapons from around the bodies, then moved to where Mitchell was pushing upright.

"What happened?" he said.

"I didn't clear the door fast enough."

"Just rest."

"You need to go check on Arkady. I'm fine."

Bolan saw the Volvo door swing open as he neared it. Greshenko swung half out of the vehicle.

"It has turned out to be a busy day," the Russian said.

"We need to get you to a doctor," Bolan stated.

Greshenko shook his head. "Doctor will mean paperwork. Gunshot—the police. First we get back to my place. In their car. Hide it. I have friends who will help. In my business it is advisable to have friends."

He reached out and took Bolan's strong hand and they walked back to the SUV. Bolan slid the body of the dead man out of the SUV. Greshenko slid onto the passenger seat and Bolan got behind the wheel.

"Arkady, are you okay?" Mitchell asked.

"You mean apart from the bullet in my shoulder?" He gave a deep chuckle. "Valentine said meeting you would be an experience. I will have to tell him how right he was."

"That bullet needs to come out quickly," Mitchell said.

"Do you have a cell phone?" Greshenko asked.

Bolan handed over his sat phone. "Try this."

He started the engine, put the drive into reverse and maneuvered the large SUV back along the way they had come.

Greshenko made a call and as soon as he was connected began a conversation in Russian. He spoke for some time without pause. Whoever he was speaking to didn't interrupt. Finally Greshenko ended his call and returned the phone to Bolan.

Bolan stopped at the trail. "Which way, Arkady?"

Greshenko took a moment to reply. Bolan saw his face was beaded with sweat. His hand was pressed over the blood-soaked patch in his shoulder.

"Go to right. The trail will join up with the road about a kilometer along. From there I can guide you to the city."

The ride had to have been uncomfortable for the Russian as each bump in the trail was causing him discomfort. He bore his pain in silence, only once letting out a subdued groan.

They reached the highway and Greshenko told Bolan which way to go. The highway was quiet. Only a few cars passed on the other side. Aktau appeared in the distance, and beyond it they picked out the gleam of water.

The Caspian Sea.

Bolan slowed as they drove into the city, Greshenko directing him along narrow streets with older buildings on either side. This was the original Aktau. The modern city rose above the rooftops ahead of them.

"The city is developing," Greshenko said. "A lot of new buildings. We do not need this Fikri making bombs. His kind does not think of others when they plan nuclear devices. Radiation released into the air has no consideration for borders. The wind blows it where it wants."

They rolled along a narrow street, and Greshenko instructed Bolan to drive into a side street. Wooden gates were set in a high wall.

"Would you open the gates, Sarah," Greshenko said.

The gates opened onto a courtyard. Bolan drove in through the gates and Mitchell closed and secured them. The courtyard was at the rear of the travel agency, with living quarters attached.

Mitchell opened the door to help Greshenko out of the SUV. As Bolan walked around the car, a door opened in the house and a figure emerged.

A tall young woman with black hair that matched her outfit.

She held a .357 Magnum Desert Eagle pistol in one

hand, handling the large weapon easily. A faint smile curled her shapely lips.

"So good to see you again, Cooper," she said. "The last time we met it was over much too quickly. I've been waiting for this moment."

It was Lise Delaware.

CHAPTER THIRTY-FOUR

Armed men showed themselves, surrounding Bolan and Mitchell. The soldier recognized Henrick DeJong and Raz Malik behind Delaware. There were a couple of armed men Bolan suspected were Delaware's hardmen.

"Nice of them all to get together in a group," Mitchell said. "Saves us a lot of running around looking for them."

Bolan kept his eyes on Delaware. Their first encounter had been brief and violent, and he had been left with the impression of a tall, physically attractive women. Seeing her close up only added to that image. There was no denying she was beautiful, though the taut expression on her face took the edge off it. The hardness in her eyes went deep. Up close now, Bolan saw her eyes were green flecked hazel; they were piercing and intense; her animosity toward Bolan was not concealed.

"Your interference has cost Hegre a great deal," Delaware said. "You have upset our plans and damaged our reputation. But that ends here and now. We have control again, and this time it stays with us." She laughed quietly. "After all your efforts you've failed. Our friend, Mr. Malik, will have his uranium. Hegre will recoup its expenses. And you, Cooper, are mine. I think overall that will give me the greatest satisfaction."

She saw the questioning look in Bolan's eyes, and it brought a brief smile to her lips.

"How did we know? Cooper, we have our sources wher-

ever we go. You were spotted the moment you stepped off
the plane. Aktau is no different from anywhere else. And
our Iranian friends here are the same. Greshenko is known
to us. When he met you…" She shrugged. "All so easy."

Hands reached out and took Bolan's pistol. Mitchell
was also disarmed. The soldier could sense the two Hegre
men close behind him. They were carrying P-90 SMGs,
the weapons pointed at Bolan and Mitchell, and as much
as he wanted to take action he realized this was not the
place or the time.

"I have a wounded man here," he said. "He needs tending to."

"We met his friends inside," Delaware said. "They will
not be able to give him the treatment he needs. They are
quite dead. So we will offer an alternative."

Delaware glanced at one of her men and flicked her
head in Greshenko's direction.

In the space of a few seconds as the man moved his arm,
Bolan understood. There was nothing he could do as the
guy freed his right hand, dropped it to his waist.

When the hand moved again it was gripping a silenced
pistol.

Greshenko wasn't even aware of what was happening.

Mitchell did and raised a hand, calling out, taking a
step forward.

The silenced Beretta homed in on Greshenko. The trigger was pulled twice and delivered a pair of 9 mm Parabellum rounds. They hit Greshenko in the center of his
forehead. The Russian's head snapped back, a dark spray
erupting from the back of his skull. He slid across the side
of the SUV. His legs collapsed and he hit the ground, blood
starting to pool from beneath his shattered skull.

"You bitch…" Mitchell screamed, all control left behind in her anger.

Ignoring the weapons aimed in her direction, the FBI agent went for Delaware. She managed two steps before the Hegre man with the silenced Beretta turned the weapon on her.

"Do it," Delaware said coldly.

The 9 mm slugs hit Mitchell in the upper body, stopping her forward motion and turning her sideways.

Bolan caught her shocked stare as she fell to the ground, her body jerking for a few seconds before she became still.

"Enough," Delaware said. "Let's go before anyone in this godforsaken town hears us. I want to be on our way in the next thirty seconds. Move, people, or get left behind."

Bolan, a hard muzzle jammed into his spine, was hustled across the courtyard and out through a smaller gate. An SUV was parked at the far end of the back street. The evacuation was swift and controlled. Delaware's men piled into the rear with Bolan between them. DeJong and Malik took the middle row, and Delaware sat alongside the driver. The SUV drove to the far end of the narrow street, hung a left and proceeded through the city, finally merging with traffic on the main thoroughfare leading out of Aktau.

Bolan heard and saw nothing. He offered no resistance as he sat between his armed guards.

He was thinking of only one thing.

Sarah Mitchell lying on the cold ground.

And he was seeing again the shocked expression in her eyes as she went down, staring at him in a mix of shock and sheer disbelief.

In his mind he was reliving everything they had been through since the moment he had met her. Her sheer professionalism in the face of deadly force. The sharpness of her reactions. The keen mind that had offered wry comments and comebacks. A young woman who had partnered him through desperate situations and traveled across the globe in pursuit of their mutual enemies.

He had not been able to save her when she needed him the most.

The memories hovered in his mind.

His anger grew and gripped him, and for a time Bolan was consumed by it.

But the rage quickly subsided and was replaced by a cold resolve.

Cold enough that it became a physical sensation. It calmed him. It did not wipe away his determination to see this thing through to an end.

An end that would leave Mack Bolan the sole survivor.

He made that promise to Sarah Mitchell.

It was the least he could do.

It WAS ALMOST dark when the SUV drove in through sagging metal gates and came to a stop outside a shabby building alongside an identical SUV. As the doors opened, Bolan picked up the scent of the sea close by. There was also the pervading smell of fish and diesel fuel. Glancing out the closest window, he made out the outlines of derelict boats. His armed guards pushed him out of the vehicle, and Bolan felt loose shale underfoot. He was pushed in the direction of the building, guided inside.

The interior was lit by overhead lights suspended from thick cables. In the background Bolan could hear the low rumble of a diesel engine that would be powering the generator for the lights.

"Only temporary quarters," Delaware said. "But make yourself comfortable, Cooper."

Two armed men were waiting. One moved to meet them. He was dark skinned, bearded and when he spoke his English was stilted.

"He killed our brothers," he said. "I want his blood now."

He was, though Bolan didn't know it, Yussef, the Kazakh who had sent his people out to take down Bolan and Mitchell.

"No," Delaware said. "This man is *my* prisoner. I'll decide what happens to him."

"You are in my country now, woman. And here women know their place. Perhaps you need a lesson in humility."

Delaware laughed, a sound expressing the lack of respect she had for Yussef.

"I can't believe I'm hearing this. If it wasn't for this *woman,* you wouldn't be in possession of your precious uranium. How do you think it was taken from that train and brought here so you could send it to Fikri? It was done by my people. *By Hegre.* Do you know why? Because you damn people could not have organized it yourselves. Do not point the finger at me, Yussef, and use your religious bigotry. It doesn't make me cower in fear. I am not one of your subservient women."

She turned her back on the man and crossed to where Bolan stood between his guards.

"Do you have anything worthwhile to contribute, Mr. Cooper?"

Bolan held her gaze.

"There isn't a thing I have to say to you, Lise Delaware. I know everything I need to know. It's enough."

Delaware searched his face in an attempt to understand his remarks. She found nothing and turned away.

"Bring him."

To Malik she said, "Let's go and look at your goods."

"Explain to me again why the goods aren't already underway," the Iranian replied.

"Patience," Delaware said. "Understand we needed to

keep the consignment out of sight until the authorities have exhausted their search. Right now they are checking every large vehicle lining up to be loaded onto a ferry bound for Iran."

"They naturally assume the uranium is bound for my country?"

"Don't be so naive, Mr. Malik. Stolen uranium is more likely to be heading there than any other destination. Your ayatollah knows Iran is on every list when it comes to being banned from importing large amounts of uranium. Regardless of his low opinion of Western ideology, the consensus is Iran needs to be watched, which is why *we* are taking precautions."

Delaware led the way through to the rear of the building. They all stepped through a door into a separate enclosure. Low lighting showed the road vehicle parked there.

Bolan's Hegre guards stayed close to him, Fikri's people to the side.

An eight-wheel tractor unit was hitched to a thirty-five-foot tanker that had triple sets of wheels. The sides of the tanker were emblazoned with the logo of the company it was masquerading as. Both tractor unit and tanker showed signs of normal wear and tear. On first inspection it looked like a regular road vehicle, scratched and dented, streaked with dirt. In all aspects it was a commercial tanker that regularly made delivery runs between Kazakhstan and Iran.

Delaware stood beside the vehicle, her hand resting on the aluminum curve.

"An example of Sergei Lubinski's skill," she said. "Two-thirds of the tanker are normal. The final section holds additional cargo—in this instance the buckets of uranium yellowcake—cleverly engineered not to be noticed. I believe our Russian friend has succeeded extremely well. It is worth the price we had to pay."

She led Raz Malik around the standing vehicle, explaining more about the construction, leaving Bolan under the watchful eye of the pair of Hegre guards. DeJong paused a few seconds before following Delaware. Standing off from Bolan's position, Yussef and Bashir waited impatiently. Fikri's men, Yussef especially, were still unsettled by Bolan's removal of their people in the SUV that had followed Greshenko's car from the airport.

And Yussef was still angry following Delaware's outburst. Her defiant words had embarrassed him. He was not used to being chastised by a woman and especially an American. Her words had struck with the force of a physical blow.

Bolan quietly observed the Yussef's barely controlled fury. He had his eyes fixed on Delaware as she walked away from him. The fact she had turned her back to him, dismissing him as she would a servant, was feeding his rage. Yussef was close to exploding, and getting closer with each passing moment. He was mouthing low words that only his companion, Bashir, could hear. Bashir was quietly attempting to cool his partner down.

Yussef was not to be placated.

He uttered a wild scream of rage, the words spilling from his lips unchecked as he reached for the pistol tucked into his waistband.

Delaware's men turned at the outburst, attention removed from Bolan.

"You stand down," one of them yelled.

Yussef ignore him.

As thin as it was, the moment became Bolan's one chance.

He took it, snapping into action and slammed his knuckled right hand into the closer guard's throat. Nothing was held back. The blow crushed the guy's larynx. He struggled to draw breath, but couldn't. His grip on the FN P-90 slackened and Bolan was able to snatch it clear. Turning on his heel, the Executioner confronted the second guard, still raising his own weapon. Seconds too late. The muzzle of Bolan's SMG was almost touching the guard's torso when it fired. A burst of 5.7 mm slugs ripped into the guy's body, tearing at flesh and organs on their way through. The spine was severed as slugs ripped into it. The guard collapsed without resistance, blood spreading out from beneath his body.

Whirling, Bolan delivered a second burst at the still-choking guy with the crushed throat. The harsh chatter of the P-90 drowned the strangled cry coming from the guard as Bolan's volley tore into him.

Seeing the Americans go down, Yussef and Bashir stepped back. Bashir clawed for the weapon tucked behind his belt.

With Delaware's gunners down, Bolan was clear to engage. He dropped to a semi-crouched position, bringing the P-90 around in a fast, hard curve that allowed him to target the men.

Seeing the SMG's muzzle tracking them, Yussef and Bashir realized they were in harm's way.

Bashir turned and ran. He had traveled no more than ten feet when Bolan's burst sent 5.7 mm slugs between his shoulders. The impact had him stumbling forward, ribs shattered and one lung punctured. Bashir struck the concrete floor on his face, the bones of his cheeks fracturing from the impact. His nose was crushed and blood gushed out in a hot stream.

Aware of Bashir falling, Yussef went for cover behind the rear of the tanker. He imagined he was safe until Bolan turned the SMG on him and fired. Slugs chunked into the edge of the aluminum tanker, easily tearing through the metal. A few, deformed by the impact, emerged from the end cap and ripped into the side of Yussef's face, exposing his gums and teeth. Blood poured from the wounds. Pain followed quickly, and Yussef would have screamed if blood had not been filling his mouth and throat.

In his agony he let go of his pistol and it thumped to the floor. Yussef clamped his hands over the gaping wound, blood streaming in hot torrents between his fingers. It spilled down over his beard and onto the front of his shirt. He failed to notice a shadow falling across him as Bolan edged around the tanker. He hit Yussef with a steady volley and saw the man tumble, stitched from waist to throat by the killing burst.

Bolan was not done yet. He turned and walked toward the front of the vehicle, pausing long enough to pick up the other fallen P-90 and a box magazine. He retrieve one of the .40-caliber Steyrs Delaware's guards had taken from him, then continued on.

Right then, as he moved cautiously forward, Bolan's feelings *were* cold.

Cold and devoid of any distractions.

He was here to finish the mission.

And that would not be done until he counted three more kills.

Henrick DeJong.

Raz Malik.

And Lise Delaware.

Bolan heard movement around the head of the tractor unit. Feet scuffling on the concrete.

A man's voice rose in panic.

Henrick DeJong stepped into view. His hands were held

over his head, his pistol dangling from one finger by the trigger guard. His face was glistening with sweat.

"I surrender," he said. His voice was hoarse, his South African accent strong, the words forced out. "No more. This madness has to stop."

Bolan kept on coming, eyes searching ahead.

He hadn't forgotten Raz Malik.

And he certainly hadn't forgotten Delaware.

"You listen, yes? You have to take me prisoner." DeJong's actions did not match his words as his hand darted to the small of his back, Bolan was convinced that he was scrambling for a backup weapon.

Bolan stayed silent, letting the P-90 speak for him. He raised the weapon so that the burst of slugs ripped into DeJong's throat, then rose to the man's head and blew it apart. DeJong stood for a few seconds, blood spurting from severed arteries in a rich fountain. He toppled onto his back, feet drumming on the concrete.

The sound of retreating footsteps reached Bolan's ears.

Damn.

A back exit.

Bolan rounded the front of the tanker and saw two people racing for the open rear door.

Delaware's black-clad shape was directly ahead, Malik a few yards behind. The Iranian turned to fire at the Executioner.

Bolan triggered a burst that caught Malik's lower limbs, blowing out his kneecaps in pulped geysers. Malik screamed as he collapsed and sprawled across the dirty concrete. Bolan stepped over him and out through the door.

The rear of the building was weed choked and littered with debris.

There was no sign of Delaware.

He realized in seconds that she was heading for the

parked SUV at the front of the building. Bolan about-faced and went back inside, ran the length of the building and burst clear from the front door.

The soldier was just in time to see the SUV picking up speed as it headed away from him, already too far for him to fire at it. Bolan watched the vehicle clear the metal gates and slide onto the road. He caught a glimpse of red taillights before the SUV vanished from sight.

Lise Delaware had eluded him for the second time.

Bolan made a promise it wouldn't end there. The next time they met, it would be the last. He would make it his priority to take Hegre down to the last man—or in this case the last woman.

It was not a Mack Bolan decision this time.

It was an Executioner promise...

CHAPTER THIRTY-FIVE

Bolan checked a nearby SUV, hoping that it belonged to Hegre. The keys were in the ignition, and it was untouched. Delaware had not thought nor did she have the time to disable it. He locked the vehicle and slipped the key into his pocket before going back inside the building and making his way to the rear. He could hear Raz Malik moaning and whimpering where he had fallen and went to stand over the man. Malik had managed to roll onto his back. His expensive suit was streaked with dirt and blood from his mangled knees. Shattered bone and pulped flesh was showing through the shredded material of his pants.

"Fikri isn't going to get his uranium now," Bolan said quietly. "It's been a hell of a waste. Good people have died because of it."

The Iranian was beyond caring about the end result. He was suffering his own personal hell. Bolan took care of that with a single mercy shot.

Bolan knew he had to move on quickly. Time wasn't on his side.

He raised the P-90 and emptied the magazine into the lower section of the tanker, the slugs tearing holes in the aluminum bodywork. When the magazine cycled dry, Bolan removed it and snapped in the second one. He raked the far side of the vehicle, blowing ragged holes in the metal where the drums of uranium were concealed.

The soldier checked out the area where the tanker stood.

It was fitted out with equipment that suggested it was used as a motor-vehicle workshop. He moved around, searching, and at the far side found a number of forty-five-gallon fuel drums. Using a tool from the cluttered work bench, he unscrewed the cap on one of the drums and breathed in gasoline fumes. Bolan slid on a pair of thick industrial gloves from the bench, returned to the fuel drums and tipped the steel drums onto their sides. He rolled them across the concrete and under the chassis of the tanker. There were eight drums. Seven went under the tanker. He removed the screw caps and let the gasoline gush out. The eighth Bolan punctured with a steel spike, letting the gasoline pour out and pool around the tanker. He spiked holes into the vehicle's fuel tank and let more gasoline run out. Heavy fumes filled the area.

When he was done, Bolan took off the gloves and threw them aside. He checked the pockets of the dead and found what he was looking for. A cigarette lighter. He took it with him as he retreated, wadding an old newspaper he found into an improvised torch.

Before he completed his demolition preparation, he climbed into the SUV and drove it well clear of the building, leaving it running when he returned.

Streams of gasoline had trickled across the floor of the building. He lit the paper torch and allowed it to flame strongly before he held it over the closest of the gasoline trails. The rising vapor caught and flared. It began to run back toward the front of the building. Bolan dropped the torch and sprinted out of the building. He made it to the SUV and climbed behind the wheel. Tires skidded on the loose earth as Bolan stomped on the gas pedal and fed power to the engine. The SUV raced out through the gates and bounced as it hit the road, cornering hard, and sped clear.

At a safe distance Bolan braked and stared back in the direction of the building. He saw a swell of flames billowing out from the structure. The fire grew rapidly. Then the mass of flames expanded and the entire building became a huge fireball, lighting up the sky. Bolan heard some muted bangs, which he suspected were the fuel drums exploding. The fire became intense, flames shooting into the air. More detonations followed.

Bolan decided there was nothing else he could do. There was no point staying around. Somewhere at the back of his mind he recalled a fact that uranium did not burn, so he would have to hope his efforts would be enough to put it beyond use. He was no scientist, but he judged that the heat from the inferno and pressure from the bursting drums would scatter the uranium powder to a degree that would render it unusable.

He dropped the gearshift into drive and touched the pedal. The SUV rolled forward and Bolan settled in for his ride.

Seconds later, Bolan felt a shock wave rock the SUV, and he heard a heavy boom behind him. He glanced over his shoulder and caught the image as the entire building vanished in a powerful explosion that scattered its remains across a wide area. The heavy vehicle shuddered. Bolan hit the brake. He turned in his seat and saw the rolling ball of fire rise skyward until it dissipated, settled, and turned into a cloud of dark smoke that became quickly lost in the darkness. He felt debris falling to earth. Light bangs on the roof of the SUV showed him how far the explosion had scattered the wreckage.

Bolan drove on, away from the area before the first responders arrived. The explosion would have been seen and heard for quite a distance, and he couldn't become involved with an official investigation.

He remembered Sarah Mitchell's face as she had fallen after being shot. Somehow he had to find out where her body had been taken. It was the least he could do He had shared too much with the FBI agent to simply walk away. Her unflinching spirit had brought her through so much it would have been an insult not to acknowledge her. He was thinking about Arkady Greshenko, too. The man had offered his help and had paid the ultimate price.

Returning to Greshenko's home could turn out to be a high risk. It was possible he might walk into a police presence if the incident had been reported. Bolan couldn't risk being apprehended by the law. He would have to consider a different approach. Somehow he would work something out.

He owed them that much.

Good people were dead because by strokes of fate they had allied themselves to Bolan. It had happened before. Allies died, becoming the friendly ghosts that peopled his dreams from time to time, while he walked away untouched. In the darkest nights he often wondered why that was. That he seemed to survive while others around him died. There was, he knew, no comforting answer. And he refused to allow it to crush his spirit. If he did, he would cease to be who he was.

Mack Bolan.

The Executioner.

And he needed to stay hard to be able to do his work.

That did not mark him as an unfeeling creature, immune to regret. He took on the loss of friends and allies. Bolan would remember them and their deaths would not be in vain. He would make sure of that. Their killers would pay. For every drop of spilled blood they would pay.

Bolan drove until he hit the highway that took him back into Aktau. He followed the main road until he spotted the bright lights of a hotel facade and swung into the parking area. He stepped out and secured the SUV, brushed down his clothing and made his way to the main entrance.

He walked through the front door and across the ornate lobby to the front desk. The young woman on duty smiled dutifully at his approach. There was a slight hint of concern in her brown eyes.

His six foot plus figure with its slightly disheveled appearance had aroused her curiosity and his having no luggage wasn't a help.

"May I help you, sir?" she said.

Bolan slipped his hand inside his leather jacket, withdrew his U.S. passport and showed it to her. She glanced at his picture and the smile remained.

"Mr. Hamilton, do you have a problem? May I help?"

"Stephanie," he said, reading the badge pinned to her uniform blouse, "I really do think you can. I need two things right at this moment. A telephone and a room with a hot shower. Preferably in that order."

"You have no luggage, Mr. Hamilton."

"That was how it all started. They lost my bags at the airport. I spent a couple of hours trying to find them. Nothing. So I decided to drive into the city. Got myself lost and then had a blowout."

Stephanie showed him a sympathetic smile.

"It doesn't sound as though you've had a very pleasant day, Mr. Hamilton." She tapped the keyboard in front of her. "We do have a deluxe room available. It's rather expensive."

"My company is footing the bill...for everything."

Bolan had his wallet out by then and showed her the credit card issued to him by Stony Man. It took only a few minutes for Bolan to be checked in. Stephanie handed him his room swipe card.

"You room is on the fourth floor, sir. If you require anything, call room service."

"Right now I just want a hot shower. I have lots to do in the morning. Thanks, Stephanie."

Bolan headed for the elevators and rode up to his floor. Walking along the carpeted corridor, he felt the Steyr pressing against the small of his back. It brought him back to his current position.

Damn Lise Delaware. Damn her ability to cause suffering and death and still walk away, Bolan thought.

Once Bolan was in his room, he placed the Steyr in the safe and scanned the room. It was well appointed, with quality furnishings. The king-size bed looked extremely inviting. He checked out the balcony with its open view over the Caspian Sea. Lights shone in both directions, fanning out from the hotel location. Bolan took a few moments to take it all in, allowing his body to wind down. A great deal had happened since he and Mitchell had landed in the country. It had all happened at breakneck speed.

Bolan ran his hands through his hair, his mind clicking through things he had to do.

He called room service and ordered a light meal and a pot of coffee.

His second call was to the laundry service. He asked for his clothing to be picked up and cleaned for the morning.

Bolan checked the room refrigerator and took out a chilled fruit juice and downed it quickly. After shedding his clothes, including his shorts and socks, Bolan dropped them into the laundry bag the room provided. The only things he didn't include were his shoes and leather jacket. He went into the bathroom and got under the shower, turning the water to hot. He soaped himself, then stood with the water spraying over him. He dried, pulled on one of the complimentary bathrobes and came out of the bathroom just as someone tapped on his door.

It was a valet for his clothes. Bolan handed them over. A few minutes later a second caller rolled in a cart with a large platter of sandwiches and a pot of hot coffee. Bolan handed the waiter several bills from his wallet. He poured himself a cup of strong, rich coffee and drank half before he sat down with the room phone in front of him.

His first call was to Valentine Seminov. Even though it was late the Russian cop picked up.

"Valentine, it's Cooper."

"My friend, what has been happening? I have not been able to get through to Arkady. Or to your phone."

"It's not good," Bolan said.

He related the events from the moment of his touchdown in Kazakhstan to the way it had ended in the derelict building.

"Arkady? And beautiful Sarah? *Dead?*" Seminov uttered a long, deep sigh. "Such a waste," he said. "Cooper, what can I do to help? Anything. Name it, and it will be done."

"I need to know where they took Sarah's body. What has happened to her and Arkady."

"Tell me where you are."

Bolan gave Seminov the hotel's number. He also added his room number.

"What happened to the woman you were looking for?"

"She's gone. Escaped while I was handling her friends."

"That one has too many lives," Seminov said. "Like the cat."

"They're running out."

"You sound tired, Cooper."

"It's been a long day."

"Then I will talk with you tomorrow."

Bolan contacted Stony Man, using the number that would reroute his connection through the cutout system designed to keep calls secure.

"Striker? What's going on?" Barbara Price failed to hide her concern.

"I'm in a hotel room in Aktau."

For the second time that evening Bolan explained. He failed to get past Mitchell's death without a moment of regret.

"I called Seminov. He has contacts here. He's going to try to find out details."

"And what about you?" Price said. "You sound so tired. I'm sorry about Sarah. By all accounts she was a top agent."

"She was. I'll be back as soon as this is all cleared up."

Price's voice became briskly businesslike again. "You said something about the uranium being destroyed. How?"

Bolan told how he had incinerated the tanker and hopefully destroyed the cargo.

"The vehicle was taken out of the picture and from the size of the final explosion, I'm hoping the uranium was scattered over the area. I don't think there will be anything to transport to Iran. At least I hope not."

"I don't think Fikri's people will be able to get near the site. If there are any still in Aktau." Price told him Brognola was not on site. "I'll update him when he shows. You should rest, Mack. No arguments, mister, just do it."

"I'll keep in contact." He ended the call.

Bolan ate, finished the coffee, climbed into bed and switched off the light.

It took some time before he slept.

SOMEONE KNOCKING ON his door awakened him.

"Laundry, sir. Your clothes."

Bolan wrapped himself in the bathrobe and opened the door. His clothes were handed to him in a zipped bag. He gave the man a tip, then hung the bag in the closet. He dropped the robe and went into the bathroom. There was a complimentary shaving kit on the shelf, which contained a disposable razor and shaving cream. He shaved, then showered and donned the robe.

The day was bright, already warm. Bolan was at the window when the phone rang.

It was Seminov.

"It is a beautiful day, my friend. Do I find you rested?"

"I slept, Valentine. Not sure about being rested."

"Good. I will be with you shortly."

"Where are you?"

"At the airport. I will rent a car and join you. Seeing it is breakfast hour, I will have coffee with you."

Seminov cut the call, leaving Bolan slightly confused.

He dressed in his clean clothing, absently noting that even his shorts had been neatly pressed. He pocketed his wallet and passport and made his way down to the lobby. The receptionist, Stephanie, had gone off duty. In her place was a smiling young woman who directed Bolan to the restaurant, which was serving breakfast.

"I'm expecting a friend," Bolan said. "A Mr. Seminov. Please tell him where I am."

Seated at a table with a view across the Caspian, Bolan ordered coffee and toast. The restaurant was slowly filling up as hotel guests filtered in. He picked up a cross section of languages.

Bolan was on his third coffee when he spotted Seminov's impressive figure. The Russian was dressed in a light suit and an open necked dark blue shirt. When he reached Bolan's table, the cop embraced him as the soldier stood. Bolan asked for more coffee and an extra cup. After the server left, Seminov poured himself a cup and nodded approvingly after he tasted it.

"Good," he said.

The Russian's cheerful manner aroused Bolan's curiosity.

"How did you get here so fast?"

"Better than that," Seminov said. "I made many telephone calls before I left Moscow. As I said, I have contacts here in Aktau. They confirmed for me that my friend Arkady is dead." Then Seminov reached out a big hand and clamped it over Bolan's on the table. "But your Sarah Mitchell is alive."

"Say that again."

"Sarah is alive. She's in hospital, recovering from the surgery to remove the two bullets that struck her. She's in critical condition, but my contact tells me it is expected she will recover. Good news, yes?"

Bolan nodded. "Is it possible to see her?"

"We can go to the hospital when you are ready. It is a fairly new one, built three years ago so it has good facilities. Sarah Mitchell is in good hands. She is one strong woman."

Bolan drained his coffee. "Let's go."

The news about Mitchell shifted some of the darkness. In his weary state the previous night, Bolan had not imagined the chance she might be alive.

Seminov's rental car had a built in navigation system, and the Russian tapped in coordinates.

"I have not been to Aktau for a few years," he said. "There is a great deal of new construction taking place. They are building a new city around the old."

Seminov had no problems with the traffic congestion. He was from Moscow, where driving was more like a rally. He pushed the rental car through the traffic with practiced ease. It took them just under a half hour to reach the hospital, a white, four-story building. Seminov parked and they went inside. As with any hospital Bolan had experienced, the moment they crossed the threshold a silence descended. Everything around them, announcements and voices, was conducted at a hushed level.

At the desk Seminov spoke to a receptionist and they were directed to a bank of elevators.

"Just to advise you," Seminov said as they stepped out. "There is a police presence. Just a precaution. I have already spoken to a colleague on the Aktau force. They are looking out for Sarah."

"And how about me?"

"We are working together as far as they know. Cooperation between the OCD and an American task force."

"You think that's going to convince them?"

"Trust me," the Russian said, "I have enough faith for both us."

They walked along the silent corridor to where a uniformed cop was standing at the door of the room. Seminov produced his OCD identification. Bolan showed his U.S. passport. The Aktau cop inspected them, stared at them both. His right hand rested firmly on the butt of his holstered pistol.

To one side of the closed door there was a wide window that allowed a view inside the room. Bolan moved so he could stare in through the glass. He had seen enough hospital recovery units to know what to expect: the electronic monitoring, the stands holding fluids that were fed via plastic tubes attached to the patient.

Sarah Mitchell's motionless form was covered by a thin sheet, tubes inserted in her arms and nose, a plastic mask over her lower face to feed her oxygen. The vital and animated Mitchell he knew was reduced to a pale shadow. Her dark hair fanned out across the pillow.

"I hope she makes it."

Seminov was at his side. "I think she will. This young woman is a fighter. She is not going to give up."

"And as much as I sympathize with your problem," someone said from behind them, "I believe you have other pressing concerns to answer to."

CHAPTER THIRTY-SIX

"Our diverse culture and our proximity to Iran can sometimes present us with—how shall I say—unique situations. The Aktau Criminal Division has a simple job to do on paper. Search out and deal with criminal activity above the normal run of things. Not unlike my friend, Seminov, here. In reality matters are not so simple."

Captain Iztak Taharun was a tall, spare man in his late thirties. A black mustache adorned his upper lip. His long, brown hands could have belonged to a dedicated pianist rather than a Kazakh lawman who had started out as a street cop and risen through the ranks to his present position. As he spoke, his dark, keen eyes were never still. He observed even as he talked of other things.

He had taken Bolan and Seminov to the hospital's cafeteria where they sat at a table close to the open windows. A fresh breeze offered some relief from the heat of the day. Over cups of dark, bitter coffee they discussed, mainly, Bolan's position.

"I believe the most urgent thing is to assist you to leave Kazakhstan, Mr. Hamilton. As a matter of interest, is that your real name and that of your lady friend?"

"No," Seminov said. "It is a cover name we used to get them into Kazakhstan. If you need someone to chastise for that, it is my responsibility."

Taharun smiled. "Ever since I first met him at a crime symposium in Paris, this man has been causing me problems. Valentine, you romance me every time we meet."

"Captain," Bolan said, "I can't let Valentine take the responsibility for this. The situation needed a fast response. I needed to make contact with the people running this deal and Ayatollah Fikri's team. The objective was to stop that cargo of stolen uranium from leaving Kazakhstan. And I had no way of doing it by the book."

Taharun picked up his cup and sipped the hot coffee.

"A diplomatic way of saying you couldn't trust anyone here."

"There has been mistrust all along with this matter," Bolan said. "Any delay and Hegre could have shipped that material out of reach. Officialdom is universal. It seldom equates with quick responses. Especially coming from someone your people wouldn't have any knowledge about."

"Ah, admittance of entering Kazakhstan illegally," he said. "Next would be the acts of violence that resulted in a number of deaths and the deliberate setting of a fire that destroyed property and an expensive commercial vehicle."

"I won't try denying any of that," Bolan replied.

"Honesty at least," Taharun said. He gestured out the window. "We have a beautiful city here. It is growing. We do not want more problems than we already experience. This scheme to smuggle out the uranium stolen from our own mines—solving it was dropped into my hands. I am angry this criminal organization—Hegre you call it—came here to Kazakhstan and caused such trouble. To find out Iran was behind it all makes it worse. That behind it all was an attempt to create nuclear weaponry does not bear thinking about. Here we are building for our future. The last thing we need is…"

Taharun shook his head.

"At least the threat has been removed," Seminov said.

"The fire service investigators have been able to inspect the tanker. What is left of it. They believe the main tank held gasoline. When the fire built to a certain temperature the contents ignited and blew. The vehicle was destroyed. They found the remains of drums of uranium in the false section. Most of them had burst open spreading the uranium around the area. It is contaminated with all kinds of debris. Unfit for any kind of use, we believe. Some was even fused solid by the heat. A specialized team will recover as much of the yellowcake as possible.

"So your Hegre has lost its cargo and so has this Ayatollah Fikri."

"Yet the woman who organized it all has gone," Seminov said. "I am sorry, my friend."

"It appears this woman has a habit of escaping justice," Taharun said.

"I keep losing her," Bolan admitted.

"Outcomes to situations do not always offer us complete solutions." Taharun looked at Bolan. "I am sorry about your companion. Let us hope her recovery is swift, and that you will find this Delaware."

"I will. It's a debt that will be collected," Bolan said.

"Your friend will be looked after, Mr. Hamilton. I promise you that. Will you want her returned to America when she is strong enough?"

"Yes."

"That will be arranged," Taharun said. "Now we come to you, Mr. Whoever-you-are. Seminov has told me you have worked with him before. That your background is as mysterious as the contents of a bottle of Russian vodka. But he says you are a man to be trusted. So *I* will trust you. If you leave Kazakhstan, this whole business can be written down as a clash between local criminals and this Hegre group. We will do our best to avoid linking it to Iran because that would only cause friction with their government, which we can do without at the present. I believe this to be a case of the least said the better." Taharun hesitated. "Are we agreed?"

He held out his hand. Bolan took it without hesitation.

"Thanks, Captain Taharun."

"Iztak, to my friends. Perhaps some day you will come back under more pleasant circumstances."

He turned to Seminov. "I will arrange for your Arkady Greshenko to be buried. It seems the wrong people are dead, Valentine."

"It happens, my friend."

Taharun offered a knowing smile.

"I knew your friend. On a casual basis."

"Knew?" Seminov was surprised.

"Yes. That he worked as a messenger for your country?" Taharun inclined his head. "He passed me information from time to time. It was a convenience for us both."

Seminov shook his head at the incongruity of the admission.

"It is time, I believe, for us to go."

"Iztak, there's a handgun in my hotel room safe," Bolan said.

"Take it with you to the airport and one of my officers will collect it from you."

Iztak stood, then held out his hand in farewell.

"To better times," he said, turning away and leaving Bolan and Seminov alone.

"What do you make of that?" Seminov said.

"I'm trying not to think about it too much."

Before they left the hospital, Bolan and Seminov returned to Mitchell's room. Her condition had not changed. Bolan stood and watched her still, pale figure. He felt Seminov's big hand on his shoulder.

"Iztak will keep me informed of her condition, and I will let you know when she can be flown home."

"This has to be finished," Bolan said. "And that's exactly what I'm going to do."

AT THE AIRPORT Bolan handed over the Steyr, in a padded envelope, to the uniformed cop from Taharun's office.

Bolan and Seminov flew back to Moscow.

Seminov pulled strings and arranged to have Bolan on a flight back to the States the next morning.

Along with Dimitri, subdued since he heard about Mitchell, Bolan had a meal with Seminov in a small local restaurant.

"I do not like to have to say this, *tovarich,* but when you leave, Moscow will become peaceful once again. I hope."

He had a wide grin on his face. He topped up Bolan's glass, Then raised his own.

"To our friendship."

"Long lasting," Bolan said.

"To our friendship," Dimitri agreed. "And to Sarah Mitchell, as well."

Seminov and Dimitri accompanied Bolan to his departure gate. When the flight was called, they watched his tall figure merge with the other passengers. Seminov waited until Bolan vanished from sight.

"So, young Nikolai," he said. "When are you going to introduce me properly to your beautiful Irina? I am sure she will be interested in some of the things I could tell her about you."

MACK BOLAN, SEATED in business class, reclined his seat and tried to sleep. It was a long time coming. The images in his head refused to give him peace. Since the moment he had first teamed up with Sarah Mitchell, a trail of death had followed them.

It had reached a bloody conclusion and had ended with the destruction of the uranium cargo.

The escape of Lise Delaware taunted him.

Yet Bolan finally slept.

When he awakened, they were only halfway through the ten-hour flight. Bolan welcomed the food and drink the flight attendants were handing out. He found he was hungry. He managed three cups of coffee.

"Would you care for anything stronger?" the attendant asked as she cleared away the tray.

Bolan declined. He wanted to keep a clear head. He had a lot to do once he reached Stony Man. The lack of communication on board the aircraft was frustrating. Despite his lack of contact, he knew the Stony Man team would be working on the Hegre problem, seeking information so Bolan would have the most up-to-date information on the organization.

The soldier would need that data.

Once back in the States he would be concentrating on the final part of his mission.

When the Executioner touched down, he would be initiating a full-on Bolan Blitz against Hegre. The organization would be taken down once and for all.

CHAPTER THIRTY-SEVEN

Three days had passed since Bolan's return to Stony Man Farm. He had been on site ever since, organizing equipment and absorbing all the data available on Hegre, preparing to leave and drop off the radar.

It meant only one thing.

The Executioner was back in action, on a mission that would involve no one else.

He was making the final act a personal one. He would not ask for help or take any direction. He would locate his target and home in for the strike.

Hal Brognola, as head of the SOG, knew enough to stand down. The day Bolan struck his deal with the President, it had come with an unbreakable proviso. That Bolan could initiate and carry out individual missions. When such a mission was activated, Mack Bolan stood alone, acted alone and accepted the consequences of his actions.

It was how Bolan had started his long campaign against the enemies of civilized society. In those far gone days he had been completely alone, pursued by his enemies and on the wanted lists of America's law-enforcement community. He had the Mob issuing vast rewards for his head. The FBI and nationwide police chased him from city to city. In those times Bolan was truly alone. Yet he began to gather a number of individuals who had respect for his ideals, who sometimes turned a blind eye when they realized the depth of his beliefs.

When Stony Man Farm was created, Bolan gathered a tight and faithful group around him, true people who understood his selfless way, who stood by him through dark days and seemingly overwhelming odds. They'd emerged victorious from countless encounters, moving on to fight the tide of enemies intent on destroying America and her allies. It was ongoing, something that had gained a life of its own. It had a motion that kept it alive, a single purpose that would never be extinguished.

Even with that strength around him, there were times when Bolan had to go solo, to walk that extra mile without assistance from Stony Man. He chose those times when only the Executioner's particular brand of justice would serve. When he meted out what he considered true justice to the enemy.

Judge.

Jury.

Executioner.

IN HIS PRIVATE quarters Bolan had prepared himself for battle. A bag held his combat blacksuit and a pair of lace-up boots, as well as a change of civilian clothing. He was dressed in a light shirt and tan chinos, casual shoes and a brown leather bomber jacket.

The business at hand would bring about a final resolution—either Hegre's—or his own. Mack Bolan had no kind of death wish. Life was important to him. Despite putting himself on the line many times over, he maintained a healthy respect for life. He refused to allow any trace of morbidity to shadow him. He accepted that his chosen path in life drew him toward violence and sudden death. That was something he had taken on board the day he initiated his first strike against the Mob. He understood then that for however long it lasted, his campaign of cleansing the world of evil, he was going to have to participate in a great deal of bloodletting. He did not relish the thought, but he knew it would be part of his life.

"Hey, mister, got a minute for a friend?"

Barbara Price stood in the open door of his room. Clad in jeans, a roll-neck sweater, and classic Western boots, the Stony Man mission controller and Bolan's sometime lover waited as he turned. She tried to hide her concern, but her eyes betrayed her true feelings.

Bolan went to her, slid his arms around her body and drew her into the room, nudging the door shut with one foot.

Price smiled. "Cool move, pal."

"I know a few more," he said.

Bolan breathed in the warm scent of her. His lips brushed her cheek.

"Is that the best you can do?"

"There are things better left for more appropriate times."

"Don't I know it."

Pushing back the thoughts crowding her mind, Price eased away. Whatever their relationship allowed, this was not the time. Bolan had matters on his mind that took precedence and she would not let herself distract him. She returned his kiss with one of her own, touching his lips briefly.

"Business, soldier," she said. "Your transport is ready. I have your paperwork, too. Standard pack. Cards. Expense money. And Kissinger is ready for you in the armory." Kissinger was John "Cowboy" Kissinger, Stony Man Farm's top armorer.

"Very efficient as always."

"We aim to please."

"And you do that really well."

Price's reserve snapped off and she backed off a little.

"Do you have to do this without backup?"

"Yeah, and you know why. People who work with me end up getting killed. I'm going in alone, and I'm going to take down Hegre. If I don't, Hegre is going to carry on, business as usual. You've read the files, and the current report on what happened out there. Too many good people have died because of that organization. FBI agents. Cops in Moscow. Seminov's friend in Aktau. Others we haven't identified yet..."

"And Sarah Mitchell," she said. "I know you still feel bad about what happened. But she's alive, Mack. And, thank God, back home at a top hospital. Sarah's going to recover. Slowly, but she will get better. Hal's keeping a check on her progress."

"It wouldn't have happened if..."

"If what, Mack? If you hadn't had her with you? She's a trained FBI agent. She wanted to do her job. You said yourself she's one hell of an agent. From what I've read in your report she proved it."

Bolan nodded.

"Aaron and the team turned up quite a file on Hegre," Price said. "Since your involvement, with Mossad's input, and all the other sources, we've got more intel on the organization. I read up on them the other day. Mercenary doesn't quite cover what they'll do for money.

"They must be really pissed at you for messing up their operations. You took away their diamond hoard. And destroying that uranium meant they couldn't complete the deal with the Iranians. So no payday for Hegre there."

"I do my best."

"I don't think they'll see it quite like that."

"So no welcome mat when I go calling?"

"I guess not," Price said quietly. "Hey, Kissinger is still waiting."

"Yes, ma'am."

They went out into the corridor. Price swung right, Bolan left.

"I'll see you before I move out."

"You'd better, soldier."

THE WARM AIR held the smell of gun oil. Bolan walked into the armory and saw Kissinger bent over his long workbench. A number of weapons were laid out across the surface.

"How goes it, Mack?"

"What can I say. Never dull?"

Kissinger laughed, turning from the bench. He wore khaki combat pants and a black T-shirt, laced up Wolverine boots. His hair was slightly mussed and he stroked a strong hand through it in an unconscious gesture.

"Heard about your partner," he said. "Is she going to make it?"

Bolan nodded. "So I'm told."

"Good to hear," the armorer replied. "I guess you'll be needing a full assault kit."

"That's about right."

Kissinger led the way over to a second bench.

Bolan saw a Beretta 93-R, a .44 Magnum Desert Eagle, his longtime favorite SMG—a 9 mm Uzi—and a sheathed Cold Steel tanto knife. Kissinger had loaded a lightweight harness with full magazines for each weapon, and there were a half dozen more to go in Bolan's carryall.

"You want to test fire anything?"

Bolan picked up the Beretta, his hand curling firmly around the grips.

"You said you'd serviced them."

A Kissinger service meant each weapon would have been fired, stripped and cleaned again.

"I did."

"Then they're fine."

"What do you reckon you're going to be up against?"

"That's the question of the day. An organized mob crew. These days that could mean anything short of battle tank."

"Better go in ready then."

Bolan stood back and watched as the armorer selected and stacked up an assortment of ordnance that included fragmentation and flash-bang grenades.

"Is this going to be a long strike or a 'hit and git'?"

"I want it over as fast as I can make it," Bolan said.

"No compound explosives and timers?"

Bolan shook his head.

"I'm not expecting an extended campaign."

"Short and sharp then."

Kissinger stowed the ordnance in a sturdy carryall.

"You want me to sign for it?" Bolan asked.

Kissinger chuckled.

"That'll be the day, Mack."

They shook hands, and Bolan headed out.

BOLAN MADE HIS way to the Annex and Kurtzman's cyber-lair. The crew was all there. The quiet hum of electronics filled the air. The rich smell of Aaron Kurtzman's quietly bubbling, and legendary, coffee percolator was there, too. His infamous brew had the strength to strip paint off the side of a battle tank, so the story went.

He placed his carryall by the door and walked into the Computer Room.

Carmen Delahunt, redheaded ex-FBI, was crossing the floor, documents in her hand. She was as vivacious as she was talented.

"Hey, the wanderer has returned," she said. "We were sorry to hear about Sarah."

"Thanks."

"Did you bring us any souvenirs from your global trip?" Akira Tokaido asked, removing his earbuds to let them hang around his neck.

"They were confiscated by customs," Bolan said.

Kurtzman swung his wheelchair around, a sat phone clutched in a large hand. "I heard you lost your other one."

"You know what it's like in the field."

"Yeah? Well, that damn field must be pretty well choked up with lost phones and other pieces of equipment you scatter around."

Bolan took the phone, examining the sleek lines.

"Full spec on that," Kurtzman said. "GPS. Email downloads. Messages. Camera and video. It will provide worldwide coverage via satellite. The power pack has triple performance." He handed Bolan a charger unit. "I would say try to hang on to it but there's no point."

"Still no digital radio?"

Kurtzman shook his head, chuckling to himself as he tapped his keyboard.

A couple of the large wall screens fired up and presented images in high-definition.

"Julius Hegre," Delahunt said. "The man himself. He runs the Hegre Corporation, which is the *legal* side of his empire. The truth is the guy is a good businessman. The companies he controls are successful. They make money. Spread across the globe, too. So why does he need to also head a criminal organization that deals in everything illegal and downright ruthless? It's the opposite of his day job."

"The old question," Hunt Wethers said. "Maybe he just gets off on playing a bad guy. Not enough excitement in his other role."

"Now Hegre has some hotshot legal people on its

books," Delahunt said. "The top man is this guy. Dominic Melchior. He's Julius Hegre's legal brain and his counselor. He's been with Hegre a long time."

"Something about him tells me I wouldn't trust him from the moment I met him," Tokaido said. "Just a feeling."

"Keep that thought," Bolan said.

Delahunt ran through a number of images Stony Man had culled from various other agency files.

"We are slowly logging faces and names of people associated with Hegre. Once we had a toe in the door, things started to come together."

Bolan indicated a pair of faces he recognized.

"Cross that pair off your list," Bolan said. "Permanently retired in Kazakhstan."

"Retired as in…?"

"As in dead."

"Just so we're clear."

"You need to see Delaware again?" Kurtzman asked.

"No. That's one image I'm not liable to forget."

"Hegre's corporate offices are in Philly," Delahunt said about the next image. "This is his main residence outside the city. There is also an office complex in New York and a couple of smaller properties in California. He keeps homes in Paris and Switzerland, and has a boat moored at Marina del Ray. He even has a private plane on semipermanent standby at a strip outside Philly. And there are a number of helicopters for personal transport."

"You wouldn't know where I might be able to find him right now?" Bolan asked.

"O ye of little faith," Kurtzman said. "Once we heard you were set to finish this Hegre group we extended our search parameters. Hal got me access to an NSA satellite and some close scans were made of Hegre properties and especially the remaining one we hadn't mentioned.

A place he had built about four years ago. A retreat you could call it that's way out in the boonies. The Cascades to be exact, up country from Seattle. Forests and mountains. Your log cabin in the hills kind of place. Only this is a little more than a regular log cabin. Incidentally it's about seventy miles upstate from the derelict house where you and Mitchell first got together."

Kurtzman tapped an instruction and the closest screen flashed up a crystal-clear image of the "log cabin." There were logs there, but incorporated with stone in a sprawling residence that stood in splendid isolation in clear ground, a gentle slope falling away from the frontage. The land around the house had been stripped of trees and bush, leaving an open area. It would offer no cover to anyone approaching the house. The backdrop of the house showed distant snow-capped mountains.

"How recent is this?"

"Latest update is three hours old. Looks like there are a few folks at home."

Bolan had seen the four vehicles parked near the house. He also noted a couple of figures moving around the perimeter. He studied the image for a while, noting details he stored away for future reference.

"Closest town?"

"There's a medium-sized town about thirty miles southeast," Kurtzman said. "I checked it out. It has a small police department with only four officers. They have a helicopter if that's what you were asking."

"You think Hegre is there?" Wethers asked.

"It's a place to start," Bolan said. "The way things have been going for Hegre, it could be time for a retreat. Somewhere for a brainstorming session." Bolan studied the image again. "I'll kick off there. Thanks for the intel."

Kurtzman handed him a folder with copies of all the data.

Bolan picked up his carryall and left.

The door slid shut behind his tall figure.

"Okay," Kurtzman said, "back to work, people. Let's catch up on Phoenix and Able. They need us, too."

JACK GRIMALDI WAS waiting for Bolan. The Stony Man pilot, a longtime ally of the Executioner, was sprawled in a chair in the lounge, a room with a view across the Farm's lush landscape. He was not alone. Barbara Price stood nearby, quietly conversational. She had a buff file in her hands. It would hold Bolan's documentation.

As Bolan appeared she turned and held out the file. "It's all here."

"Thanks."

Price leaned forward and whispered, "Be safe." Then she left the lounge.

"Wheels up when you're ready," Grimaldi said as he uncoiled his lean frame from the chair.

He took the smaller bag holding Bolan's clothing and led the way out. The soldier followed with his ordnance carryall. They exited the outside door and walked across to where a helicopter stood on the pad.

Farm buildings around the area concealed various vehicles, including Grimaldi's deadliest piece of hardware, *Dragonslayer,* the state-of-the-art combat helicopter. *Dragonslayer*'s design and electronics made the aircraft as close to perfect as was possible. Grimaldi had been involved in the development, customizing the aircraft to his own specifications. The mechanics of the machine were upgraded often, so that Grimaldi needed to update himself on a regular basis. Bolan had flown in the aircraft on a number of missions. He had seen for himself the fearsome capabilities it offered. Coupled with Grimaldi's superb piloting skills, *Dragonslayer* had no equal.

This time around there was little need of the combat helicopter. Grimaldi was simply transporting Bolan to his location in one of Stony Man's regular helicopters.

They both donned headsets and Grimaldi started the preflight procedure. He flicked switches, checked readouts almost casually. Bolan knew otherwise. Grimaldi was a consummate pilot. Nothing was taken for granted. He would pick up on the smallest fault.

"Hey, Sarge," Grimaldi said, "you sure you don't want me to tag along?"

Bolan shook his head. "This is on me. No one else."

Grimaldi said no more. He understood Bolan's strictly hands-off decision. This was going to be an Executioner deal all the way. No quarter asked, no quarter given. The people Bolan was going after had, by their actions, shown they didn't give a damn about the rights of their victims. They chose their targets and went for the heart.

They dealt with the devil.

The jury had already been out.

So Mack Bolan was about to hand them the verdict.

THE FLIGHT ONLY lasted a half hour. Grimaldi put the helicopter down at a small field upstate. He had a twin-engined Beechcraft on standby, fueled and ready to go. The pilot had already filed his flight plan. During an eleven-hour flight, they would traverse the U.S. from east to west, two stops to refuel, then land at Bellingham Airport in Washington State.

They touched down midevening. While Grimaldi had the Beechcraft refueled and checked over for his return flight the following morning, Bolan picked up the rental vehicle Price had organized. He stowed his luggage and drove the Volvo XC70 around to pick up Grimaldi. The plane was parked in the area reserved for private aircraft.

"Nice wheels, Sarge," Grimaldi observed as he took the passenger seat.

"I have connections."

Grimaldi chuckled.

Aware they would need accommodation for the night, Price had also secured a couple of rooms in a Comfort Inn. It was no more than a couple of miles from the airport. Bolan parked and they made their way to the reception desk, the soldier slinging his weapons bag from one shoulder. They checked in and went directly to their rooms. Neither of them wanted anything more than a shower and bed.

They met in the breakfast buffet early the next morning and helped themselves to coffee and food. Checking out, they returned to the Volvo and Bolan dropped his friend off at the airport. Grimaldi wanted to check out the Beechcraft for the return flight.

"Good hunting, Sarge," Grimaldi said. "I'll be waiting at the hotel when you get back."

"Thanks, pal."

Grimaldi watched Bolan drive off then turned and headed back into the terminal building to prepare for his flight back to Stony Man.

CHAPTER THIRTY-EIGHT

From Bellingham Bolan took the highway heading north. A few hours later he branched off on a road that wound its way through high forest terrain—the single lane highway took Bolan into a magnificent landscape. Mountain peaks showed above the evergreen trees. Water glinted occasionally through the lush forest. The road was climbing gradually. The Volvo XC70 cruised the elevated road with ease, barely a murmur from the powerful six-cylinder engine. With the amenities built into the SUV, driving was a luxury. Bolan allowed himself to relax in the soft leather seat, feeling the cool stream of air from the climate control unit.

Memory played one of its subtle tricks then and reminded Bolan it had been a Volvo Arkady Greshenko had driven, but an older, less sophisticated car, the man's final drive before being executed.

As he came around a curve in the road, Bolan saw a break in the trees on his left and pulled the SUV to a stop. He took out the file he had received from Kurtzman. Printouts and maps. He rechecked the coordinates. He had read through the information in his room before sleeping and had memorized the details. Bolan stepped out of the SUV and walked to the rear where he had placed his bags. From his large carryall he took out a pair of binoculars and scanned the distant landscape. He finally located what he was looking for.

The image sprang into sharp relief: a sprawling structure, timber and stone, no more than a half mile from where he was parked. The only difference now was a couple more cars were parked out front.

And a helicopter.

It looked like a family gathering.

In this case a criminal family.

Bolan studied the layout. He saw people moving around the area, and he could see the men were carrying SMGs dangled from shoulder straps. He guessed that visitors would not be welcome.

Hegre was in a for a surprise because the Executioner was planning to drop in.

Without an invitation.

Bolan drove to within a few hundred yards of the Hegre stronghold. He found the narrow service road that would eventually bring him to the house and maneuvered the Volvo into the trees, easing it through the greenery until it was deep in cover. As he changed into his blacksuit and boots, he noticed the sky darkening overhead. Dark clouds were scudding in from beyond the peaks and he felt a sudden chill in the air.

Rain?

That could help. Cover as he moved in.

He slipped on his combat harness and jerkin filled various pouches with extra magazines for his guns. One pouch contained several plastic ties, ready looped, that he could use as restraints if it proved necessary. The combat knife in its sheath was threaded onto his belt. His grenades and canisters were attached to the harness. The Desert Eagle and the Beretta 93-R were primed and holstered, the Uzi suspended by a nylon strap.

Bolan secured the SUV, pocketing the hand activator. He used the combat knife to cut a number of leafy branches from the undergrowth and arranged them around the Volvo as added camouflage. When he walked away and looked back, the vehicle was only noticeable on close inspection. He felt confident it would be safe. He doubted if any of Hegre's hardmen would be coming out this far from the house. They were bodyguards. Not long-range scouts.

The temperature had dropped a couple more degrees. No problem for Bolan, but he was thinking about the sentries outside the house. He didn't know if they were seasoned professionals or city guys who might not enjoy the mountain climate. Most likely the latter, brought along to protect their bosses.

Bolan had the position of the house fixed in his mental map as he started to move. He could keep in cover until he reached the cleared patch surrounding the property. He would need to gain an advantage then.

Hopefully before he made any physical moves on the house, Bolan would need to gain intel on the occupants, who they were and how many. The more information he gained, the higher his chances of success.

That would be the ideal, if he had unlimited time and resources. All he actually had was himself. It wouldn't be the first time he might have to go ahead in possession of thin intel.

He moved steadily, cautiously. His senses were attuned to his surroundings. The forest sounds were close. Birds making their noise. This was their domain and, provided nothing in nature alarmed them, they provided a background that would warn him if anyone was moving around clumsily.

Bolan caught a glimpse of the house a quarter mile ahead through the trees. He slowed his approach now, using the timber and bushes as cover as he closed in on the cleared section. As the trees opened up, he noticed the line of stumps where the timber had been cut back.

He spotted the first of the sentries. The guy wore dark clothing and a buttoned overcoat. A ball cap was pulled low over his forehead. The thick gloves he wore would restrict his hand and finger movements if he went to use the MP-5 he was carrying.

Bolan watched the guy tramp awkwardly through the rough stubble where grass and brush was starting to establish itself again. He looked around, head movements jerky and too fast to really take in what he was observing. The guy was out of his element, doing what he had been instructed but not in tune with his surroundings. The guy stopped, let his MP-5 hang by its strap as he banged his hands together, working his fingers even though he wore gloves. Bolan could tell that he didn't enjoy the mountain chill.

The soldier watched him turn his back to the trees. The guy was looking in the direction of the house, most likely wishing he was inside with a mug of something hot in his hands, Bolan thought.

None of the other sentries were in sight. They were spread out around the house, covering other sections, which left this guy on his own for the moment.

An opportunity?

Bolan couldn't manufacture such a moment. It had presented itself unannounced. He had to take it.

He let the Uzi dangle from its strap, slid the combat knife into his right hand and moved up behind the sentry. The Executioner eased forward, knowing the guy could walk away at any second. The moment he had the guy directly in front of him Bolan rose to his full height. He reached out with his left hand and curved it around the guy's head, clamping it over the man's mouth. At the same time he pressed the tip of the Cold Steel tanto knife against the sentry's lower back, pushing hard enough so that the blade sliced through the guy's clothing and nudged flesh. Bolan felt the softness of flesh, increased the pressure so that the blade penetrated a fraction more.

"Your choice," Bolan said. "Cooperate, or piss me off and I push this blade in up to the handle."

The man stiffened. Bolan wiggled the combat knife a fraction to emphasis his threat. He heard a mumble of sound, felt the guy nodding.

"Back up. Keep both hand at your sides."

The guy complied, aware that the knife pressed to his back could cut deeper if he made any sudden moves.

The trees and undergrowth closed around them.

"Okay," Bolan said. "I'm taking my hand away from your mouth. If you make one sound other than breathing, I use the knife. Understood?"

The guy nodded.

Bolan dropped his left hand and fished out a plastic zip tie.

"Hands behind your back. Wrists together."

As soon as the sentry obeyed, Bolan slipped the loop over his hands, above the gloves and jerked on the loose end. The plastic loop closed tightly against the guy's wrists. With the man secured Bolan stepped back, withdrawing the knife.

"Turn around," Bolan said.

The guy was of average height and build, his brown hair cropped. He had a gold ring in his left ear. Day-old stubble darkened his jaw.

He let his prisoner see the combat knife, the tip moistened with fresh blood. "Same rule applies. You make any noise that causes me concern, I'll use the knife again. Got it?"

The guy nodded again. His eyes darted left to right, then back to Bolan. The soldier unclipped the MP-5's strap and removed the weapon. He unbuttoned the man's coat and searched him for a handgun, removing a Desert Eagle from a shoulder holster.

"Emulating the boss lady?"

The man actually offered a sneering twist of his mouth. "She's been waiting for you. She's going to rip you a second asshole."

"You know me?"

"We all do. My guess is she has that picture of you on her wall to throw knives at."

"Then you know that I don't play games."

Bolan sheathed the knife and tucked the Desert Eagle behind his belt. He checked the MP-5.

"Do you think she does?" the guy asked. "Is she sitting watching TV? Reading girlie magazines? It's like a command center up there."

"And you guys are out in the cold."

"I guess that's why she earns top dollar and we get plenty of exercise."

"I'll remind her when I see her."

"She won't run."

"From my perspective you people already have. All cozied up here in the back of beyond. Hegre is running scared of something. Me? Or those Iranians you messed with? I hear they don't like being screwed."

"That was down to you jacking around with the cargo back in Kazakhstan."

"It appears it's worked. Hegre must be worried. Get the Iranians on your case, and it's a big-time headache."

"We can handle them."

"You're not doing so well with me."

"One guy?"

"Who has *your* hands tied?"

"I could still yell. Bring my buddies running."

"I warned you what would happen."

"Maybe I don't scare so easily."

Bolan took out the Cold Steel tanto blade.

"Remember what I told you at the start?"

"Huh?"

"Your choice."

The guy's head turned away, eyes searching. Bolan glanced in the same direction and saw two figures moving along the open ground. They both carried MP-5s. Something had drawn their curiosity, and Bolan figured it was the missing sentry.

He wasn't going to be allowed any more time to gather his intelligence.

His captive had decided the appearance of his buddies made all the difference. Whatever he thought, it prompted him to take action.

He opened his mouth and let loose a bloodcurdling yell, attracting the attention of his armed friends.

It was a wrong move.

Bolan cut off his warning shout with a powerful sweep of the combat knife, the keen edge of the steel slicing the guy's throat from left to right. The severely deep cut opened the guy's throat and released a burst of blood that splashed down his front. The shout ended in a wet gurgle of sound.

The knife was slipped back into its sheath. Bolan quickly checked the MP-5, saw it was cocked and flipped the fire selector switch to full-auto.

He saw the pair of armed sentries closing on his position, alerted by the shout from their missing partner. They were well inside the MP-5's range now, still not sure what was happening, but not holding back.

Bolan put the sentries in the picture, the H&K spitting out a 9 mm welcome as he engaged them.

The Executioner was familiar with the H&K MP-5. It had been his weapon of choice during many previous combat situations. He knew the weapon and was able to draw on its performance capabilities. He held the muzzle under control as he unleashed a couple of bursts, preventing it from rising and losing his intended target area.

He caught the first guy head-on, the 9 mm Parabellum slugs hammering into the target's upper torso. The guy's forward motion was halted as the slugs hit home. He faltered, then went down on his knees, face a blend of astonishment and then shock. Before the guy fell facedown Bolan had switched to the second guy who was still advancing. Unable to respond fast enough, the sentry took a burst that cored into his chest, his own weapon discharging too late to do any harm as the shooter went down in a heap, flipping over onto his back as he jerked against the pain invading his body.

There was no going back. Bolan was fully committed now. The gunfire was going to attract the rest of the crew, so he could expect resistance before he even reached the house.

He chose to head in the direction of the parked helicopter, the need to disable it of paramount importance. The same went for the parked vehicles. He had to keep the Hegre crew isolated, unable to leave the area. As long as he managed to keep Hegre from leaving, his strike would have a higher body count.

As cold as that might have sounded, to Bolan it was the aim of this hit. He wanted the Hegre organization taken apart.

No exclusions.

The crackle of autofire reached him. Bullet bursts chopped at the cleared earth, falling short. The shooters were firing on the move, the action of their movement denying them accurate fire. Bolan turned and saw three moving figures, muzzle-flashes winking as they exhausted their magazines.

Bolan halted, leveled his SMG and laid down accurate fire, catching the advancing shooters in the open. He put the farthest guy down with a hard burst that cut the man's legs from beneath him. Nine millimeter slugs plowed into his upper thighs, drilling into flesh and shattering bone. The guy screamed as he went down and his yells distracted his partners as they saw him fall, legs bloody.

As the guy bled out, Bolan acquired his targets. He wasn't about to grant time for the opposition to reload. He placed a burst into one guy that shredded his throat, then ranged in on the surviving shooter and placed his shots in the guy's heart, knocking the man over backward.

Bolan cast aside the empty MP-5 and brought the Uzi into play. He moved on, angling in the direction of the helicopter, circling to come up the side away from the house. As he neared the aircraft, the soldier caught a glimpse of a moving figure hidden by the aircraft. He didn't pause, simply dropped to a running crouch, aiming the Uzi under the body of the chopper.

His auto burst clipped the concealed figure and the guy lurched upright from his hiding place. Bolan moved around the tail of the helicopter and faced the guy. The bullets had torn across the sentry's hip and left a bloody mess of a wound. It slowed the guy down and he had little chance to raise his own weapon before Bolan appeared. The Uzi chattered again, this time full on its target, and punched holes through the target's chest.

Bolan let the Uzi hang on its sling as he paused by the helicopter. He took one of his fragmentation grenades, popped the pin as he opened the side door and tossed the grenade inside. Bolan cut around the front of the aircraft, powering forward and fisting the Uzi again.

He was counting down the seconds and dropped to the ground just before the grenade blew. It ripped open the helicopter, filling the air with debris. The fuel tank blew a couple of seconds later, spewing flame and smoke. Bolan felt the heat across his back.

He pushed to his feet and left the flaming wreck of the chopper behind as he sprinted for the side of the house. As he cleared two of the parked vehicles, the soldier blew out the windshields and tossed in a couple more armed grenades. He dropped beneath the underhang of an encircling gallery as the twin blasts rocked the area. The blasts disabled both vehicles. One was further rocked as the gas tank detonated. Flames swept up and out, the expensive cars reduced to smoking wrecks. Bolan used the Uzi to lay down a burst that shredded the tires on the remaining vehicles.

From where he was briefly concealed, Bolan swept the area, looking out for more targets.

He picked up one guy cautiously approaching, eyes searching as he surveyed the scene of burning helicopter and cars. He was unable to see much through the drifting smoke and curling tongues of flame, disbelief written all over his face.

He was still looking when Bolan swapped the Uzi for the Desert Eagle. He double-fisted the big pistol, aiming and holding his target before he fired the 125 grain jacketed round. It was a solid hit. The powerful Magnum slug slammed into the guy's head and blew out a big chunk of bone as it exited. The impact threw the guy's head back, brain tissue and blood spurting out as the bullet passed through. He had no time to react as his pulverized brain shut down. He collapsed without a sound.

Before he moved from his temporary cover, Bolan stripped out the exhausted Uzi magazine and snapped in a fresh one. He holstered the .357.

The rain Bolan had been anticipating came on. It drifted in from the distant slopes, quickly building. Within a few minutes the fall had become heavy, soaking the ground.

Bolan chose that time to move, skirting around the base of the house and across the rear. There was access there to what looked to be a basement area. He saw metal ducting angling out through the wall. An exhaust outlet, most likely for the diesel plant driving the generator for electricity.

Palming a grenade, Bolan took out the pin. He went down the short flight of concrete steps to the basement door, which swung open at his touch. He picked up the muted sound of the generator. Leaning inside, the soldier sprung the lever and tossed the grenade in through the door. He heard it land and roll across the concrete floor. Bolan eased to the side, protected by the outer wall. The explosion had a hollow, echoing sound. He heard the patter of falling debris. When the noise abated, Bolan could no longer hear the sound of the generator.

CHAPTER THIRTY-NINE

The crackle of gunfire alerted the group inside the house. The exploding helicopter drew everyone's attention. In the large main room Julius Hegre moved slowly toward the window. To his left he could see the blazing aircraft, the debris scattered across the ground.

"The helicopter," he said.

Lise Delaware reached him in long strides. She caught his arm and dragged him away from the window.

"Stay away, Julius. Don't go near the glass."

Four of Hegre's men were inside the house. They were all armed.

"You want us to stay inside?"

"Yes," Delaware said. "Make sure the front and rear entrances are covered. Get someone from the ground crew if you have to. Kelso, you and Boyd stay with me. You protect Julius and Dom."

Melchior was standing by the open hearth, a glass of whiskey in one hand. He listened to the grenade detonations as the first of the cars were hit.

"Who is out there? Fikri's people?"

He appeared calm. No sign of any agitation.

Delaware dispersed the crew, then guided her uncle to a recliner well away from the main window. She turned her head as she picked up another rattle of autofire.

"What do you think?" she asked Kelso and Boyd.

"One gun," Boyd said.

"Just the one," Kelso agreed.

Delaware actually smiled. Not from joy. It was simply an affirmation that she had just confirmed something.

"It's him," she said. "Cooper."

"Persistent," Hegre observed.

His voice held a weary note, as if, despite his influence and power, things were slipping away.

Delaware slid her Desert Eagle from its hip holster, checking it.

"Tenacious," Melchior murmured into his whiskey glass. "Julius, maybe we were a little hasty decamping to this godforsaken place."

"I have a feeling that man would find us wherever we were."

"Do I detect a degree of defeatism?"

Hegre made a tired gesture.

"Nobody is giving up," Delaware said.

"Perhaps we should pool our checkbooks and make the man an offer?" Melchior said.

"Dom, no jokes," Delaware said.

Melchior sat and faced his old friend across the stone fireplace. Movement outside the window caught his attention. It was the rain striking the glass.

They all heard the muted sound of an explosion from the rear of the house. Wall lamps were extinguished.

"He's hit the generator," Boyd said. "Cut the power."

"Son of a bitch," Kelso said. "Let me go after him."

"Hanson is at the rear. It's his job," Delaware said. "We stay together. That's our job."

She crossed the room, jamming her Desert Eagle back in its holster, and picked up one of the P-90s leaning against the wall. She took up a position at the window and peered down. Even through the pouring rain she could see the cars that had not been destroyed had their tires shot out.

Anger rose, hot, threatening to overwhelm her. She clamped down on it. Losing control was not going to help. She needed to stay focused. She regulated her breathing, kept her emotions steady.

She glanced across the room at Melchior. He was still sipping his whiskey, and seeing that took her back to when she was younger and he had taught he how to control her temper. Even now she remembered his gentle voice as he instructed her.

Allow your emotions to control you and any problem will grow out of proportion. If that happens, your ability to think clearly will be lost. In a stressful situation you have to remain detached, as if you were separate from your body, able to stand outside and see the problem. Remain calm, assess the moment and make a decision based on what you see, not what you feel. Push anger and uncertainty aside. Deepen your breathing and look at your problem again....

"Keep this window covered," she said to Boyd.

Boyd moved to stand at one side, away from any threat from being shot.

The rain increased, becoming a heavy downpour that reduced visibility. Now Boyd was unable to see very far.

He looked across the room at Delaware. She was motionless, her face calm, the P-90 held across her chest. Waiting.

Melchior inspected his whiskey glass, gently swirling its contents.

Switching his gaze to Julius Hegre, Boyd was surprised at the man's appearance. In all the time he had known his employer, Hegre had been in total control. He had always been ahead of the game, unflinching in his decisions, a powerful man who held his destiny in his own hands. Looking at him now, Boyd saw an aging figure, almost shrunken in his expensive clothes. Boyd had always had respect for the man. Observing him now, he experienced a degree of pity for him.

An exchange of autofire sounded from the rear of the house.

Boyd looked in Delaware's direction.

He saw no reaction except for her eyes moving toward the sound.

More gunfire.

Delaware turned and crossed the room, through the open arch at the far side, heading in the direction of the front entrance. She wanted to make sure the man there was still in position.

THE DOWNPOUR INCREASED. The rain was icy. A rising wind pushed it into Bolan's face.

He had remained pressed close to the basement wall, smoke drifting out the open door. It was whipped away by the wind and sheeting rain.

Bolan assessed his position. The outside crew was dealt with. The unknown factor remaining was how many of Hegre's people were inside the house. The only way he would know would be to go inside and face them.

He moved, heading up the concrete steps, the Uzi angled up at the house.

Movement on the upper level alerted him.

An armed figure leaning over, weapon extended.

The shooter triggered a short burst that chewed at the concrete. Bolan felt the chips strike at his legs. He returned fire, raking the area above him as he ducked back out of sight, back to the wall again.

He paused as, out the corner of his eye, he caught a glimpse of flame coming from inside the basement. If the fire spread, the occupants might be forced out of the house.

Bolan's thoughts returned to his current situation. The shooter above him was his prime concern.

A sudden gust of wind drove the rain in at him, soaking his clothing even more. He closed his mind to the chill invading his body.

He moved at that moment, figuring the waiting shooter would be in the same situation. It might throw him for a few seconds.

Might.

Perhaps.

Chips in a gamble.

Bolan's life against the shooter's.

He continued up the steps, twisting his body and holding down the Uzi's trigger, sweeping the upper level with a sustained burst. Nine millimeter slugs slammed against the house wall, chipped stone, splintered timber, shattered a window.

And found human flesh.

The shooter arched his body as the rounds hit, tearing into his body. He returned fire in a reflex motion.

Bolan had the guy in his sights now and burned off his magazine. The high angle of his shots caught the target in his upper chest and the lower part of his face. The slugs ripped through the flesh of his jaw, tore at the bone and plowed up through his skull to lodge in his brain.

Bolan's Uzi clicked empty. He reloaded automatically, dropping the spent magazine and snapping in a fresh one. He worked the cocking bolt to load the first cartridge.

That, he decided, *had been close.*

As he stepped away from the basement again, he saw that the flames inside the door were growing.

He crouched and moved quickly around and up to where the shooter lay on the concrete outside a partly open door. Through the gap he could see a well-appointed kitchen.

At the far end of the room, tiled steps led up into the main body of the building.

Bolan stepped inside, Uzi tracking left and right as he advanced. He cradled the Uzi against his body, snagging one of the flash-bang grenades from his harness. Reaching the base of the steps, the Executioner pulled the pin and threw the canister hard. It curved up out of sight and landed in the room above. Covering his ears, he bent over and pulled back from the steps, into the room behind him.

He heard someone shout.

The flash-bang detonated.

When the hard sound and the blinding light faded, Bolan went up the steps fast, the Uzi probing ahead.

THERE WERE TWO armed men in the room, reeling from the effects of the flash-bang. One was only a couple of yards away, the other at the far window. Bolan brought up the Uzi and burned them both with fatal bursts. The guy by the window tumbled against the glass, his weight cracking it as he slid, bloody, to the floor.

Bolan brought the Uzi round to cover the seated figures.

He recognized Hegre from the image Stony Man had produced.

Julius Hegre.

The man was responsible for so much. The man had engineered thefts and death and suffering reaching around the globe, ever intent on increasing the wealth of the sprawling organization he had created and now ruled. And he was indifferent to the pain he inflicted. Blind to it all.

The man facing Bolan looked less than his image: pale faced, smaller in reality than in the photos Bolan had reviewed.

Across from him the quiet, urbane figure of Dominic Melchior stirred in his seat. He stared at the tall, dark-haired man with the ice-blue eyes and knew with certainty he was looking into the face of death. The fingers of the hand holding his whiskey tumbler lost their grip, and it dropped to the stone fire surround. The glass shattered and the pale liquid spread. A thin smile edged his mouth.

"Accensa domo proximi, tua quoque periclitatur," Melchior whispered. There was the hint of a smile on his colorless lips.

When the house of your neighbor is in flames, your own is in danger.

As he stood, intending to at least try to protect his old friend, the savage chatter of the Uzi ended his thoughts and his life in a blinding moment. Melchior was pinned to the back of the chair, his lean body torn open by the sustained burst.

"Am I allowed a plea for my life?" Hegre asked.

Bolan turned and drew the Uzi into position.

"Do you really expect me to even consider that question?"

"Does a fortune in untraceable cash not interest you?"

Bolan's expression turned even colder.

"To forget about the people you have slaughtered? The lack of consideration for the lives your greed has shattered? Your indifference to the most basic human right of your victims?" Bolan shook his head. "There's only one payment you can offer, Julius Hegre."

Bolan triggered the Uzi and took out Hegre with a sustained burst. He felt no malice; he was judge, jury and executioner, and was carrying out a sentence that was long overdue. Hegre's body jerked and twisted as his life was ended in blood and ravaged flesh."

Slinging the Uzi, Bolan drew his Desert Eagle.

There was a flurry of movement as a Hegre sentry raced into view, his P-90 rising in his hands.

Bolan swung around, the Desert Eagle coming on line, his response faster than the other guy's.

The moment the guy appeared in the archway the Magnum pistol thundered twice. The powerful shots took the guy directly between the eyes, bursting out from the back of his skull. The guy kept coming forward a couple footsteps until his body shut down and he fell facedown on the floor, bloody debris leaking from his shattered skull.

LISE DELAWARE HAD registered the gunfire. There were no return shots. She took that to mean Cooper had taken out the men she had left behind to stand watch over Hegre and Melchior, and when, moments later there were two separate bursts she knew Hegre and Melchior had been killed.

"Make sure that bastard is dead," she said to the hardman at the door. She hefted her P-90, reaching to open the front entrance. "I'll circle and come in through the kitchen. Let's do it."

As the man ran toward the main room, Delaware hauled the door open.

She had barely taken a couple of steps when the crash of gunfire reached her.

Not the crewman's P-90.

It was the unmistakable sound of a Desert Eagle, Delaware's favorite weapon. She would have recognized its distinctive sound anywhere.

Damn you, Cooper. Damn you to hell and back.

She screamed the thought in her head as she darted through the door. Icy rain hit her the instantly. It shocked her with its intensity and she gasped in shock. She moved forward, shoulders hunched against the downpour. She knew the vehicles parked yards away had been rendered unusable.

Delaware kept moving, circling the disabled cars, using them as cover. She ducked, shaking her head to clear away the rain. She was already soaked through, her black clothing sodden and clinging to her.

There was no need to circle the house. Cooper would be coming out the front looking for her.

She crouched, watching the open door.

He would come. She knew that as certain as she knew everyone in the house was dead.

All of them.

Julius.

Dom.

The Hegre crew.

The finality had not truly struck her yet. She felt nothing.

She knew she would, later, and then she could grieve over the loss of the two most important men in her life.

Julius Hegre, the man who had taken a young girl and molded her into the woman she was now. He had provided security. A reason for her to live and to become his protector. Which she had been until now. When he had needed her the most, she had let him down, failed to stand at his side. He had died without her. Just as her mother had died alone.

Lise Delaware would be a long time coming to terms with that fact.

And it would be the same with Melchior. Her confidante, the man who had always been there to advise, always ready with a gentle word, the simple pronouncements that settled her doubts and cleared her mind when she was unsure.

She was on her own again.

And it was all down to the man called Cooper.

Cooper.

CHAPTER FORTY

She saw his tall, imposing figure step outside. Cooper was dressed all in black like herself. He was fully rigged for combat. The Uzi he had was suspended from a strap around his neck, and a .44 Magnum Desert Eagle filled his right hand.

This was the man who had destroyed Hegre's operations. He'd screwed up the diamond deal, ended the uranium deal with the Iranians, had killed her crew.

And now he had taken away Julius Hegre and Dom Melchior. She knew that Cooper was here to wipe out all traces of Hegre.

She pushed back the rage that would have engulfed her, the anger she needed to control if she was going to deal with him.

She gripped her own Desert Eagle, feeling her fingers ache under the pressure she was applying.

"Just who are you, Cooper?" she called out.

She needed to understand him before she killed him.

As an enemy he had proved himself over and over. In his way, he was as good as she was.

If things had been different, they would have made an unbeatable team.

Not now.

Not since he had killed Julius and Dom.

For that he had to die.

But she wanted to know.

"Tell me, Cooper."

"I'm the one who stops you. Puts an end to you and the Hegre organization."

She moved from cover until she was standing in the open. The chill of the rain made her shiver.

"Why?"

"You have people killed because they stand in your way."

"Business, Cooper. They were interfering."

"You did it without a trace of regret. I saw it in your eyes when you had Agent Mitchell shot. Not a second of hesitation."

"She was in the way. In the way of Hegre business. Just as you have been."

"It's good then that your business has come to an end. It's over, Delaware."

"Never," she said. "I'll come back bigger than before."

Bolan recognized the look on her face.

She had made her choice. She was committed.

Bolan saw the big pistol in her hand move, rising to track in on him.

Her move was fast—but by no means fast enough.

There was no hesitation as Bolan brought his own Desert Eagle into play, his finger already curled across the trigger.

Delaware fired in the same instant.

The shots were muffled by the sheeting rain.

The woman's eyes registered shock as the slug cored in between them. It was a clean shot that rocked her dark head back, and she was dead by the time she hit the ground.

Bolan felt the searing streak as her slug jarred his left side, over his ribs. It was a hard enough blow, and the impact forced him to his knees. The pain registered seconds later, and Bolan grit his teeth. The blood felt hot against his cold skin. He lowered the Desert Eagle and reached around to clamp his hand tightly over the ragged wound. He remained where he was for a moment, oblivious to the rain that was as cold as any grave.

"No comeback, Lise Delaware," he said. "Hegre is officially closed for business."

He climbed slowly to his feet. He was not looking forward to the trek back to the hidden car. When he walked past Delaware's, body he saw her eyes were wide open, staring. The rain had washed her face clean of any blood from the hole in her forehead. The black Desert Eagle lay close to her right hand.

He had just reached the tree line when he heard a dull thump of sound. Over his shoulder he saw a roll of flame rising from the house.

As BOLAN TRUDGED ALONG, HIS side throbbed with pain. But at least the blood flow had almost stopped. Once he was in the cover of the forest, the rain's power abated. Bolan kept on walking, his only thought to reach the Volvo and get inside.

Overhead he heard the rumble of thunder. The storm had settled in for the duration.

It took him a couple of hours to reach the SUV. He dragged away the camouflage, unlocked a door and crawled in the rear seat. It would have been so easy to simply lie back and close his eyes. That was not about to happen.

His bags were in the trunk, so he had to exit the vehicle, open the rear and reach them. He took off his weapons and dumped them in the bag. Everything went except the 93-R. He would keep that in the glove box. Bolan took the smaller carryall and closed the trunk.

Back inside the SUV he stripped off his blacksuit and

boots. He had to move carefully because he didn't want to start the wound bleeding again. He tore a T-shirt into ragged strips and bound his torso, covering the gash in his flesh. Dressing was a slow process, but he finally succeeded. The effort left him exhausted. He rested for a time, then hauled his aching body into the driver's seat. He put the 93-R away, fired up the engine and set the heater to maximum. The flow of warm air felt good.

Bolan reversed out of the trees, back onto the narrow trail where he turned the Volvo around and headed back to the regular highway. He gave silent praise for the engineers who had created power steering and automatic transmission. He followed the road back the way he had come in, settling in the comfortable seat, and drove.

JACK GRIMALDI WAS NO doctor. Still, years of involvement with the Executioner had given him some skill with emergency medical treatment when it came to dealing with the aftermath of Bolan's missions.

The tap on Grimaldi's door had a familiar cadence to it and he opened it to see his longtime friend standing there.

"Jack, is the doctor's office open for business?"

Bolan walked into the room and collapsed in a chair.

Grimaldi closed the door and turned to his friend.

"You got a bandage?" Bolan asked. His voice sounded tired.

Bolan barely recalled the drive back to Bellingham. He had taken it slow, conscious of the heavy rain swamping the tarmac. Only two vehicles passed him on his return to the town. When he had finally braked in the hotel parking lot Bolan had simply sat there. He hadn't moved for some time. He had little energy left. The pain from Delaware's bullet wound had increased during the drive. He was certain now that he had at least a cracked rib. He had eventually eased himself out of the Volvo, crossing to the entrance. The rain was still falling and the heavy clouds overhead threatened more.

Grimaldi noticed the way Bolan was holding his hand across his side. He moved the hand clear and slid the zip down and opened the leather jacket. There was a semi-dry patch of blood staining Bolan's shirt.

"Souvenir?"

"Runner-up prize," Bolan said.

The Stony Man pilot went to the kettle and flicked the switch. He opened a sachet of instant coffee and dropped the granules into a mug.

"You get it done?"

"Slate's clean, Jack."

"No leftovers?

Bolan shook his head. "Not this time. Hegre has been canceled."

Grimaldi handed Bolan the mug of coffee. He waited as he took a drink. There was a question ready to be asked but Grimaldi hesitated.

"Just say it, Jack."

"The woman—Delaware."

"Like I said, Jack, Hegre's done. Totally."

And that was it. Grimaldi nodded. No need to take it any further.

"Finish your coffee," he said. "I'll get your key from the clerk and get your bag from your room. Then check us out and we can head for the airport."

Twenty minutes later Grimaldi was driving them to the airport. Bolan waited in the car while the pilot readied the Beechcraft. He loaded their luggage and arranged for the Volvo to be picked up by the rental company.

"You set, Sarge?" Grimaldi asked.

Bolan looked out through the rain-streaked windshield.

"Let's go home," he said.

"You sure you don't want to hang on for treatment?"

"I'm sure," Bolan said.

Grimaldi had picked up a few bottles of water and a pack of pain killers. Bolan swallowed a handful and washed them down.

"I'm good."

"Good? I'm not so sure," Grimaldi said. "Crazy I'm certain about."

He taxied the Beechcraft across the apron and positioned it on the runway. A voice came through his headphones. Grimaldi smiled at the question.

"Rain? Hell, son, this isn't rain. Storms are my specialty."

He powered up and rolled along the runway. The Beechcraft rose from the tarmac in a textbook lift off. Grimaldi set his course and settled in for the long flight.

Beside him Mack Bolan watched the wipers raking back and forth. The steady rhythm of the blades held his attention. He let himself relax, the effect of the tablets he had swallowed taking the edge of his pain. He was coming down now from the powerful adrenaline surge that had engulfed him during his Hegre strike. It took time. Right now that was what he had.

Time.

A break from the hell grounds.

Time for him to let his mind and body recover.

Bolan closed his eyes and the world eventually rolled away and he achieved a semblance of peace.

THERE WERE MATTERS to be resolved over the next few days.

Bolan spoke to SAC Drake Duncan. He asked for a face-to-face meeting with the man. It would have been easy for

Bolan to have simply spoken to Duncan by phone. That was not Bolan's way. He faced up to his responsibilities.

Duncan was in a somber mood when they met in a quiet corner of one of Washington's parks. He held out a hand and Bolan took it.

"I can't say I'm entirely happy with the way this ended," Duncan said.

"Mitchell deserved more," Bolan agreed. "A hell of a lot more than being shot down like that without a chance to defend herself."

"Damn right." Duncan cleared his throat. "Cooper, you said she held her own all the way through until that time?"

"Every step of the way. Let's say I would never want her angry at me. I'd have her by my side on any mission."

"Happy to hear that," someone said from behind Bolan and Duncan.

The lean, gray-haired man who had come up behind them, quietly, spoke with a determined tone.

Bolan saw a middle-aged man, conservatively dressed. He held himself erect and gave off an air of controlled vitality.

His eyes were fixed on Bolan.

They were Sarah Mitchell's eyes, as much as the mouth was Mitchell's.

The man was her father, Jonathon Mitchell.

"You're Cooper," Mitchell said.

"Sir."

Mitchell held his gaze and Bolan was trying to establish just what the man was thinking. Whatever else Jonathon Mitchell was, he was good at keeping his emotions in check.

"Drake, here, has given me all the relevant facts," Mitchell said. "At least the facts he is allowed to divulge.

It seems anything beyond your name is somewhat not for my ears."

"I did explain…" Duncan said.

Mitchell held up a firm hand. "Drake, you made your case and it's fine."

He turned to Bolan again. "Mr. Cooper, my reason for joining Drake is so that I can say my piece here today. I understand fully the covert nature of your business. That aside, my prime concern is my daughter. From what I have learned her accompanying you on your mission was down to her dedication to the FBI, her overwhelming need to follow through on a case involving the deaths of her fellow agents and the desire to see criminals brought to justice. Now I was ready to take you to task because you involved Sarah in dangerous business. When I had time to think, I realized that would have been unfair. My daughter knows her own mind. She would not have volunteered, as Drake put it, for anything but the right reasons. She is a trained, dedicated FBI agent. Putting herself in harm's way comes with the badge."

"It was still my responsibility," Bolan said. "She was hurt on my watch."

"Sarah told me you would say something like that," Mitchell said. "She also said if I tried to put the guilt trip on…well, I'm sure you'll be able to figure that out."

"She's awake and talking?" Bolan asked.

"Yes, and making life difficult for everyone around her. If you want to do something for me, son, go see her. She's asking for you every five minutes."

"My next call," Bolan replied.

"Just to set my mind at rest," Mitchell said. "Did it all end successfully?"

"Yes," Duncan said. He could sense Bolan's unwillingness to become involved in a discussion. "The Iranian threat has been resolved. And Hegre will not be causing us any more problems."

"And Sarah?" Bolan asked.

"Her job is safe. I will see to that. She did the FBI proud."

"Thank you, Drake," Mitchell said, still watching Bolan. There was a quiet nod from Mitchell that brought a barely noticeable response from the soldier. "And thanks again to you, Mr. Cooper."

"I'll see you later, Duncan," Bolan said and moved on.

"A good man," Mitchell said.

Duncan smiled at that.

You will never know, he thought.

BOLAN MADE HIS way to the intensive care unit where Mitchell had been brought after her flight from Aktau. That had been almost a week ago. Bolan would have visited sooner. He had been tied up with details at Stony Man and he had decided not to call and see Mitchell until he had cleared the air with Duncan and, especially, Jonathon Mitchell.

The intensive care unit was bright and decorated in muted pastel colors. Mitchell's room was at the far end and had a large window at one side that looked out on the manicured grounds. Beyond was the Washington skyline. The solid buildings declared the permanence of the city. Traffic could been seen moving silently along the wide avenues.

Pausing to look through the viewing window, Bolan was reminded of seeing Mitchell in the Aktau hospital. Unmoving. Pale and lifeless. Not the vibrant woman he was used to. Now it was different. Mitchell was still lying down, still attached to a number of tubes, but at least she was able to breathe on her own again.

She saw him after a few seconds, her lips curving into

a smile, and she beckoned him to join her. Bolan pushed open the door and stepped inside the room.

Mitchell watched him, noticed the way he moved, still favoring his side where Delaware's bullet had hit.

"What happened?"

"A parting gift."

"Mmm." Mitchell eyed him solemnly. "The way you said that makes me think you don't want to talk about it."

"Still the hotshot agent. Never miss a thing."

"What can a girl say?"

"I talked to Duncan earlier," Bolan told her.

"Is he still mad at you?"

"We kind of came to an understanding."

"Did my name crop up?" Mitchell asked.

"Yes."

"I hope you didn't screw things up for me."

"I think you'll still have your job when they let you out of here."

"Only *think?*"

"Don't worry, Agent Mitchell, Duncan will have your badge safe."

"That's something, I suppose," Mitchell said in her usual self-deprecating manner.

"There's one other thing I have to tell you," Bolan said.

"What?"

"I had a serious talk with your father today."

Mitchell stared at him, unsure what he was saying.

"My God, you didn't ask if you could marry me?"

"You make it sound the worst thing that could happen."

"I didn't mean it like… Cooper, what *are* you talking about?"

"I said I was responsible for what happened to you."

"Dammit, Cooper, why did you say that? He'll think I'm not safe out on my own now."

"You should give him more credit, Sarah."

"What about you, Cooper? What do you give me?"

Bolan leaned over and placed a gentle kiss on her cheek. He slid something from inside his jacket.

"Mitchell, you're a trained FBI agent." He walked back to the door. "Go figure it out...."

When he had gone, Mitchell saw the thick envelope lying on her bed. She drew it close, fingers tracing the shape inside. She started to smile then laughed as she recognized the outline of her Glock pistol.

"I BELIEVE WE can keep a fairly tight lid on this," Brognola told the President.

"I've heard a few rumblings," the President said. "Nothing confirmed and no one is making much of them. So give me the rest of the story."

"There was trouble in Moscow when Hegre and Striker clashed. The trail led him and Agent Mitchell to Kazakhstan where the stolen uranium was in the hands of Hegre and the Iranians. Striker got to them before they were able to ship the cargo off to Iran."

"And it was in Aktau that Agent Mitchell was injured?"

"Yes, sir. She and Striker were compromised. From what Striker told me, the shooting was done out of hand, ordered by Lise Delaware against an unarmed target."

"Thank God Mitchell survived."

"When matters were settled in Aktau, Striker returned to the U.S. and made his final move against Hegre. My people had located Hegre bases and with the loss of their deal with the Iranians, the Hegre top people went to hide in a bolt-hole in the Northwest. Pretty isolated place." Brognola paused. "The next part of Striker's mission was a personal strike against Hegre."

"Don't spare my feelings, Hal. I understand Striker's way

of handling certain, shall we say, operations. I may not be a fan of his methods, but I see his motivation. He has a strong sense of justice and a unique way of administering it. In truth, Hal, haven't I given the go-ahead to dark ops? Sent our people out to administer what we believe is best for America? Striker does his own cutting out of the deadwood. Removing those who are doing their best to rip our society apart."

"He would be pleased to hear those sentiments."

"Well, keep them to yourself. I wouldn't want what we discuss here to end up on the news."

"The same goes for local law enforcement," Brognola said. "I've been talking to the law up in Bellingham. They aren't having a good time with what happened. SAC Duncan has an FBI team there after I suggested the local sheriff might need help. The FBI will move in and smooth things over. Sidelining the Bellingham cops will keep the matter out of the spotlight."

"Let's pray it does."

"Iran hasn't mentioned anything about the uranium," Brognola said. "Ayatollah Fikri wouldn't want his backdoor deals being made public. He's been made to look foolish enough with his big plan going belly up."

"The problem there, Hal, is it will make him even more determined to succeed. Fikri will try again."

"Then we need to keep an even closer eye on him, sir. Mossad will be relieved the uranium was destroyed. They will increase their surveillance and harden their stance against Iran."

The President said, "And so it goes on. Threat and counterthreat. Secrecy and back-door deals. It doesn't seem there's an end to it all, Hal."

Brognola said, "Maybe one day, sir. When we all make

the choice to sit down and admit what a bunch of idiots we all are."

"That's not going to happen soon, though, is it, as much as I would like to see that happen. So in the meantime we stand with our backs to the wall and keep the wolves at bay."

"Or send out our own wolf to deal with our enemies. Let him off the official leash for a while?"

The President smiled.

"Are you making a plea for Striker? There is no need, Hal. I admire what that man does for his country. The shame is he has to do it all under a cloak of secrecy, forced to cover his tracks because if he was exposed it would all be over. He's a shadow man, Hal, who deserves to be honored but never will be."

"Striker wouldn't want to be put under the spotlight. He does what he does because he has to. It's not for personal gain. It's for what he considers true justice. His war is against those who turn their backs on civilized society for personal gain."

"Let's hope he continues to think that way. If he put aside his arms and called it a day…"

The President didn't want to think that might happen.

It was one man.

One man who had put his personal life on hold because he felt the need to carry his War Everlasting on his shoulders. Who asked nothing for himself.

Striker is one hell of a man, the President thought.

One hell of an American.

BOLAN WAS IN his quarters at Stony Man, on the phone to Valentine Seminov.

"My friend, it is good to hear that Sarah Mitchell is recovering. Will she be able to return to her work? I do not feel she would be very happy if that was not possible."

"It'll take time. She isn't going to sit back and do nothing."

"I will tell young Nikolai. It will, as you say, make his day."

"Is Arkady resting peacefully?"

"His body lies in the village where he was born. It seemed only fitting."

"So we all have ended up where we should be."

"You also, Cooper?"

"I'm back home. "

"Nikolai sends his regards."

"Thank him for me."

"Always remember that you have friends here in Moscow. Come visit us one day—but leave your gun at home."

The Russian's booming laughter echoed from the phone as he signed off.

Bolan heard the door open behind him. He knew who it was before he turned.

"You do realize we have hardly spoken since you got back," Barbara Price said. "I suppose you'll tell me you've had things to do."

"Would I lie?"

"You don't look busy right now."

Price stood just inside the room. She pushed the door shut with the toe of her boot.

"Remember that move you used the last time we spent time together?" she said.

"Only just."

"Soldier, I'm here on a refresher course, so don't you even think about ducking out on me."

Bolan saw he had been outflanked. He stood his ground and followed orders.

* * * * *

The Executioner

Don Pendleton's

SLAYGROUND

A cult holds a senator's daughter captive, endangering government secrets...

National security is on the line when a senator's daughter disappears in Florida. The leader of the cult responsible is desperate to boost his sect's influence by gaining access to the sensitive government information the girl possesses. Needing to act fast, the White House sends in Mack Bolan.

Bolan's mission is to rescue the girl before she gives up any secrets, but infiltrating the leader's stronghold is no easy feat. Nevertheless, the Executioner has put his faith in justice, and he won't quit until his enemies are converted.

GOLD EAGLE®

Available November wherever books and ebooks are sold.

GEX432

JAMES AXLER

DEATH LANDS®

POLESTAR OMEGA

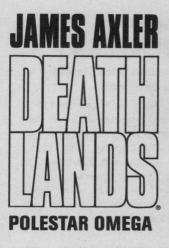
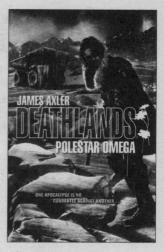

One apocalypse is no guarantee against another...

Ryan and his crew become the subjects in a deadly experiment when they're taken captive inside a redoubt at the South Pole. A team of scientists is convinced the earth must be purified of mutants, and now they have the perfect lab rats to test their powerful bioweapon. Filled with toxic chemicals and faced with Antarctica's harsh and unstable conditions, the companions must fight the odds and take down the whitecoats before millions are killed. But in this uncompromising landscape, defeating the enemy may be just another step toward a different kind of death....

Available November wherever books and ebooks are sold.